Praise for the works of Laina Villeneuve

Cowgirl 101

Cowgirl 101 is a slow-burn romance between two very different personalities set in the beautiful High Sierras of California in summer. The story is well rounded with good conflict, and a lot of interesting information about guided mule trips in the wilderness of High Sierras trails. I was very happy with this book and could easily recommend it.

-Pin's Reviews, *goodreads*

I really enjoyed *Cowgirl 101* by Laina Villeneuve. This book has all the elements of an exceptional modern Western romance with two unique and individual main characters. The setting, of course, is gorgeous. The romance is kind of an enemies-to-lovers tale and definitely a slow-burn romance, but sweet and satisfying. This is the first novel I've read by this author, and I'm definitely going to be looking for more of her work. If you love modern-day Western romance with distinctive and engaging characters set in a stunningly beautiful land, then I can recommend this novel for you.

-Betty H., *NetGalley*

This is a gorgeous book. Everything about it is gorgeous, from the setting to the writing style. Her writing is so readable, so beautiful and lyrical, that it makes the story flow even better. The first half was very slow for me, but I knew that this was a deliberate choice. We needed all that background, all that time to pass, to understand how Daisy and Jo would fit together.

-Karen R., *NetGalley*

The Right Thing Easy

The Right Thing Easy is a well written romance. The writing is clean, the characters are charming, and the story keeps you entertained. Villeneuve wrote the characters with a finesse and grace that I enjoyed, especially when they were struggling with tough choices. Laina Villeneuve writes nicely. The thoughts and feelings the characters had were real…I could not help but understand what they were going though.

-The Lesbian Review

Kat's Nine Lives

…is a friends-to-lovers romance about putting in the time and energy to figure out who you are rather than accept what others think you should be. …Villeneuve does a superb job with the pacing of this story. It is clearly a romance novel, but there are elements to it that made me feel like I was reading a mystery. She reveals clues about Kat's past bit by bit. As each new piece of information was revealed I was surprised over and over again. All of these tidbits lead up to a better understanding of Kat's fears and understandings.

-The Lesbian Review

Such Happiness as This

The novel describes Robyn's journey from grief and disappointment, through the joy of new friendships and the uncertainty of potential love. Characters are skillfully drawn, and interweave in a plot with enough realistic problems, local references, and surprising twists to satisfy.

-The L-Word

Cure for Insomnia

Other Bella Books by Laina Villeneuve

Cowgirl 101
Kat's Nine Lives
Return to Paradise
The Right Thing Easy
Such Happiness as This
Take Only Pictures

About the Author

Laina Villeneuve leaves all things science to her wife of sixteen years. They live in Southern California with three children and are very grateful to the professionals who help build educational plans for their autistic son, dyslexic daughter, and ADHD son.

Cure for Insomnia

Laina Villeneuve

BELLA
B O O K S

2021

Bella Books, Inc.
P.O. Box 10543
Tallahassee, FL 32302

This is a work of fiction. Names, characters, businesses, places, events and incidents are either the products of the author's imagination or used in a fictitious manner. Any resemblance to actual persons, living or dead, or actual events is purely coincidental. The publisher does not have any control over and does not assume any responsibility for author or third-party websites or their content.

Printed in the United States of America on acid-free paper.

First Bella Books Edition 2021

Editor: Cath Walker
Cover Designer: Kayla Mancuso

ISBN: 978-1-64247-201-1

Acknowledgments

This book has not been the easiest to wrangle, and I have so many Bella women who helped me along the way. I am beyond grateful that Jessica said no to the first draft. I'm also grateful for Linda suggesting I talk to KG MacGregor about the problems with that book and for all her brainstorming to help me understand the structure needed to weave intrigue into the plot. (With apologies for sucking up her time for ideas I didn't end up using!)

Thanks to Becky Harmon for reminding me I write romance. While I was still trying to figure out how to keep the intrigue plot, I thought I could make two books out of this story, separate ones for each character. I am so glad I listened to Jaime Clevenger's argument that Karla and Remi were meant to be together. (She deserves an award for reading through that first awful draft!) Many thanks both to her and my friends Heather and Samantha Coughlin for slogging through multiple drafts and offering encouragement as I chopped and added and rearranged and added and changed POVs and resurrected old scenes.

Thank you, Rae Rae for tracking down what I hope are the last pesky pronouns and for the enthusiastic texts from you and Paul about the content.

Thank you to the ladies who helped my own romance with Louisa blossom and thus brought science to my humanities-driven world. Margaret and Valerie, my characters are smarter and more grounded because of your presence in my life.

I thought my editor would be of help making my Aussie character more authentic, but as it turned out, her expertise in research and clinical trials has made this a much better story.

And Louisa, my own scientist, is proof that an intelligent lady in a lab coat is hot as hell. Eighteen years, and I still love listening to you talk about your work.

Dedication

For Dr. Rosa
In gratitude for all you have taught me about patience

CHAPTER ONE

Not one more second to spare, I saved my updated file for our lab's application to the FDA to fast track the drug we had developed. As I shrugged out of my lab coat, the reddest lips I'd ever seen caught my attention. The way she'd penciled the perimeter mesmerized me. Rosa's voice whispered *that could be her, the answer to your sleeping problem*! I cringed and extinguished her idea with a loud internal *WAY TOO young*!

Wanting very much to encourage my niece Rosa's interest in science, I'd allowed myself to become her research subject for the middle-school science fair, her goal to cure my insomnia. The eleven-year-old's conclusion? That I needed a girlfriend. The oh-so young woman was peering into the real-time thermocycler, making me anxious that she didn't know how to use it. Relief swept through me when she walked away from equipment so expensive our lab had to share it with the neighboring one. I grabbed my bag from the drawer and said a prayer that our Principal Investigator was at lunch or deeply absorbed in her work. I needed to get over to Rosa's science fair, now.

Passing through the lab benches, I saw Red Lips return to the machine. Scowling at it again, she started to lean forward with her lips pursed as if she was about to blow out birthday candles.

"Stop! Stop! Stop!" I hollered, startling the woman as she let loose a puff of air projecting all sorts of contaminants toward a machine that cost in the tens of thousands of dollars. "No more blowing!" I said, hustling around the bench. "What the hell are you doing?" Up close, I could see a fine sheen of sweat on her forehead.

"The tray got stuck, and when I opened it..." She looked away.

"What?"

"The cap on one of the tubes came off. I was trying to get it out."

"By blowing in there?" The younger woman cringed. Young. Inexperienced. I took a breath to calm myself. "Ask for help."

"Sorry! I couldn't find the postdoc who asked me to run the samples."

"Look harder! Use your eyes, not your mouth. And for heaven's sake, find gloves for those," I said, pointing to the woman's hands.

Red Lips nodded vigorously.

"Now!"

Fear in her eyes, the woman spun around and ran toward Dr. Bautista's lab. Burning with frustration that they had left someone so green unsupervised at the bench, I considered following to make sure that a staff member would come back to assist her with the thermocycler, but I was already late. I turned, only to spot my boss, Dr. Judy Vogelsang talking to a research scientist just inside our lab. My heartrate spiked as it always did. Was it because of how intimidating she was? Attractive? No, it was definitely how intimidating she was. There was no way to slip by unnoticed, so I said a prayer, held my breath and hoped that she was so involved that she wouldn't interrupt her conversation. Hand on the doorknob, I was practically free when my boss's voice froze me in my tracks.

"Karla! Are you finished with the report?"

"I will have it finished tonight," I said.

"Something is keeping you from it at the moment? It is essential for the meeting I have with the sponsors tomorrow morning."

"I will have it finished…" I wanted to leave it at that, but the air in my lungs puffed out of my chest when I realized I had to explain my errand. Knowing I would be gone longer than it would take to grab a late lunch, I had to admit where I was going. "I'm on my way to the county science fair."

"Are you a judge?"

The idea had not even occurred to me, but I quickly saw how I could run with it. "Not this year because I was my niece's research subject. It's something I'd like to do, though."

"The Miracle Center sponsors the Innovation Award. See what sort of projects the students are doing these days. Talk to the judges. It wouldn't hurt for them to see us out in the community."

"I'll make sure to find them." Relieved the exchange had gone so well, I pushed the door, but Judy's voice caught me once more.

"Good. I'm in the clinic seeing patients this afternoon. I'm hoping to recruit some volunteers. Check back with me when you return as I may have some samples for you to process."

I froze. I had promised my family that I would join them for the celebration dinner following the fair. I'd been in the lab hours before anyone else that morning since I hadn't planned on coming back. I'd hoped to finish the report at home, but I couldn't do that if Judy did collect samples. "I'll check with you when I'm back. It may not be until this evening."

"It's no matter," Judy answered. "I'll be here."

Stuck again, I agreed and jogged down the stairs.

It took me twenty minutes to cross town and ten more to park and walk to the fair site. The room was swarming with teachers, parents, and students. I impatiently navigated through the displays until I found my family.

Antonia glared when she saw me. "So happy you could make it, Dr. Hernandez," she whispered. Rosa was running through her project with someone, her expression anxious. I felt terrible when Rosa saw me and visibly relaxed.

"Hi. I'm the research subject," I said, in case the man was a judge. I didn't know if they made themselves known or tried to blend into the crowd. As Rosa continued explaining her experimental method, I leaned toward my sister. "I'm so sorry I wasn't here when it started. I ran into all sorts of problems trying to get away from work."

Antonia waved off my excuse which was somehow worse than the punctuality lecture I usually received from our mother. "This is the first person to ask questions," she said.

"Judge?" I whispered.

"What do I know?" Familiar taunting edged her tone.

"What would you do differently next time?" the man asked. He was tall and lanky and wore running shoes with his loose-fitting suit.

From what I'd researched about how the judging worked, the question positively identified the man as one of assessors. A knot of anxiety formed in my belly, but I was impressed with Rosa's poise as she discussed trying multiple methods to cure my insomnia. Rosa concluded that she either needed more time to gather data or needed to omit one of her experimental arms, so she could dedicate a week to trying two of the potential remedies paired.

I knew from my own poster presentations how hard it was to keep it succinct and as clear as possible when the curious wanted to know more about my work. It had taken me a while to learn to keep my mouth shut, thereby masking my insecurity and making me appear confident and collected. All of this seemed to come naturally to Rosa, who appeared at ease with the man now offering his thanks. After he left, I swept her up in a hug.

"That was a judge, wasn't it?" Rosa asked.

"Probably, and I'm so, so impressed with how you answered all his questions. Keep doing that, and you're going to knock their socks off!"

A group of students stopped to ask questions, taking Rosa's attention again. As she explained her project to cluster after cluster of attendees, I realized how little she needed me. I scanned the nearby projects, listening in on some of the students. The boy to the right clearly had no idea what his parents had done for his effects-of-an-oil-spill project. His setup with a huge tray of water with oil floating on top amid coated bath toys looked great, but he had trouble discussing both his method and the relevance of his project. When asked about recent oil spills, the kid's silence and his parents' tension spoke volumes about who actually had the investment in marine wildlife.

I could see myself being a judge for the event sometime. I itched to walk around the hall and see more projects and hear the young scientists talk about their work.

Across the aisle, a gorgeous woman in a tailored suit and heels caught my attention. My body zinged with the probability that she was a judge. Her attire made her stand out as loudly as her actions. She took a seat in the student's chair, putting her at eye level with him, and listened as if the child was the only person in the auditorium. I appreciated the length she went to make the student comfortable. To be honest, I appreciated a lot more. Every aspect of her screamed professional. Her wedge-cut black hair accentuated her slender neck and flawless jawline. Her features were delicate but her expression sure and strong. When she reached out to shake the student's hand, I felt the urge to offer my own.

The woman stood and turned, reading the projects on Rosa's side of the aisle. I watched as the woman's gaze went from the flawless project next to us to Rosa's project before stopping on me. Caught staring, I should have looked away, but I couldn't. Warmth flooded my chest as if I knew the woman, yet I was sure I'd never seen her before. She moved in my direction, every step accelerating my heartrate. Only when she was directly in front of me did the woman's gaze drop to Rosa. A wide smile graced her face as she gestured to Rosa's chair.

"May I?"

Rosa nodded vigorously, as tongue-tied as I was. She nudged the chair toward the visitor.

The judge, because surely she was a judge, tucked her perfect legs to the side, a picture of elegance. "Tell me how you chose this particular project." She had an accent that I couldn't quite place. The cadence and pronunciation suggested that English was not her first language.

By now, I had heard Rosa's answer many times and was accustomed to nodding politely when Rosa pointed me out as the research subject. This time when the questioner's eyes turned to me, my body reacted again. I cursed the person who had decided that judges would not wear name tags and myself for not removing the elastic I typically used to keep my hair out of my face. My thick black curls would have covered the blush creeping up my neck.

"Not being able to sleep sounds terrible," the woman said. "What did you find?"

Though her question was directed at Rosa, her eyes stayed on me. She frowned sympathetically as Rosa explained that the suggested remedies of melatonin and meditation grew less effective. Next was the question about what Rosa might have done differently, but instead of giving the answer she had for the whole afternoon, Rosa went a completely different route.

"If I did this as a project in the future, I'd try to find more people who have trouble sleeping and compare how the treatments work, but for my aunt, I just have to find someone to sleep with her."

CHAPTER TWO

I gasped because my niece was speaking the literal truth.

Three weeks earlier, after a very frustrating day, I had just succumbed to gravity, sinking into the soft couch right inside my door. The way the cushions embraced my exhausted body, I knew I'd made a big mistake. I never should have stopped moving. Sitting felt too good, the quiet too much of a blessing. I released my hair from the elastic and tilted my head side to side. The pressure in my shoulders and scalp eased slightly. Petri leapt to the couch and kneaded my thigh when I stroked her slick black coat.

My phone rang. I was late. I groaned as I reached for it.

"Karla!" My mother's voice boomed the moment I swiped the screen.

"Ma."

"You've had time to pee or do whatever you need to do. Your family is waiting."

I should have known my mother would be watching the street. Her voice got me to my feet and to the door. When I opened it, Rosa was already there. I couldn't help but return her smile. She smelled like home.

"Beef *cocido* tonight?" I asked my mother, still on the phone.

"Ah! Rosa made it. Be a good example. Do not make that child late."

I clicked off without saying goodbye, pocketed my phone and held my arms out. "You smell good enough to eat." I buried my nose in Rosa's hoodie, eliciting a laugh.

"I was helping *Abuela* in the kitchen."

"Before you went out to spy on my driveway?"

"I wasn't spying. *Abuela* saw you drive by and sent me."

"It's my lucky day to have an escort." I locked my door and followed Rosa to the sidewalk for the two-block walk down the street to my parents' house which they shared with my sister's family.

"My mom said you could help me with my science project."

"Me? I suck at science."

Rosa pushed into me with her shoulder. "No, you don't."

We passed my condo complex and crossed the street entering an older neighborhood with single-story homes. Rosa did not set the pace of a kid sent to retrieve the last member of the family. Her feet and mouth were set at opposite speeds as she attempted to fill me in on her project. Once we arrived, it would be hard to complete a thought without being interrupted. I could see Rosa's agitation when we reached the olive-green stucco house my parents owned. "Let me say hi to *Abuela*."

She nodded wordlessly as we entered through the side kitchen door. I kissed my mom on the cheek and reached past her to stir the soup simmering on the stove. The rich aroma eased some of the tension in my shoulders.

My mother stood a full head shorter than me and had twisted her dark hair up off her neck for her kitchen work. She patted my shoulder in greeting and took the spoon from me. "Go help your niece. She has been moping around the house all day waiting for you."

In the bright living room, my brother, Luis, popped his chin in my direction, absorbed in the video game his son was playing. Though he dwarfed his six-year-old son, Beto, the two otherwise looked like twins in their white shirts and black jeans. Luis's girlfriend, Giselle, waved before returning her attention to her phone.

"Why aren't you punks helping Rosa with her project?" I sat next to Rosa on the brick hearth of a fireplace they never used. The mantel was lined with wedding photos: my parents, Antonia and her husband, Gustavo, and both my maternal and paternal grandparents.

"You're the brains," Luis said.

"What did you do to cure diabetes today?" Antonia said, entering the room carrying a toddler already leaning in my direction.

"What's your mama doing carrying you, big girl?" I asked. The second Olivia was in my arms, she wiggled down and across the room. "When did you get so fast!"

"That's why I carry her. Keeps her out of trouble," Antonia said, plucking her up before the toddler pulled herself up on her cousin Beto's pants.

"You know I'm not curing diabetes," I said, returning to my sister's jab. The baby of the family, I had almost thirty years of their pretending they didn't understand what I was talking about. You'd think I'd know whether she was teasing me or testing whether I could let an inaccurate statement slide. I couldn't. "The drug we're creating to prevent retinal damage will…" Rosa interrupted me with a pat on my shoulder.

"They don't listen, *Tía*. I tried to explain how your lab is making a pill to reduce blindness for people with diabetes, but they just pretend to sleep. See?"

As she said, both my siblings had closed their eyes. Olivia delighted in the game, patting her mother's cheeks, and Luis quietly snored.

"At least one person in my family listens."

"Two!" my mother shouted from the kitchen.

"Three," my father added from the bedroom where he was watching TV.

"The important ones." I winked. "Have you brainstormed ideas for your project yet?"

"*Tío* says I shouldn't be wasting my time on science projects, and Mom says I should Google a project."

"Google isn't a bad place to start."

"But none of it's relevant. I want to do something that could help people, like what you do."

"You sure she's your kid, Antonia?" Luis asked.

"I know, right? You think she wants to talk about makeup? Boys? Curfews? Any of the stuff I cared about in the fifth grade?" She shook her head. "Only reason I don't think they switched her at birth with some other baby in the hospital is that she sounds exactly like Karla when she was this age. Remember how we used to think she was messed up somehow?"

"Hey," I squawked, "look at how I turned out. Still think science is a waste of time?" My brother refused to take his eyes off Beto's tablet. When Rosa mirrored my exasperation, I stage-whispered, "He'll be the first one claiming that the cure for diabetic retinopathy was all his idea."

"The way I remember it, that first science project *was* all my genius," he said smugly.

"Oh, yeah! The fart project! That was a winner," Antonia laughed.

"Farts?" Rosa's shoulders drooped.

"It was actually your uncle's idea. He had the worst smelling farts."

"Had?" Antonia interrupted.

"Has," I conceded. "So I decided to test whether what he ate affected how bad his farts smelled."

"You smelled his farts?"

The room filled with familiar laughter. They were always laughing at me. I'd always been an outsider to them, an oddity. Sometimes it rubbed more than others. "You pay a high price for science."

Rosa crossed her hands over her chest. "Well I want to do something important. Something that could help people."

"You want to do something to help, help your *mamá* get some sleep." Antonia nodded at Olivia. "This one still gets me up at least once a night. I don't get how Rosa sleeps through her screaming her head off."

"At least you know why you're not sleeping," I said. "I have no excuse. I just can't find the off-switch for my brain."

Rosa jumped up and ran to the computer on the desk across from the fireplace. I caught Antonia's eye, but she shrugged and gave me the look that said since my niece was more like me, I was the one who should get her. "Like I said, she's no mini-me. She's a mini-you." She dropped her voice. "Still waiting to see if she digs chicks. You knew when you started crushing on your seventh-grade math teacher, right?"

"I never should have told you that."

"Jackpot!" Rosa shouted. "Have you tried taking melatonin?"

"I tried valerian root once, but it didn't do anything. Plus it tasted nasty."

My niece's fingers flew on the keys. "Tea or pill?"

"Tea."

"We could try the pill form."

"What's this *we*?"

"For my science project. Since you didn't like the tea, we'll try the pill form. Web MD says to take four hundred to nine hundred milligrams. You're not pregnant, right? It says that you can't take it if you're pregnant."

"No worries there," I deadpanned.

"How about lavender?" Rosa said, unfazed. "This site says you can try rubbing it on your feet."

"Sign me up for that," Giselle said.

"You have trouble sleeping, too?" Excitement flashed on Rosa's voice.

"Could be your uncle snores too much."

Rosa's brow creased as she considered Giselle's idea. She blinked and shook her head. "Snoring would be a different study. I could search up remedies for snoring that we could try."

"Give her the valium root," Luis said, never taking his eyes off the video game. "I'm not takin' anything."

"It's not valium, idiot," Giselle said. "It's..." She pointed at Rosa.

"Valerian root," Rosa supplied.

"Yeah. I don't need valerian root. I sleep fine until you fall asleep." Giselle tucked her phone away and directed raised eyebrows and pursed lips at my brother. Although they weren't married, Luis had lived with her ever since Beto was born.

I waited for Luis to react, not surprised when the silence after Giselle's remark lengthened. "So far, it sounds like babies and boyfriends ruin sleep. There's your research angle. I can see your paper title: 'Studies show that sleeping alone improves your sleep.'"

Rosa frowned at me. "But you sleep alone, and you said you don't sleep."

"Giselle doesn't sleep alone," Luis said, clueless.

"She will if she doesn't get a lavender foot rub," Giselle answered.

"Pshaw," Luis said. "None of you ladies askin' how I sleep. I'll be a lot safer sleeping by myself."

"Oh, no. You're not blamin' that on me," Giselle said.

"She didn't tell you, did she? How she pushed me outta bed?"

Rosa's eyes widened. "You pushed him out of bed?"

"He sleeps on his back. Look at him. He's a big guy. I was trying to push him onto his side. I couldn't budge him. I'd push. He'd rock back. I pushed again and got him further. Then I thought one big push would do it. How did I know he was going to turn over on his own?"

"Freakin' launched my ass onto the floor."

"You didn't hurt nothing. You're such a baby. Karla, you got it wrong. Antonia and me, we both sleep with babies. You're the only smart one sleeping alone."

"Work hours are unforgiving," I said. My grad school commitments had strained my previous relationships, but they were nothing compared to the hours Judy expected of me as a research scientist.

"Did you ever try sleeping with someone, Aunt Karla?"

Luis doubled over laughing, and Antonia turned to hide her smile. I tried as hard as I could to clear my brain, to picture my parents chastely lying side by side in their own bed. Instead, a vivid memory of my ex, naked and very much not sleeping, flooded my mind and my senses. I turned a deep shade of red.

"What?" Rosa demanded.

"Your mom and uncle are crass, that's what," I said, wishing it wasn't so hot in the room. "You are a way better big sister than some of us had."

"Mom says I'm the best."

"Must be you have a good role model," I said from the side of my mouth.

Antonia pushed her lips out like she did when she got defensive. "Okay, you be the role model. You explain."

That hadn't redirected the conversation as I'd hoped it would. How to put this? Rosa crossed her arms, waiting. "Okay. In your head, when you ask 'have you slept with anyone,' you're asking with the idea of a slumber party?"

Rosa nodded, all innocence.

"And I have." I struggled to continue the thought. I tried to keep the idea of a slumber party in my head to push away my blush by telling myself that whether we'd had sex or not, I'd always slept better with Ann in my bed. Just thinking the words sex and Ann restarted the tape in my head, embarrassingly heating other parts of my body.

Antonia cackled as if she could tell what was happening in my pants. "The kind of sleeping together your aunt's thinking about now gets you one of these." She tipped her head toward Olivia. "Well, it gets me one, but your auntie is lucky. Doing the nighttime tango doesn't get her knocked up."

"Oh," Rosa said, flushing as red as me.

Luis, not blushing at all, pointed out the deepening red on both of our faces. "I swear that kid is really Karla's."

"I don't think finding a girlfriend qualifies as a science project," said Rosa.

Thankful we were finally back on the subject at hand, I said, "You don't have to find me a girlfriend. There are lots of other things we can try."

"None of which will be as fun," Antonia tsked.

CHAPTER THREE

Thus, when my niece said that all she needed was to find someone to sleep with me, my mind went directly to picturing the beautiful judge naked and in my bed.

My gasp carried a tiny bit of saliva to my windpipe. I tried to disguise the cough as merely clearing my throat, but that made my lungs panic more. Antonia thwacked me on the back and shoved a bottled water at me. Her big smile told me she was remembering exactly what she'd said three weeks ago. Her eyes danced as her eyes drifted from me to the judge. "You okay, *hermana?*"

"Fine. Sorry. I'm fine," I sputtered.

"You sound certain that you solved your subject's sleeping problem," the woman said with a twinkle in her eye.

"When we were working on the poster, I stayed at her house. She slept so well, she had me stay over again."

"So your aunt wasn't simply your subject? She helped with the project as well?"

"She's a research scientist at The Miracle Center. She

showed me some of her posters to give me ideas about how to present my research."

"I logged my sleeping data onto a spreadsheet, so I printed that out for her." I hesitated, realizing I probably sounded like the parents at the poster next door. "The rest is all her."

"Sounds like she has a good role model." The soft edges of the woman's professional voice melted into something much more intimate.

"She is!" Rosa agreed. "She's a real scientist. She studies diabetes. I've been to her lab. She showed me her dark room, her hood, and…"

I wanted to die right on the spot. Rosa's unintentionally suggestive description pushed the judge's sculpted eyebrows higher and higher on her lovely forehead. I interrupted her before it got worse. "You keep your focus, and you'll be a research scientist yourself someday."

Rosa beamed at me.

"She certainly has a good start," the judge agreed.

"A pleasure to meet you." She grasped Rosa's hand and then looked at me. "Both of you."

With a smile, she was gone. I was certain that under different circumstances, I would have received a handshake as well or maybe even something more. I could see myself intertwining my fingers with hers to pull her into a private conversation. Though I did my best to stay present for Rosa, the woman had thoroughly captured my attention, and I found myself searching for her repeatedly.

"What's with you?" Antonia bumped me after I'd been caught distracted.

"I promised my boss I'd check out who is representing The Miracle Center."

Antonia shook her head and sucked air through her teeth. "Thought you were here with your family. But you're always working, aren't you?"

"I'm sorry."

"Go."

"No. I'll do it later."

"Did you hear me ask you? Go do your thing, and then you can come back and be here."

I heard the sister-mom Antonia had been when our mother was at work and she was in charge. "I'll be right back."

Guilt wove through the crowd with me as my thoughts remained on the judge instead of my brief from Judy. What was I doing? I came to an abrupt halt realizing my foolishness. As it was, I had to flake on my family to get back to work. I didn't have time for distractions. I turned an about-face to head toward the check-in table to talk to an official and nearly collided with the judge.

"I'm so sorry!" I said.

"Please excuse me," the judge said at the same time.

Caught face-to-face with the exact person I was hoping to see, words failed me.

"Were you looking for something?"

How could I answer that when all I wanted to say was "some*one?*" "Yes. My boss asked me to find out how to become involved."

The beautiful woman in front of me swept her eyes up and down my body. "You would like to be involved?"

Her delivery was decidedly flirtatious, which put seeking information for Judy even further from my thoughts. My stomach surged like a tumble of leaves pulling together in a dust whirl. I struggled to find a witty response. "It seems like a good opportunity."

"As I'm sure you guessed, I am a judge. I would be happy to talk to you. I can offer some personal insights."

"That would be wonderful!"

She pulled a small notebook from her pocket and tore out a sheet on which she jotted her phone number. "My name is Remi."

My mouth dry, I accepted the paper, folded it and slipped it in my pocket, so I could extend my hand. "Karla. So glad I bumped into you again."

"Nearly." Remi squeezed my hand warmly. "I had hoped we would."

"Bump into each other?"

"That I would see you again. I have some ideas of how to further your niece's research."

A zing of desire zipped through my core. "Do you?"

"Indeed. Sadly, right now I have more projects to judge."

"I'll call you."

"I look forward to it." Remi grasped my bicep as she passed. She glanced over her shoulder before she turned down an aisle of projects.

Dazed, I returned to the entrance to gather information for Judy. I nodded in the correct places though most of the deluge of information washed over me. Remi. Her name was Remi, and she had ideas about my insomnia. My body recalled Remi's hand on my arm. I could think of little else beyond wanting to feel that hand elsewhere.

* * *

With a knot in my stomach from disappointing my family yet again, I reluctantly returned to the lab instead of joining my loved ones for dinner. They had complained as they always did when I'd told them Judy had called me back to the lab, but I knew they would have accepted my bailing if I'd said I had a date. I certainly wished I could have called Remi to see if she had dinner plans.

Judy's light was on when I reached the second floor, so I swiped into the office space before heading to the lab.

"Were you able to introduce yourself to the judges for the Innovation Award?"

"I was. They were very excited about the projects they had seen and thought it was an excellent idea to have additional participation from The Miracle Center. I have several contacts I'll follow through with next week." Remi's number burned in my pocket. I wanted to follow through on that much sooner.

"Wonderful. Definitely something to pursue. I collected samples from two new volunteers. You'll be able to process them tonight, yes?"

"Yes, I'll get to them after I finish the report."

"Excellent." She dismissed me with a crisp nod and returned to her work.

I ducked out of Judy's office to grab my laptop. While it booted up, I pulled the paper from my pocket. I smoothed it on the table and wiped my palms on my jeans. I took a deep breath, surprised by how nervous I felt. Dial the number, I told myself. An unknown number, it's likely to go to voice mail anyway. All you have to do is say it was lovely to meet you and…what? I keyed in my password trying to think of what to say after that. I had no idea whether it was too soon to ask to get together on the weekend, but with a steady stream of patient samples coming in from the clinic, it wasn't likely that I was going to have any early evenings for a long time.

I berated myself to just leave a message and get on with my work. Nice to meet you and I hope to talk to you soon. That sounded fine. I punched in the number and held my breath, my mind racing forward to the story I would have for my family and friends about how Rosa's research had led to my finding a girlfriend.

Before the first ring ended, an automated message cut in. *The number you have dialed has been disconnected or is no longer in service. If you feel you have reached this recording in error, please check the number and try your call again.*

I frowned and held the screen next to the paper to check for an error. The numbers matched. My heart sank. She'd punked me? That didn't make any sense at all. Remi had definitely been flirting. She had said she hoped she would see me again. She had ideas about how to solve my insomnia. She wouldn't blow me off, would she?

Disappointed, I sat down and stared at the screen. An idea came to me. I opened my email and typed in the address the person at the welcome table had given me and jotted a message letting him know how much I would appreciate the opportunity to volunteer. It didn't hurt to show some follow-through there. I added that Remi had offered to give me insights about volunteering and asked if they might be able to put me in touch with her since the number she had given me mysteriously failed.

This was good, I told myself. Better to not spend the weekend wondering about her calling back. I turned my full attention to the report and Judy's samples, confident that Monday would bring an answer to the question of Remi's number. If luck was on my side, by next Friday, maybe I'd have alternate plans.

CHAPTER FOUR

Luck clearly not on my side, I headed home late, choosing my route to avoid passing my parents' house. I plopped down on my couch and Petri jumped up beside me. Her gentle kneading made me pine for someone to rub the sore spots on my shoulders. My eyes slid shut imagining deft fingers massaging my scalp.

My stomach screamed at me to get up and slap together a sandwich since I'd missed the family dinner. Instead, I sat there mentally arguing with my family about what everyone in the lab understood: Judy Vogelsang prioritized research over all else. I wondered whether there was an excuse Judy would have accepted. An emergency out of my control? Something like a ruptured appendix? Maybe. But if I'd said family member? Forget it. It would have to be my life on the line for her to see the need. She'd probably drive me over to the hospital, hover over the operating team, and return me to the lab as soon as the anesthetic wore off. No, factoring in that Judy was an MD as well as a PhD, she'd more likely sterilize a counter, give me something local for the pain and take out the offending organ herself, so I could return to work immediately.

Then she'd use my appendix for some scientific discovery, and I'd be known not as the brilliant protégée but as the one lucky enough to be saved by the great Dr. Vogelsang. That's what I wanted, wasn't it? To be known as a brilliant scientist? For so long, I had made my career my first priority. Now my thoughts kept returning to Rosa's conclusion, that I needed a girlfriend. That, of course, reminded me of Remi. I still couldn't believe she'd given me a bogus number.

I pushed myself to eat. I toasted some frozen waffles and smeared a good amount of peanut butter in-between. I felt the shadow of Ann beside me and realized how little I'd thought of her since we'd broken up. I'd been so thankful that I didn't have to explain my hours any more, but on a night like tonight, I missed how she would have chastised me for not eating earlier. And whether or not we had sex, she would have been next to me in bed, guaranteeing a sound sleep.

Rosa had outlined three test remedies to treat my insomnia. One involved ingesting something—melatonin. The next was topical—the lavender foot massage. Neither had worked at all for me. The last was breathing and meditation and while it hadn't seemed to improve my sleep, I had developed a routine that soothed me.

Snack finished, I changed into pajamas and found my notebook. Rosa's protocol included listing all the things I was thinking about and giving myself permission to dismiss them all until the next morning. After that I had to stretch. Pen and paper in hand, I settled at the kitchen table and listed out the ideas for my current experiments. The small notepad filled quickly. I hadn't realized how many ideas constantly swarmed through my thoughts until I had started keeping track. Ann had often complained that even when I was at home, my thoughts were still at work. The notepad forced me to admit she'd been right. I held the pen perpendicular to the table and dropped it. The spring engaged, pulling the tip in and returning the pen back to my hand. I clicked it again, dropped it and caught it on the return.

My family had liked Ann and agreed with her complaint that I worked too much. She would have given me a hard time for returning to work tonight. I owed Ann an apology for disregarding her opinion for so many months. I spun the pen around, turned the page and wrote down the apology Ann deserved. I probably wouldn't send it, but it felt good to get it on paper. I placed the pen down and my palm on top of it giving myself permission to leave the thoughts and disengage my brain with my nightly mantra.

When Rosa had assigned the week of meditation, she had sent me home with a handful of ideas, which I'd quickly dismissed. Playing relaxing music made no sense to me. Memorizing a poem sounded like torture, not relaxation, especially when she'd suggested her four-line bedtime prayer. I'd thanked her for the idea, knowing that I'd never be able to use it. The *if I die before I wake* part was too creepy for me.

In place of that, my father had given me a mantra that he said he'd been using for years that clicked with me instantly. He repeated four simple phrases: *Be well. Be content. Be calm. Be at peace.*

His suggestion had surprised me. He'd never mentioned it before. But I did have memories of waking up in the night and finding him sitting in the glow of the TV.

As I'd been doing for weeks, I put my feet up on my bedroom wall and stretched my arms out from my body, hearing all four phrases in my head. I felt my heart pushing blood through my veins. I was well. And yet there were so many sick people counting on science to make them well. That was what pulled me back to the lab tonight.

Not thinking about it! I reminded myself.

Be content. I held the pose and thought about how excited I was to have a sponsor for the drug we had developed in our lab. Many were not as lucky.

Be calm. I breathed in. I breathed out. I would not think about the disappointment of the call that didn't connect.

Be at peace. This was my message to focus on work. It was probably for the best that Remi's number had not gone through. I didn't need another factor in my life to compete for my time.

Keeping my movements as quiet as possible, I used the bathroom and tiptoed to bed as if I were trying not to wake Ann. And now Ann was back in my brain. Great. I resisted the habit of looking at the clock.

Be well. Be content. Be at peace. Be calm, I repeated.

I climbed into bed, lay still and listened to my breath waiting for sleep to claim me.

* * *

Of course sleep didn't claim me. On a typical night, it took me hours to drift to a restless sleep. On good nights, I'd get a four-hour chunk and then spend from three-thirty to five wondering if it would be more productive to get up and read papers than stay in bed and try to sleep. This was one of the nights I glanced at the clock every single hour.

My thoughts kept exploring how well I had slept when I was with Ann. Scientist to the core, I wondered whether I'd slept more soundly on nights we'd had sex, but I had no data from back then. Based on my sleepover with Rosa, I did sleep much better with someone next to me. In the wee hours, I fantasized about how nice it would have been to start new data collection with Remi. After hours of that torture, I came up with two options: call Ann or text my sister and ask to borrow Rosa again. I texted my sister the next day.

That evening, we walked to my house after dinner. I carried leftovers, and Rosa carried a knapsack packed for a sleepover.

"You're not missing your mom and dad, are you?" I asked Rosa when she came back from changing into her pajamas and brushing her teeth.

"Are you kidding me? I was calling them to tell them they can pack my stuff. I'm going to come live with you."

"You already got my old bedroom. Now you want me to give you the spare room here?" I didn't say more, but I could see the wheels spinning in her mind as she fantasized about moving in.

I thought about my own sister and the distance our eight-year difference created. Antonia's girls were also eight years apart. "Nice to have some space from your sister?"

Rosa looked relieved. "It's not that I don't love her, but she's so annoying! Now that she pulls herself up on the furniture, she's always in my stuff."

"Your mom protects your stuff, doesn't she?"

"She tries. With Olivia, I can put things out of reach. But now *Abuela* is watching Beto after school. He doesn't like to do his homework, and he's always into my stuff, too."

"Maybe your mom needs to put something on your door handle, so Beto can't get in your room."

"I don't want to make more work for her."

"Then I'll do it."

"You will?"

"Sure. You can call me when you need help with anything. You know that, right?"

"But you're busy with your research. I can usually figure it out."

"I'm not too busy for you. And I kinda owe you for the sleep study. Not everyone has an award-winning scientist working to solve their problem!"

She blushed at the mention of the prize she'd won. "None of it helped you, though."

"It's okay. Sleep is a tricky thing."

"Not as tricky as your job. You have to do things like test your drug's efficiency."

"Efficacy. How do you know about that?"

"I like to listen when you and *Abuela* talk."

"You were listening when we were doing the dishes? I thought you were watching TV."

"I learn more when I listen to you, especially when you talk to *Abuela*. What's—"

"Efficacy? It means that our drug works the best it can."

"And now you're the boss, so you don't do as many experiments?"

"I'm not the boss, but as the lead research scientist I analyze data and write about it."

"Do you miss the experiments?"

"A little. Now that people are starting to take our drug, I'll be testing to make sure the drug is helping them. Then I'll be at the bench more."

"You have to know how to do a lot of different things."

"That's what makes it fun." I watched Rosa's eyes flutter as she struggled to stay awake. In the year I'd dated Ann, we'd never talked about what I actually did at my job as much as Rosa and I just had, and she'd certainly never tried to keep herself up longer to ask more questions. "Ready for lights out?"

"Yes. I can do my prayer in the dark."

I snapped off the lamp on her bedside table and pulled the blankets around my shoulder. Nine o'clock on a Saturday night, and I was in bed. My bestie Valerie would be disappointed that I wasn't out in public where I might actually meet someone to spend the night with. I nudged the thought away and lay still, not wanting to interrupt Rosa's prayer.

"I prayed that you sleep better tonight," Rosa whispered a minute later.

"Thanks. I appreciate that."

"I didn't pray for you before because I didn't want to mess up the data, but after I finished my project, I added you in."

"You're a natural researcher."

She flashed a smile which faded quickly as her breaths deepened. "Goodnight, *Tía*."

Like a pace car, Rosa's breaths guided mine, and my eyelids grew blessedly heavy. Though I knew I should bid Rosa goodnight, all I could manage was a hum of acknowledgment before sleep claimed me.

* * *

The next morning, I awoke from the deepest sleep I could remember since Rosa stayed over to work on her poster. I started to sit up but remembered Rosa who was still fast asleep beside me. The light outside already conveyed how late I'd slept, but I turned carefully to peek at the clock anyway. Seven. I'd slept ten solid hours without even getting up to pee. That's what had woken me, so I carefully slipped out of bed.

Being in bed so long had made my body ache, so after I finished in the bathroom, I grabbed my phone and lay down on the floor to stretch.

Slept ten solid hours. I'm keeping your kid forever.

Antonia replied immediately. *Is she already up? That one usually sleeps in.*

She's still crashed out. I'm stretching quietly.

She'll sleep through anything. You could do your whole aerobics routine and she'll stay dead to the world.

Still dopey from sleep.

Go back to bed.

Too late. When do you want Rosa back?

Monday morning.

Are you serious? Because I will absolutely keep her for another night of sleep like that.

Ask her. Let me know later.

Sure!

I threw on a sweatshirt and went to grab the newspaper. I had already finished my toast and juice while I read when Rosa emerged from the bedroom.

"You should've poked me when you got up," she grumped and settled onto the barstool next to me. "Abuela will be mad at us for missing mass."

"She will have forgotten about it by the time you get back home tomorrow." Rosa blinked in confusion, so I added. "Your mom said I could keep you today and collect more data for this breakthrough with your sleep study."

"Breakthrough?" Rosa's face lit up.

"I slept alllllllll night, so your first sleepover wasn't a fluke. We've got more evidence to back up your hypothesis."

Rosa threw her arms around me. "I was right!"

"What do you say to spending the day here?"

"Don't you have to go to the lab?"

"With no new samples coming in over the weekend, I don't have anything to check. I can analyze data and write reports anywhere. I could even write at the beach." The ability to work without having to be in the lab all day was fantastic, especially since it made spending the day with my niece possible.

"Yes!"

"Ready for breakfast? You want cereal?"

"Sure." Rosa's brow furrowed.

"What?"

"I'm happy that you slept well last night, but that means that we should have been looking for a girlfriend instead of having you meditate or take melatonin."

"I told you it's not your job to find me a girlfriend."

She poured cereal in her bowl, looking thoughtful. "Maybe we'll find her at the beach. I can do my homework while you work, and we'll both be on the lookout."

"Now you sound like a detective."

"Detectives search for answers too. It's not so different."

"I can't argue with that. You sure you're okay if I do some of my work?" I couldn't help hearing Ann's complaints hurled my way at the suggestion of taking a laptop with us to a coffee shop, let alone the beach.

"As long as you promise to look up once in a while. Maybe the pretty judge will be there!"

When she said that, my stomach fluttered. Was that possible? Here I was thinking about the past. Rosa had a much better idea to keep my focus on the future.

CHAPTER FIVE

"G'day." Valerie gave me a squeeze around the shoulders as she sat down next to me on the patio outside the small campus café that sold snacks, sandwiches, salads, and soups. It was the tall Aussie who had observed the place's predilection for food that started with the letter S. Valerie had just begun her postdoc, the low-pay entry point on the path to being a Primary Investigator with a lab of her own. Many shared lunch tables led to a friendship that had supported me through my breakup and celebrated Valerie's marriage to her wife, Emma. "You look well rested," she said.

I scowled at the sarcastic inflection. "I never should have told you about the sleep study."

"I disagree. We've all lucked out."

I laughed. When I'd been in the rub-lavender-on-your-feet week of Rosa's sleep study, I'd complained about the smell. After the first night of my hands stinking of the oil, I took home some gloves, but I did not find snapping them on to smear oil on my feet at all restful. I'd quickly passed it on to Valerie having barely made it through the week.

"Emma finds it very soothing."

"Like that helps me." My thoughts flitted to Remi. Her solution for my insomnia would probably not involve lavender oil.

"I think you didn't expect anything to help."

"You try taking melatonin. It makes everything taste awful, almost as bad as valerian."

"I don't have trouble sleeping."

"No, but you have Emma."

"I do, and, sorry to say, mate, I'm with her on this. Nothing helped you because you didn't even give it a chance to help." Emma taught interpretive dance and believed in esoteric things like miracles. Valerie and I often talked about the irony of a hundred scientists grounded in replicable data working at a place called The Miracle Center.

I sighed heavily. I would have taken a chance on giving Remi's idea a try in a heartbeat. "I tried to give something a chance…" I stopped. I hadn't wanted to tell Valerie about Remi, but I couldn't stop thinking about her.

"What?"

"At Rosa's science fair, I sort of met someone."

"What's that mean, sort of?"

I described the flirtatious exchange and the embarrassment courtesy of my niece, ending with my disappointment with the phone call.

"Crikey, you're a researcher. How hard is it to find out who the judges were? You should be able to find her in a snap!"

"I already tried that. They said they don't have a judge named Remi."

"She's got to be affiliated with one of the schools in the area. Couldn't you hang about and see if you spot her again?"

"Sure. That's not at all creepy."

Valerie slapped her knee and laughed as she shook her head. "What I would have given to see Rosa telling that hot judge that she needed someone to sleep with her aunt!"

"She meant someone to sleep in my bed. She made a prediction and early research suggests she's accurate. She slept over a week ago, and I was dead to the world the whole night. Once she was back home, I fell right back into restless nights."

"Well you need to do something because you look like shit."

"I know. I thought I was managing fine with the amount of sleep I was getting. Since I started trying to sleep better, though, I realize how messed up my sleep pattern really is. I thought once I finished my PhD I'd sleep better. Or once I figured out where I was working I'd sleep better, but I've hit those goals, and my mind keeps spinning."

"And now it's spinning on how you can't sleep. That can't be helpful. I'd offer to come over, but I don't think Emma would be keen on that."

"No. You've got your own stresses. Any luck this month?" Valerie and Emma had been trying home insemination for three months.

Valerie pushed her pasta salad around with her fork. "No. I was so ready to break out the 'third time's a charm,' but…"

"I'm sorry."

"Me too. I told her I thought we should try going to the clinic in San Diego, but she wants to try one more time at home. She says that a sterile environment doesn't exactly inspire the miracle of life."

We ate in silence. "I'll worry for you while I can't sleep."

"You're a good friend. I'm going to get some tea. You want anything?"

"Tea doesn't start with 'S'."

"I'll get soda, then."

"You mean sugar water. I'll pass."

Valerie returned with her drink and set a chocolate cookie in front of me. "They had your favorite, so I grabbed one for you."

"Thanks. You have to split it with me, though. Unless I find time to exercise, I can't afford the calories."

"Run the campus with me. I'll kick yer arse."

"No surprise there."

* * *

"I hate this." I pushed on my knees as I climbed the third flight of stairs two days later when I joined Valerie on her exercise routine. "And I hate you."

"Arms up, you twit! You're burying yourself there!" Valerie trotted back down the stairs, pivoted and climbed the stairs again. "Chest up, legs up!"

I swatted at my friend and stopped at the landing, chest heaving.

"Don't give it away, mate. You can make it!"

"You go."

"Like hell." Valerie did jumping jacks as she waited.

I knew that the longer I stopped, the more difficult it would be to climb the next set of stairs. My friend's endurance was maddening. I should take comfort in knowing that Valerie worked for her toned body, but I didn't, at least not when she seemed to climb the stairs of The Miracle Center's main hospital effortlessly. I took a deep breath, lifted my torso and faced the next flight.

"Here we go!"

"Remind me why we're doing this?"

"You're the one who said how bad it would be for someone studying diabetes to be diabetic."

"It's more than..." my need for oxygen punctuated my thoughts, "...diet and exercise. That study..."

"I know all about the study. You and your epigenetics. Save it for the ladies. I won't let you turn into a pudgy, pale lab rat."

"Pudgy, maybe, but pale?" My panting echoed in the stairwell. My parents were Hispanic. I could stay inside all day everyday and never be considered pale.

"You know what I mean. Stay inside, it doesn't matter what skin tone you have. You've got to get out of the lab. Your skin misses the sun. Vitamin D. Come to the house this weekend. I've got my doubles volleyball tourney. You can help me warm up and catch some rays."

"Can't."

"You're not in the lab Saturday."

"No."

"You have a date," Valerie fired back so quickly I had a hard time answering.

"Not really."

"What's that supposed to mean, not really?"

My muscles screamed. I waved away Valerie's question, focused only on getting more oxygen to ease the burn.

"Got it. Save your breath. Let's see. You have a research strategy to find your hot judge and start this weekend."

"Nope," I gasped.

"The spring interns roll in, and you're doing a walk-through of the lab?"

"No."

"Your sister needs you to babysit?"

I shook my head, instantly regretting the action as a wave of dizziness swept through me.

"One of the little people has a game?"

"No."

"Family barbeque? If that's it, why am I not invited?"

All I could manage was my best glare.

"Step it up then. I'm out of guesses." Valerie dropped behind me and gave me a nudge from the back.

Swatting at her again, I made the last few steps up to the fifth floor. Gasping for breath, I rested my head against the railing waiting for the lightheadedness to pass. How could my feet feel like lead when my head felt like it could float away?

My so-called friend squatted and kicked her feet back as if she was going to do a pushup but then hopped back up. She smiled wickedly every time she stood, and I knew that she expected me to join in.

"I really do hate you. I should've taken that position at Johns Hopkins."

"You were never leaving. C'mon. Let's get our view."

I followed her to the panoramic window where we could see the sweep of the research center a half-hour north of San Diego. My building, which housed diabetes research, sat three hundred and fifty yards southwest of the hospital. I knew the exact measurement because Valerie had mapped out a precise two-mile walk around the campus. Valerie's building, which contained the cancer research labs, sat below mine and had no view, and though the coastal breeze made her twice-a-week afternoon walks pleasant, Valerie liked to climb the stairs to see the ocean beyond the campus.

Valerie said, "Out with it. Why can't you come out to the beach with us this weekend?"

"My brother won tickets to the Padres game."

"Called the radio, did he?" When I confirmed, she mumbled, "Unbelievable. The luck in your family!"

"He's got a special knack for sure."

"It's your whole family. Your drug might be going to a clinical trial! It's going to be huge. Put you on the map. Dr. Vogelsang's been trying for how many years, and when you decide to stay, she finally gets a sponsor? You've got it, too."

"Maybe."

"Maybe? What does that mean, maybe? The sponsor is excited, yeah?" Valerie asked.

"The research is going well. We've got steady volunteer recruitment. We're culturing their white blood cells. Looks like our treatment is reducing retinal adhesion molecules which hopefully correlates to decreased white blood cell adhesion to retinal tissue associated with blindness. Judy is meeting with the sponsor to discuss dosage and delivery of the drug, and the FDA Fast-Track application."

Her gaze out on the ocean, Valerie's expression put her miles further than anything she could see on the California coast. "What I would give to work with her."

"You hate diabetes research. And it's creepy how you crush on my boss."

"Who wouldn't? She's beautiful, intelligent, and driven. I don't know how you get any work done at all. If I worked in that lab, I'd stare at her adoringly all day."

"Even if it wasn't unethical and inappropriate to date your boss, she's not gay."

"You don't know that. You've never seen her *partner*..."

"Judy lives at the lab. Her partner never sees *her*. And I'd put money on that being a man that she keeps in his place by using 'partner' instead of 'husband.'"

"I wouldn't mind being put in my place by…"

"Enough. You are so gross! I'm going to tell your *wife* that you have a thing for my boss."

"Go right ahead. She feels the pull of Dr. Vogelsang's magnetism as well."

I looked out at the ocean and wished we were staring at the waves from where we could hear them pounding on the shore. The campus bustle inhibited the peace that should come with such a view. "I didn't stay in her lab because she's hot."

"Ah! Finally you agree that you've got a crush on her."

"No way do I have a crush."

"Then why is it so hard for you to say no to her?"

"Because she's my boss! I'm sure you don't say no to your PI!"

"I do when it counts; like when Emma miscarried and needed me at home."

Her words snuffed the lightheartedness from our conversation. I knew that she disapproved of my working relationship with Judy, that I should stand up for myself more, but I also knew that she was jealous of the trajectory of my career. I didn't know how to respond.

She waved her hand as if to erase her last comment. "Crush or not, your involvement in this clinical trial is your ticket. With your name associated with a drug that's a potential blockbuster, you'll get your own lab for sure!" By unspoken agreement we turned and headed for the stairs to continue the workout.

"That's still what you want, isn't it? Your own lab? Your own research? Your own team?"

"Of course," I said, my eyes on the stairs.

"You don't sound very excited." Jogging with ease, Valerie continued, "Have you finally realized that no matter how great success is, it's nothing if you don't have someone to share it with?"

I grunted.

We pushed through the ground-level doors, inhaling deeply. Gardenia hedges perfumed the air. Freshly cut grass gave a new-day tang even though the sun was dipping toward its coastal sunset. Purple jacarandas shadowed the path back to our buildings.

"Still hung up on the judge?"

"It doesn't make sense. She wouldn't say that she had some ideas for the sleep study and then give me the wrong number."

"But what are you supposed to do? Wait until next year and hope she judges again?"

"There's an idea," I grumbled.

Valerie smacked me. "That's no solution! I was messing with you! Come to dinner. We'll ask Emma." We stopped in front of Valerie's building.

"How's she going to help?"

"She has herself tuned into things like energy and fate. If you're meant to find this Remi, she'll have some ideas."

Valerie disappeared into her building, and I slowly made my way back to my lab wishing I felt as enthusiastic about my research going as well as it was. I had what I had always told Ann I wanted, but if that was true, why was it so hard to stay focused?

* * *

I took a deep breath as I pushed through the heavy glass doors and did my best to bound up the stairs, still hearing Valerie's earlier prodding. I stopped at the bathroom to change and splash water on my face before I went back to my bench. I was still sweaty and red-faced when I heard someone clear her throat behind me and say, "Dr. Hernandez?"

I turned and found Red Lips wringing her hands and damnit if my stomach didn't do the dip and spin. I blushed before I could help it. *Stop!* I scolded myself. *So young!* I yelled at myself hoping that being overheated hid the blush I felt warming my face. Confronted by her again, I could see just how very young she was. Only a few years out of high school. She had a roundness to her face, baby-fat chubbiness that, I was embarrassed to admit, often lifted a "prediabetic" flag of concern. I spent so much time researching the disease it was hard to tell my brain to give it a rest.

"I wanted to apologize," Red Lips said.

"Accepted." She wasn't part of our lab and taking time to work out with Valerie meant I needed to buckle down and get back to work. It was hard enough after discussing Remi. The chiseled bob that set off Remi's delicate jawline flashed in my mind once again, and I imagined her approaching from behind, interrupting me with a kiss. Startled by the image and the heat I felt, I turned back to my pipettes, hoping that having delivered her apology Red Lips would leave. She didn't. "Are you interning in Bautista's lab?" I asked.

"I go to Beachside Community College. My biology professor has this service-learning project, and The Miracle Center is easiest to get to. But I wish I was in your lab."

"Something wrong with Dr. Bautista's lab?"

She scouted over her shoulder before she said, "The guy I'm supposed to work with hardly ever speaks English, and when he does, I still don't understand him."

I frowned. I knew how different cultures could affect how smoothly a lab ran. Before meeting Valerie, I would have argued that anyone could communicate through science, but cultural conflicts made work difficult for Valerie, and it seemed this young woman was experiencing the same thing. I hadn't signed up for this service-learning project, but I didn't see enough young Latinas interested in the sciences and didn't want to turn my back on this one. "What's your name?"

"Maricela Gonzales." She extended her hand.

"At least you found gloves. Not that you'd want to contaminate them shaking my hand."

Maricela pulled her hand back making me want to kick myself, knowing how easily young women could be discouraged. And if women in the sciences were rare, Latinas were even more so. That alone was a reason to encourage this woman. I resolved to behave more like a mentor and less like a critic.

Red matching her lips the day she'd nearly destroyed the lab equipment crept across her cheeks.

"Sorry."

"Mistakes are part of learning. Don't be afraid to ask for help, okay? I practically live here."

"I have a lot of questions."

"Questions are good. Keep asking them. That's what science is about."

Her smile was hesitant.

"You have a question now?"

She nodded, and I sighed, I hoped not too loudly. I put my samples on ice and hoped it was something I could answer quickly.

CHAPTER SIX

Valerie and Emma lived in a Spanish bungalow a block from the beach. At least twice a month, they invited me for dinner. I stowed my Pacìfico beer in the fridge and offered to help. As usual, Emma said she had it all under control, but said I could serve up the beers. I held up two fingers and then flashed three. Emma shook her head, so I popped two caps while I listened again to her plans to remodel the house. Built in the mid-twenties, it had a tiny kitchen she wanted to expand by taking out the wall that separated it from the dining area. That part stayed constant, but Emma often had a new twist she'd picked up from a magazine or a TV show. Tonight, she talked about counters—granite versus composite.

"As if we have money for either," Valerie said when I handed her a beer in the tiny dining area next to the kitchen.

"Doesn't cost anything to dream," Emma said.

Emma's tone was light, but Valerie looked away. I immediately thought of how expensive their pregnancy project was, and I knew that, ever so much more than a new kitchen, they dreamed of having a baby. Valerie was awfully intent on her beer label, making me wonder where they were in the math, counting days until ovulation or until they would find out whether they were pregnant. I felt exhausted for them.

"How's your research going?" Emma asked, probably trying to direct all our thoughts away from her uterus.

"Great! It's still early, but the human studies are looking very promising, which is getting the sponsor excited."

Emma walked to the doorway, her hand on her hip. Strangers mistook Emma and Valerie for sisters all the time. Both tall, blond, and athletic, many people labeled their closeness as genetic instead of romantic until Valerie revealed her Australian accent. "Are you still working with your fat little diabetic mice?"

"We're finished with them for now. We might come back to them. I have one of our postdocs working with the mice exploring other therapeutic targets. My boss is already riding my ass to help with the fast-track status with the FDA. They seem to think this drug has huge potential, since there's nothing out there at all to treat diabetic blindness. All the complaints Ann had about the time I spent at work are even more valid now. Judy's made it very clear that she expects me to live in the lab."

"You can't use work as an excuse. I work just as much as you do," Valerie said.

"More," Emma interjected.

Valerie rolled her eyes good-naturedly and continued. "And it's not a problem because Emma has her own life. The problem with Ann was that she counted on you to be home. She was too needy. That's her fault, not yours."

"Val's right. Ann was not driven enough." Emma set bread on the table and squeezed my shoulder.

I attempted to defend Ann. "She was an entrepreneur."

"She said she was going to start a dog-walking business until she figured out that walking a dog meant going outside where she had trouble seeing her phone," Valerie reminded me. "She filled your garage with books that she picked up at thrift stores and said she was going to sell online. Did she ever actually *make* any money or just manage to spend yours?"

Emma brought a colorful quinoa salad to the table. "You need someone with the same energy you have."

Emma talked about energy a lot. I smiled and accepted that she more freely embraced the unknown and classified any inexplicable phenomenon as "energy" even though I felt more comfortable with something that could be scientifically proven.

"What you call drive," Emma revised. "I know where your brain goes when I say energy."

Valerie and I shared a guilty look.

"I will say, though, your energy is great. You're finally projecting that you're available."

Valerie scrutinized me. "She's exactly the same as the last time we saw her."

Emma rolled her eyes. "Trust me. She's radiating desire."

I peered down at myself and then to Valerie who raised her shoulders and then dropped them. "Don't see it."

"You wouldn't, and not just because your science brain has locked that door tight. You, of course, only have eyes for me."

Valerie tipped back to accept a chaste kiss from her wife. "I won't argue with that."

"Back to you," Emma said, setting down a plate of crispy baked chicken and gesturing to begin serving ourselves. "I mean you need someone with her own drive. Someone who understands that being a professional comes with demands. Someone who doesn't expect you to hold her on the couch every night."

I pictured Remi again. Her image alone was the polar opposite of Ann. Ann, who could spend an entire day in her pajamas, whereas my whole day felt off kilter if I wasn't dressed by eight. I would bet Remi was the type to get up early without an alarm and go for a run to clear her mind for her day's work.

"You're thinking about this judge again." Emma held up her glass of water. Valerie and I held up our bottles, and we clinked our drinks. "To energy."

There was something inexplicable about the energy I'd felt at the fair, something that had crackled between me and Remi. "To energy," I agreed.

"Okay. Now back to where to look for her."

"I thought we were trusting my energy."

"That only gets you so far. You can't sit back and passively wait for her to come to you. You have to get out there. I have a suggestion. Go to a MeetUp for science professionals. They have them. I checked."

"Why do I feel like I was tricked into a spot where I can't say no?"

"Because that's Emma's thing. Welcome to my life." She leaned over for another kiss. "When's the next MeetUp?"

"I'm so glad you asked. It's tomorrow in San Diego. I can put the address in your phone after dinner."

"My phone?" Valerie asked.

"If you don't go, Karla will promise to go and then say that her PI made her work."

Valerie glared at me. "She's got you pegged, mate."

"Is there any way out of this?" I asked.

"Nope!" Emma said. "Your job is to be here at five. Valerie will navigate you."

"What exactly do I get out of this?" Valerie asked.

"Are you kidding? Karla is your designated driver, and you have a chance to get shnockered."

"Excellent!"

"You've figured everything else out, so you might as well tell me what to wear while you're at it," I grumbled.

"No plaid."

I looked down at my plaid shirt. "I don't *always* wear plaid." I looked to Valerie for support.

"Ah, you sort of do, mate," Valerie said apologetically.

* * *

As instructed, I met Valerie the next night dressed in a forest-green blouse and black slacks. Having passed inspection, I made the drive south to San Diego with Valerie.

"I'm doing this purely because Emma went to all this trouble. What are the chances that we'll see this woman in San Diego? Who drives down to San Diego on a Saturday night?"

"Judging by all these cars, a lot of people. Including us."

I navigated the traffic wishing I had gone into the lab and told Emma and Valerie that I'd had too much work to make the MeetUp. "Any progress on your dream?" I said to break the silence.

"Speaking of chances." Valerie sounded downtrodden. "You know what they say! Out of the millions of sperm per ejaculate, it only takes one!"

"Thanks for getting me thinking about ejaculation."

"You're not the one warming a vial of sperm in your armpit."

"No, I'm not. And I'd rather not picture the details."

"So no talking about what syringe to bring home from the lab?" Valerie asked.

"You don't!" I shot her an incredulous look.

"No. The clinic actually sends a whole kit with…"

"Again, don't need to think about it."

A few minutes passed before Valerie added, "You probably don't want to hear about how orgasm can help the sperm enter the uterus. You see…"

"Don't want to know! Don't need to know!"

"How can this bother you? You're a scientist. Don't the details fascinate you? Think about that. All those little swimmers, and your job…"

"I'm sure the procedure is very interesting minus the details that make me think about you having sex with your wife."

"That's fair."

I felt bad for cutting off my friend. "Will Emma try the clinic next time?"

"Nope."

"But you said the success rate is higher when they do the insemination."

"Yes, well. She'd rather us try switching ovens before we go to a lab."

"Switching ovens? What does that mean?" I looked over at Valerie, but she was staring out the window. "You mean you? Your uterus? You'd carry the baby?"

"That's the idea. Can't very well get me pregnant and move the fetus to her uterus."

"Is that okay with you? I thought she was the oven because it was easier for her to take time off from the studio. Wouldn't Dr. Seonwoo flip?" It was easy to predict how Judy would react if I were to get knocked up.

"You know what they say. I'll jump off that bridge when I come to it."

"I don't think that's how it goes." I glanced over again and saw Valerie's worried look. "You're that scared?"

"The whole time, it's been Emma wanting to be pregnant. I want a family and her being pregnant made sense. This…"

"It's bigger?"

"A hell of a lot bigger."

The rest of the hour-long drive was quiet until Valerie's phone chirped out directions to Sloan's Grill and Arcade. I wasn't sure what to say to Valerie, but she jumped out of the car before I could think of anything. The noise inside obviated talking anyway, so I braced myself for the screeching of the video games and the big-screen TVs and tried to calm my anxiety. I hated places like this. "How are we supposed to talk to anyone with all this noise?"

"The restaurant side isn't so loud. But let's find the bevies first," Valerie said, heading to the bar.

Valerie ordered a pale ale for herself and a virgin margarita for me. Drinks procured, we headed into the restaurant and found a small group socializing awkwardly in the corner. I was immediately grateful to Emma for sending Valerie. The moment she introduced the two of us as scientists from The Miracle Center, everyone was asking about her accent and how long she had been in the United States. As long as she had a beer in her hand, chatting with strangers did not sap her energy as it did mine. It was easy to fade into the woodwork, especially when, as I'd suspected, the universe had not placed Remi in the group.

"Are you cancer as well?" a member of the group who had clearly consumed a good deal of beer leaned over to ask.

"Diabetes."

"Oh, I heard that Miracle Center might be collaborating with a biotech on a hot clinical trial. Do you know Dr. Vogelsang?"

"Yes," I said honestly.

"Devon," the man said, thrusting his hand into mine. "I would kill to postdoc in that lab." Getting the attention of others in the group, he gave a rundown of the work my lab was doing. "And she knows her."

Valerie gave me a questioning look. I ever so slightly shook my head. If I admitted that I actually worked with Judy, there would be no way to dislodge myself from the discussion. I didn't want to talk to a guy about work. I wanted to talk to one specific woman about sparks. "I heard her talk at a campus symposium. Her postdocs were grousing about how unreasonable her hours are."

"Oh, I thought you knew her."

I knew her all too well. I saw her more days than not. It didn't matter how early I got to work or how late I stayed, Judy was there. And present. "You're studying diabetes as well?" I asked, hoping that switching the focus to him would at least end his inquiry about Judy's lab.

"Tying up loose ends in the lab where I did my grad work at UCLA." I got what I'd hoped in terms of him not digging for more information about Dr. Vogelsang. However, he launched into tedious details about his methodology on a paper that had recently been accepted. I kept looking for a way to dislodge myself politely from the conversation. Still nodding noncommittally at Devon, I startled when Valerie elbowed me.

"What?" I snapped at my friend, her eyebrows high on her forehead, and nodding in Devon's direction.

Devon waited expectantly. "Have you read Hyperglycemia-Induced Damage to Target Proteins Leading to Retinopathy and Blindness in Diabetes?" he asked. "Hernandez and Vogelsang's paper. I've read it through a half dozen times looking for an angle to build on."

"I haven't had a chance yet," I lied. I pulled on Valerie's sleeve. "But Valerie's been talking about it, too."

"Seeing a similar correlation in human cells would be exciting, wouldn't it?"

Had I come clean about knowing Judy, it would have been fun to talk with such a thorough reader about my findings. Why had I lied? I was a terrible liar and kicked myself for putting myself in a position where I would have to carefully monitor what I said for the remainder of the evening. Stuck now, I listened to Valerie fake her way through the conversation based on the scope of knowledge she had from our chats.

"I owe you a beer," I whispered, taking Valerie's empty glass. I wished I could convince Valerie to turn around and leave, but after fighting traffic to get there, Valerie wasn't about to get back in the car anytime soon. While I waited at the bar, I started to text Emma about my predicament. As I typed, I breathed in a sweet scent that sent my mind spinning. I closed my eyes and inhaled again, willing my memory to place it. I breathed in the lazy days of vacation. I breathed in purple, and my mind snapped to the scent. Lilac.

"Ale and a water," the bartender said.

I opened my eyes and pocketed my phone, message unsent. Accepting the drinks, I raised the glass of water to take a sip and at the same moment recognized Remi. I inhaled sharply, and I was seized by a coughing fit. I clumsily set down the glasses as I tried to catch my breath.

Remi reached out and placed a hand on my shoulder. "Are you okay?"

I am now, almost left my lips. Not trusting my voice, I nodded and blinked. "I don't seem to be able to breathe around you." Yeah, that was better. I almost smacked myself in the forehead.

"Karla!" Recognition shifted her tone. "Oh my goodness! Are you okay? Do you need to sit down?"

"I'm fine," I uttered between coughs. I risked a sip of water and cleared my throat. "Just a little water down my windpipe. I really do quite well with this whole breathing thing most of the time."

"I guess I'll take your word for it." Remi glanced at the arcade and then back to me as if she was trying to decide whether to say something more. Her eyebrows pulled together, and she said, "You never called."

"I did!" I insisted. "You gave me the wrong number."

"I did not!"

I pulled my phone from my pocket and pulled up my call history. I tipped the screen toward Remi for her to see. Remi crossed her arms over her chest. "You dialed wrong. That's not my number. You reversed the seven and the three."

"But I checked, and my friend checked! I'm sure I dialed the number you gave me." I wanted to throw my arms around her. Squabbling over her number wasn't what I'd imagined happening when I saw her again. My heartrate surged. I'd found her!

"Oh." Remi bit her lip. "Did I mention I'm dyslexic?"

My defensiveness dissolved. All could be forgiven since we now stood in front of each other again, couldn't it? "I don't think we got past talking about my insomnia."

Remi opened her mouth to reply, but then stopped. I jumped as an arm slung around my shoulder.

"Way to leave me in the lion's den!" Valerie said, plucking her ale off the bar, oblivious to the woman next to me.

Remi took in Valerie's close proximity, immediately taking a step back. I quickly disentangled myself. "Valerie, this is Remi, the judge I was telling you about."

Valerie's jaw literally dropped.

"And this is my *colleague* and *friend* Valerie."

Remi extended her hand. "Nice to meet you."

Valerie whooped louder than necessary. "I can't believe this worked!"

"What worked?" Remi continued to look between the two of us.

"My wife sent us here to find you when Karla here hit a dead end asking the science fair people for your contact info."

"You asked the school?"

"I told you. The number you gave me didn't work."

The bartender set two drinks in front of Remi. She closed her beautiful eyes for a moment as if she were collecting herself. "I was a last-minute substitute for someone who got sick, and the principal at one of my schools volunteered me. They had my given name, Andromeda."

I wanted her to say her given name again. I maybe thought I'd read a story with the name Andromeda in it before, but I'd never met anyone with the name. "Andromeda?" I tried my best to mimic her pronunciation.

"Yes. Remi is a childhood nickname that stuck."

"So you teach science?" Valerie asked.

"Oh, no. I'm a behavioral psychologist. I work at several district schools with special-needs children." Remi's gaze slipped away to the arcade once again and her sparkle faded for a moment. She was with someone, I realized, remembering the drinks waiting to be delivered. I felt as if I'd been punched in the gut. As if reading my mind, Remi picked up the two glasses.

"Do you want to join us?" Valerie asked. "It's quieter here at the bar than it is in the arcade."

"I'm sorry I can't. I've been away too long." She held up the glasses in a subtle toast as she left.

"She didn't want to go, right?" I asked Valerie. "She looked reluctant, right? Not excited to get back to whoever's in the arcade?"

"You twit," Valerie snapped as Remi walked away. "Did you even get her real number?"

"No. The wrong number thing probably blew my chance. She's obviously here with someone. Two drinks. Nice to see you. Goodbye. I'm such a dork. Can we go now?" I rubbed my eyes with my fingertips, groaning audibly. "We can't go back to the MeetUp after I lied to Devon about whose lab I work in."

Valerie jabbed me.

"Don't. I know I'm an idiot."

Valerie pushed me harder. I opened my eyes to see Devon standing at the bar.

"You do work in Dr. Vogelsang's lab?"

I hadn't anticipated my lie snapping me in the ass so quickly. Devon stood there like an excited puppy. His dark hair and goatee were immaculately groomed, and beneath that pristine layer, he vibrated with energy waiting for direction. I had no time for puppies jumping for attention and following me nonstop. I was caught, though, and I knew it. I ground my teeth, knowing I had to come clean about everything. "That was my paper you were talking about."

"You're Dr. Hernandez?" Now he looked like a kicked puppy. "Why didn't you say so?"

My gaze drifted toward the arcade. Why had I lied to Devon when I hadn't even known that Remi was there? For the first time I could remember, I didn't want to talk about my research. I wanted to talk to a beautiful woman about lilacs and summertime.

When Remi reappeared in the doorway, I thought my imagination had conjured the image, but my imagination would have only gone as far as offering a lingering look. I wouldn't have dared to go as far as seeing Remi walk back in my direction.

"I don't get it. Why wouldn't you want to talk about your paper?" Devon asked.

I had to answer Devon, but I was very distracted by Remi whose every step made my heart beat harder. "Like you said, the collaboration is in its early stages. It's all confidential, and I can't speak about it. Dr. Vogelsang has put us in lockdown for now."

"Come on. Your paper was in *The Journal of Cell Science*. That's clearly not hush-hush. Can't you talk about that?"

Remi extended her hand. "I forgot to correct my number on your phone."

I typed in my code and handed the phone to Remi. She tapped in her number and handed it back, lingering for a moment. "I wish I could stay. I'd like to share my ideas about your sleep study."

"Sleep study?" Devon asked as I watched Remi slip back into the arcade. "I thought you were in diabetes."

I wondered if this could be my out for the evening. "I really can't talk about it."

"Sleep or diabetes?"

"Neither. Look, I promised my friend I wouldn't talk about work." Though Valerie looked confused, I leaned closer to Devon and whispered that Valerie had received news that she'd just had a paper rejected. "We were already scheduled to come out when she got the letter. I'm sure you understand that I don't want to rub salt in her wound. Honestly? We want to drink and forget work."

"That is rough. I get it. Maybe next time." He waved and walked away.

"What did you say to get him to leave?"

"That your paper was rejected and you want to drown your sorrow in beer."

"Wow, I'm a downer!"

"I'm sorry! What was I supposed to say? All I want to do is go home. I wanted to talk to Remi, not some guy who will eventually ask me to set up an interview with Judy. I want a girlfriend, not a colleague."

"'S'okay, mate. You've got Remi's number, and you saved us some earbashing. It'll come good. But I was promised a shnockered night out and look what they've got on the telly!" She pointed to a flatscreen behind the bar. "The Wallabies are playing the NZ All Blacks! We're not leaving until someone's chanting Aussie, Aussie, Aussie! Oi! Oi! Oi!"

"You're the only person who ever does that."

"Well then, let's get started!"

Seeing that Emma's plan had worked to find Remi, I couldn't begrudge Valerie more time out. I kept my eye on the arcade, hoping to catch sight of Remi when she left.

"Bloody hell, go on and call her now," Valerie said when I failed to keep up with the conversation.

"But what if she's on a date?"

"Then it's with the wrong person. Seems to be going around."

"I'm sorry I'm not better company."

"I'm just razzing you. You could text."

"You think?"

She shrugged. "Why not? I think she's into you. Could be girl's night out for her, too, but she doesn't want any of her mates to see you and get any smart ideas."

I didn't reach for my phone. "Tomorrow. Otherwise I look desperate."

"Might as well let her know what she's signing up for."

"Some friend you are," I said.

"Love you too." Valerie smiled devilishly as she tipped her pint back again.

CHAPTER SEVEN

Even though I knew my phone hadn't rung while I changed into my workout clothes, I couldn't help swiping the screen to confirm I hadn't missed a call. I'd waited until mid-morning to call Remi and had left a message. Was that lame? Maybe I should have texted instead?

I pushed myself into a vigorous walk to warm up my muscles on the way to meet Valerie. Between our buildings, there was a bronze statue of a man sitting on a bench reading a paper. It unnerved me enough that I'd programmed my brain to ignore the bench altogether. I'd nearly passed it when I realized an actual person sat next to the statue, and I had passed by entirely before recognizing the waterfall of thick, black hair. I stopped and turned to watch the young woman engrossed by her phone. I hadn't seen Maricela in the lab since her apology and my awkward offer to help her, which had resulted in a surprisingly satisfying tutorial on the purpose of the spectrophotometer.

Given the amount of time I spent in the lab, I had expected to see her again.

If I stopped, I'd be late. If I continued, I worried that I wouldn't see Maricela again. Curiosity got the best of me. "Maricela?"

She looked up, surprised. Then guilt flashed across her face. "Hey." She switched off her phone and tucked it into the front pocket of her gray hoodie.

"Are you finished with your service-learning project?"

Maricela looked away. "I'm dropping that class, so I stopped going."

"What?" I couldn't mask the disappointment in my voice.

Maricela shrugged. "It was too hard."

I looked at my watch. I couldn't afford to linger. I barely knew Maricela. What did it matter if she dropped science? Still, I found myself feeling a little maternal toward the younger woman. The way she refused to look at me, I figured she wasn't happy about her decision. "Did you drop already?"

"I haven't figured out how to yet."

"Have you talked to the professor?"

Maricela's "No" fired back so quickly, it gave me an idea. "Hang on." I pulled out my phone and called Valerie. "Go on without me," I said without preamble.

"You're skipping?" Valerie said, accepting the baton of disappointment that I'd picked up from Maricela and passed to her.

"No. I'm walking. But I can't do your pace today. I'll explain later."

"I'm intrigued. If you don't get good cardio, do that aerobics DVD I lent you."

"I hate that aerobics DVD."

Valerie dismissed the complaint with an exaggerated kiss and was gone.

"If you're not doing the service-learning project, why are you here?"

"My mom's diabetic. She's a patient here and has an appointment."

"How long does that take?"

Maricela shrugged. "Maybe forty minutes."

"Let's go."

"Where are we going?" Maricela asked, standing.

"Being Latina, I have twice the chance of developing type two diabetes as a white person. You know that, right? I know what side of that percentage I want to be on, so I exercise. I promised my workout buddy that I would walk, so we'll circle the campus while we talk."

"I don't walk."

I bit back the *you should* that sat at the tip of my tongue. I started walking, stewing over Maricela's stubbornness. I smiled when I felt her jogging to catch up with me. We walked in silence while I weighed out all I wanted to say.

"How many classes are you taking?"

"Three. Biology, math and English."

"How are math and English going?"

Maricela shrugged, and I wanted to shake the indifference out of her. I rephrased. "You said you're not passing bio. Are you passing math and English?"

"I think I'm passing English," she answered. Already her breath was labored, and we had barely begun to walk through the beautifully groomed campus.

"You think? If you shrug again, I won't be able to help myself. I'll have to pop you."

Maricela turned wary eyes my way.

"I have two older siblings. I know what it takes to keep a punk in line."

Maricela acquiesced. "I've gotten C's on most of my papers. I turn in my homework."

"The teacher must make your grade available."

"There's this school website she says we can use."

"But you haven't."

"No."

Though the young woman's lack of student skills frustrated me, at least she hadn't shrugged. "What are you hoping to get out of school?"

"A degree?"

What was it with young people delivering statements as questions? Did she have any idea why she was in school? "In what?" I pressed.

"I haven't picked a major yet."

"Knowing what you're working toward helps with motivation."

No response.

"Do you mind if I make a suggestion?"

"Does it matter?"

"No. I'm going to tell you because you need to hear it from someone, and it might as well be me. Talk to your teachers. Ask them for help. Get this English teacher to show you how to check your grade so you *know* you're passing. Then check your math grade. Make an appointment to talk to your biology teacher to see if you can salvage your grade. I'm sure the campus has tutoring. Go. Put some effort into it. Do you have a job?"

"I have to bring my mom to her appointments."

"So the rest of your time you can dedicate to school. Do you know how many of your peers have to work *and* find time to study or go to tutoring?"

"Yeah."

"Why wouldn't you try to figure out how to pass if you have the time to dedicate to it? That's what I can't figure out."

"I'm not stupid," Maricela shot back.

"I didn't say you are."

"But you said go to tutoring. Stupid people go to tutoring."

Baffled, I stopped. "Smart people go to tutoring."

"Smart people don't need tutoring."

"I failed organic chemistry." I enjoyed the disbelief on Maricela's face.

"Isn't that an important class?"

"One of the required ones, yes. That's why I'm asking if you talk to your teachers. I wouldn't talk to my teacher the first time I took it. Like you said, I didn't want to look stupid. All my friends were passing, and they didn't go to tutoring." Maricela looked away again, so I knew I'd hit on something. "I thought that I should be able to get it as long as I was doing the homework, but I was wrong. The next semester, I was in the teacher's office every week, sometimes after every class. I went with a list of questions. I accepted that I needed help."

"And you passed?"

"I passed. Barely. I'm no chemist, but I passed."

"I don't want to waste the teacher's time."

"You think that's what the teacher thinks?"

"They're busy."

"They always have time to talk to someone who cares, and if they don't, then you should drop the class and take it with a teacher who has the time. If you see it as wasting their time, it is. You control that. If you already decided to fail biology, then nobody can help you, not me, not your teacher. Only you can pass it."

"Why do you care? You don't know me. If I'm not in the lab, I'm not screwing up your stuff."

"I care because I'd like to see you in my lab. There are at least more women in science these days, but I'd love to see more Latina women. You have a science brain."

"How do you know?"

"You've got the natural curiosity any scientist needs. When you were measuring your protein concentrations, you could have walked away after I helped you calculate the answer, but you didn't. You wanted to figure out how it worked. That kind of focus and interest could take you somewhere. You could transfer…"

"And do what? More college?" she interrupted.

I ached for what I heard in Maricela's voice, the belief that she didn't belong in academia, not community college and certainly not a university. I knew it because my family had met me with the same kinds of questions. Why did I want to go to college? How did I expect to pay for it?

"Why wouldn't you go to college? Money?" I asked.

"Yeah."

"There are scholarships, especially for women in science. Does your college have a STEM center?"

"I think my teacher talks about it."

"Science, Technology, Engineering and Math. All areas that minorities are encouraged to pursue. And they are encouraged with money."

"Those are all the hard degrees."

"If you think it's hard, you've already sunk yourself. Why not think about it as a challenge? You think anyone here is doing anything easy? What if doctors thought it was too hard to figure out how to cure cancer? What if my PI thought it was too hard to figure out how to preserve sight for people who struggle with diabetes? But I see what you mean. It's all too hard. Let's play games on our phones instead."

Having worked myself into a state, I turned on my heel and began walking again.

"Wait up," Maricela said.

I was mad enough to be mean and picked up the pace. Make her work for it if she wanted to talk to me. I was tired of being nice.

"Wait!" Maricela was jogging now and came up on my shoulder. "You think I could get a science degree?"

"It doesn't matter what I think," I said, pumping my arms, pushing my body until my calves ached.

Maricela fell back again. I wanted to scream at her that what mattered was whether she believed in herself. She had to change the way she looked at her education. She had to want to succeed. Had she not heard a word I'd said the whole walk? And then I thought about myself in community college. It was easy to guess that Maricela's family questioned her in the same way mine had. What I would have given to have someone in my life to say, "Ignore them. Trust yourself." I felt a wave of compassion for Maricela and turned to see her retracing the steps we'd taken.

"Come here!" I called. Maricela kept walking, but I easily made up the difference. I grasped Maricela by the forearm. "You're going the long way. We're making a circle. If we go this way, we're almost back to your bench with the creepy guy."

Maricela laughed. "My mom gets confused. That's the one spot she can find when she's finished."

"What did she say when you told her you stopped going to the lab here?"

Maricela didn't answer.

"Oh. She thinks that you come together, so you can go do your service-learning while she's at her appointment." Maricela's continued silence confirmed my thoughts. "Why haven't you told her?"

"She thinks I can be a scientist and cure diabetes."

"Now I'm really confused. I would have loved to have a family who believed in me. You do, and you still don't think you can do it?"

"They don't know that I'm not passing. They'll be disappointed."

"Then you pass."

We walked together, and I didn't say anything more. I'd already given her a lot to think about. "Do you know about handicaps in horse racing?" I laughed at Maricela's expression, understanding how far off from our conversation horse racing was. "My brother is super lucky. Sometimes he goes to the track. One of the things he talks about is the handicap they put on a horse. They want an exciting race, so they put extra weight on the faster horses. That's the handicap. You put a handicap on yourself letting your test scores go down, but that doesn't mean that you can't succeed. Sometimes, the horse with the biggest handicap still wins, and the good news is that in college, you don't even have to be the student with the highest score. All you have to do is pass. But you do have to race. If you stop, you lose."

"Okay."

"You're in the race?"

"I'll stay in the race."

"The next time I see you, I'm going to ask what your teacher said."

"What if he says I've already failed?"

"Then you ask him if you can stay in the class to learn what you can to make repeating it easier. If he says there's still a chance, then you run toward the finish line for all you're worth. You promise yourself you will give it your all."

"What if I need help?"

"Bring your homework to the lab. I'll see if I can help." Almost at our starting point, I glanced at my watch and saw that I still had some time to do stairs if I jogged over to the hospital. "I'm cutting out here, but don't you dare stop at the bench. You have time to check in with Bautista about your project to see what he expects you to do."

"Okay."

"I'm checking up on you," I said, jogging backward.

"Okay."

Would a thank-you have killed her? I shook my head and broke into a jog. I was pretty sure that I could at least get in one trip to the top floor of the hospital, and wherever I caught Valerie coming down, I could convince her to do a few more stairs. The high I felt from the conversation spurred me to a faster pace than I usually took the first two floors. When I hit the landing of the second floor, I was already as out of breath as she would be at the last if I was following Valerie's steady pace.

My phone rang. I was expecting Valerie, so when the number I'd been waiting to see lit up my screen, a thrill of adrenaline hit my system. I filled my lungs deeply three times. I didn't want to answer the phone sounding like I was about to collapse, even though I truly felt like I might, but I wasn't about to miss the call.

"Hello," I finally managed.

"Hi, it's Remi."

My breath was still coming fast. "I know." The adrenaline combined with the stairs I'd run made it impossible to catch my breath. I felt light-headed and reached for the stair rail to steady myself.

"Wow, you weren't kidding about that not being able to breathe around me," Remi laughed.

"You caught me…running up…the stairs."

"Should I let you go?"

"No! Don't let me go!" My heart and lungs would not cooperate with my desire to talk to Remi.

"Don't let you go?" Humor continued to warm her voice.

I heard how dorky I sounded and smacked my forehead. "You talk. I have to catch my breath."

"Are you running because you're late?"

"For a workout with Valerie."

"We can talk later."

"No. It was ridiculous to try to catch her." My breath coming more easily now, I descended the stairs anxious to get out of the echoing stairway.

"You work out a lot?"

"Trying to. Valerie guilts me. She says it'll help me with the ladies."

"You do not seem like the kind of person who would have any trouble with the ladies."

"I've been told I spend too much time at work."

"By your girlfriend?"

"Ex," I quickly clarified. "When I was doing my postdoc."

"You have more time now as a researcher?" Remi asked.

Should I answer honestly? Valerie would tell me to lie, but what the hell? It wasn't like I could invent time for dates that I didn't have. "Not really."

"Oh good!"

"That's good?"

"My ex was always on my case about how little time I had for her, too. Maybe we should set them up."

"I hope you're not serious about that!"

"Not in the least." Remi's voice felt good in my ear.

"So you have no time this week?" I asked.

"None at all!" Remi said, her voice equal parts amused and relieved. "And I was so worried about explaining that. I want to see you, but Saturday is the earliest I could swing it."

"Saturday sounds great," I said. We arranged a time and place and chatted a little more before disconnecting. Valerie pushed through the door as I slid the phone back in my pocket.

"You're here!"

I started to do jumping jacks, but Valerie narrowed her eyes. "You don't fool me for a second. You haven't been working out at all."

"No, but I have a date!" I squealed.

Valerie released the leg she'd been stretching and punched the air. "Yes! You could have told me you were ditching me to speak to Remi, you know. I would have understood."

"Actually, I ditched you to talk to that student intern I told you about. That's a different story, though. I was on my way to meet you when Remi called, and I had to take it."

"Of course you did. Where are you going?"

"She invited me for ice cream, that place you and Emma like."

"Where you never get anything. What were you thinking?"

"It's fine. It's no big deal."

"You're going to have to eat something. Otherwise, weird."

"I know. I've got this. Don't worry about me."

"I'm your best friend. That's my job!" She hip checked me.

So much felt right in the world as we strode across campus. At the spot we parted ways, I gave Valerie a quick hug. Happy to lose myself in thoughts of Remi as I walked to my building, I was jolted back to reality by the sound of my name. I saw Maricela standing wide-eyed next to an older woman who shared her daughter's stricken countenance. Both of them looked from Valerie to me and back again.

"I'm late getting back. Hooroo, mate!" Valerie waved as she quickly trekked away.

I waited for Maricela to say something. She was the one who had called out to me, but she stood frozen and silent. I awkwardly waited for her to speak, maybe to introduce me to her mother, but one look at her mother's dark expression made me anxious to leave. "I'm expected back at the lab as well. See you this week?"

"I checked in with the lab. I'll be there Thursday afternoon."

"Find me. I want to hear what your bio professor had to say."

Maricela's mother scrutinized her daughter and then me during the short exchange, and it bothered me that she seemed so upset. Surely she would appreciate me trying to help her daughter. Then I remembered Remi's expression when Valerie threw her arm around my shoulder. I could see how others might easily see us as a couple. The way we had been walking together could have produced the tightness on Mrs. Gonzales's face. If that was the case, I said a little prayer that Maricela wasn't a lesbian.

CHAPTER EIGHT

I knew the ice cream parlor Remi had suggested. It sat directly across the road from the beach and always had a line outside from the moment they opened. At one o'clock, the beach was packed with families and sunbathers. A handful of boogie boarders chased waves, and younger children played in the sand as gentle waves rolled in. I rested against the patio railing telling myself to watch the waves instead of the people on the sidewalk. However hard as I tried as I waited for Remi, any movement at my periphery caught my attention. I closed my eyes for a moment, trying to figure out whether our phone conversation setting up this date moved us into hug territory.

Remi's voice brought a smile to my face.

"So sorry I'm late. I have no excuse since I'm the one who picked the spot!"

Of course Remi would pick the one moment my eyes were shut to materialize. "I hardly count two minutes as late." I admired Remi in her cream capris and flowing blue blouse. Her hair was as perfectly styled as it had been at the science fair.

"You didn't even look at your watch. You knew I was late. I hate to be late. If I'm not early, I'm late."

I made note of that and smiled at the babble that made me think Remi could be nervous. "Being on time is a thing. Got it."

"My whole day is meetings. People who show up late to meetings ruin the entire day. I don't want to be the cause of someone's ruined day."

"You haven't ruined mine," I said, thinking of how Remi's mere presence lifted my spirits. I wanted to throw my arms around her, but we'd been talking so long, it felt like the time to hug her had passed. We stood awkwardly. "Are you ready for ice cream now, or did you want to worry more about being late?"

"Now that you've admitted I was late, we can have ice cream. Hello, by the way," she added, stepping forward to hug me.

Our embrace was brief, the self-conscious negotiation of how much contact was acceptable. The barest brush of bodies and slight pressure of hands on shoulders. Still, I drank in the lilac perfume I remembered from the bar. Now I was close enough to notice how sweet her hair smelled. Too soon, the hug was over and we were inside.

I'd been to the shop with Valerie and Emma whose sweet tooth often dictated an after-dinner walk down to the beach for a cone. The first time I had tagged along and hadn't ordered anything, Valerie assumed my diabetes awareness made me avoid the sugar. I couldn't very well decline ice cream now since Remi had picked it for our meeting place. I compromised by ordering the smallest serving hoping that Remi wouldn't even notice.

I felt Remi's eyes on me as I ordered a small cup of strawberry and didn't choose any of the vast array of toppings. Cup or cone wasn't up for debate at all. There was no way I was going to lick a cone in front of Remi. Remi ordered the same size but chose vanilla, also leaving it unadorned. I reached for my wallet, but Remi already had hers out and was waving off my offer to pay. Glad for Remi's distraction, I fished a pill from my pocket and swallowed it quickly and then accepted the cup of ice cream from the teenager behind the counter.

Remi followed me outside and we found an empty table.

"What was that?" Remi's voice was too cool to be merely curious.

"What?" I said, stalling.

"The pill you took."

It wasn't a big deal, but I hated to say. I would have taken it earlier, but it was most effective if I ingested it right before I ate ice cream.

"While I was paying," Remi prodded. I wasn't ashamed, but I knew telling her would make her feel bad. Remi crossed her arms, scowling. "I do not like secrets."

"It's nothing." Her scowl deepened. "I'm lactose-intolerant," I finally said, chagrined.

"What?"

"My system doesn't deal well with dairy." Now my face flushed.

"I grasp the meaning of lactose intolerance. I'm simply… Oh, how embarrassing! Why ever didn't you suggest a different place to meet?"

"This is what you picked. I didn't want to argue with your choice."

Remi laughed and pointed at the small serving of strawberry. "So that's why you got the small."

"You got a small, too," I tossed back.

"I thought you must have decided things might not go well." She gestured between the two of us.

"You're joking, right? I've been thinking about you since I met you at the fair. Please tell me you didn't get less ice cream than you wanted because you were worried that I didn't actually want to be here!"

"No." She took a bite of her vanilla and grimaced slightly. "I don't particularly like sweet things."

"Get out! You could have picked coffee!" I said.

"Coffee seemed too…"

"Boring?"

Remi bit her lip, searching for a word.

"Hot," I guessed. Remi blushed, so I leaned forward and added, "intimate?"

Remi swatted me, and I savored the short amount of contact between her hand and my skin. "Unmemorable."

"That was my next guess." She rolled her eyes playfully, making every cell in my body hum. "I am certainly going to remember your willingness to subject yourself to something you don't even like purely to be in my company."

"I've never met someone who didn't love ice cream. I've always been the odd one out."

"Stick with me, and we'll be the even ones out," I said.

Remi's eyes rested on me, reading me. I could see her picturing me by her side at future events and hoped we looked as good together in her mental projections as we did in mine. "So the ex liked ice cream?" she asked.

"Quite a bit. If she was angry, a pint of something rich helped smooth things over."

"But not enough to fix everything."

"No. There is a limit to what ice cream can fix. What about you? Did you know of this place because of an ice cream-loving girlfriend?"

"No. There are times I like to listen to the waves, and I've seen the lines here and construed that it must be good."

"Valerie told me to come clean and ask to meet somewhere else."

"Did she? She is aware of your lactose intolerance?"

"Yes. She and her wife live a block away. After dinner, they like to come down and walk along the beach. They stop for ice cream here often enough that I couldn't find an excuse every time."

"You and Valerie seem close."

It wasn't an accusation the way it would have been had Ann delivered the words. It was merely an observation. "She says we were bound to be friends because we're the only two lezzies on campus."

"That isn't the case?"

"I don't think shared sexuality predicts friendship. It gives us something in common, but it would be like someone from Australia hearing her talk and assuming they'll be best pals because they both lived in Australia."

"So why are you best pals?" Remi asked.

"I'm a sucker for accents. Even if she were boring, which she isn't, I don't mind listening to her talk." I grinned widely.

"Is that why you called? Because of my accent?" Remi drew out her words, teasing me.

"Maybe." I smiled. "Could be I needed to talk to you longer to figure out what it is."

"How are you doing with that?"

My brows tipped downward, and I studied her intently. "I'm going to need to collect more data."

"A scientist to your core."

"That's me."

"Or you could simply ask what languages I speak."

"Languages!" I exclaimed. I paid the price for talking around a bite of ice cream and fell into my familiar coughing fit.

"Do you need water?"

I nodded, and Remi disappeared into the store. She returned a few moments later with two bottles of water, one extended. I drank from the bottle and cleared my throat. "Sorry about that."

"I keep taking your breath away. That can't be a bad thing. You're surprised I speak more than one other language?"

"I struggle enough with Spanish. My family says that science takes up too much room for me to remember another language."

"They speak it, then?"

"Mostly my sister because her husband is fluent, and he wants his kids to grow up knowing Spanish. I was picking up some when the kids were little, but I have to say that Rosa blew by me and I gave up. I remember enough to say hello to my nieces and ask how they are. And swear."

"At your nieces?" Doubt laced Remi's voice.

"If they deserve it, sure!"

A chortle lifted from deep within Remi catching the attention from every table on the patio. Most smiled along to her obvious delight. When she was finished, Remi relaxed in her chair. "You've never sworn at your nieces."

"How do you know?"

"You don't have it in your voice. That and you said your siblings teased you. You might say something like that to them to try to keep up with them, but convincingly? No. You are too innocent."

"And you?"

"Not so much in English. Greek, yes."

"Greek! I never would have guessed that."

"But it is so obvious!" she gasped.

I tipped my head, not following.

"My given name is Greek."

I smacked my forehead. "Andromeda." We were talking about her accents but had not discussed her ancestry. "Are your parents Greek?"

"My father is of Greek ancestry. He was pleased when he was able to move his family to Greece though none of his relatives were there anymore."

"And your mother?"

"Telling you would reveal another of my languages."

"Then don't tell me. I'm going to guess the next one."

"Three."

"Three more?"

Remi nodded.

"Five in total!" I was impressed. "Okay. No hints."

"You think you can guess?"

"That means it's not something obvious, like Spanish."

Remi lifted her shoulder. "Is that an official guess?"

"No. I'm going to need more time listening before I take another guess."

"That may be possible." Her head was inclined toward the cup, and when she glanced up and flashed me a smile, my insides melted.

I so wanted to spend more time in this captivating woman's company. "When did your family move to Greece?"

"When I was ten. I still remember it so vividly. There was a man who lived near us who owned burros. I still have this image of him herding them down a narrow, cobbled road. I can't imagine where he was taking them, but it is one of my favorite memories."

"How long did you live there?"

"Three years. My father was a diplomat for the United States. I'd tell you where else he served, but it will give away the other languages I speak."

"I'm not ready to give up yet," I said. "What else do you remember about Greece?"

I could have listened to Remi forever as she talked first about the mainland and then about the beautiful Greek isles. "It sounds amazing," I said when Remi finished a story about visiting ancient cave paintings that were being restored. "Why did your family leave?"

Remi took her cup and reached for mine. "Finished?"

"Yes," I said, startled by Remi's abruptness.

When she returned from throwing their our away, she picked up her water and drank half. "We had to leave because of my brother." Her eyes caught and held mine. She seemed to be assessing me, weighing her choice of words. "My brother's behavior necessitated our return to the States. My parents... What is the expression? Hit a wall?"

I nodded.

"They could not handle it, him, any longer."

My mind whirred, and I intuited that my response was important. I was at a loss. "Oh."

"Yes. Oh." Remi looked away.

"I'm sorry."

"Don't be. We cannot choose our parents."

Her statement shocked me. I had never once wished for parents other than the ones I had and said so.

"You had better luck. I am glad for you."

"I've never thought of myself as lucky. That's always been my brother. He's the one to take to the track."

A smile returned to Remi's lips. "Do you go?"

"Hardly ever. Is it something you enjoy?"

"I'd rather be on the horse than watching it run." She looked across the street. "Do you have time for a walk?"

"Absolutely." Once we'd crossed the street, I removed my sneakers and tucked my ankle socks down into the toes before stepping into the warm sand. We walked together toward the surf, turning horizontal to the tide when we reached the more tightly packed sand.

"You were with your sister at the fair, and you allowed yourself to be the subject for her daughter's project. Are you as close with your brother?"

"We get along okay. I see my sister more often because she and her family live with my parents. I see my brother at Sunday dinner." We walked in silence, Remi's eyes on the mirror-like surface of the sand at the water's edge. "Are you and your brother close?"

The quiet stretched before Remi answered. "We are."

"You see him often?"

"Yes."

"Wait." I remembered the way Remi had looked at the arcade. The two drinks. "Was your brother with you at Sloan's?"

"He was there, yes."

"Valerie was sure you were there with a date. She wanted me to go in and scope out the competition."

Remi laughed without humor. "Depending on the perspective, that is a very accurate statement."

"He's important to you."

Remi paused at this, and something inside of her relaxed. She reached for my hand and continued walking. "My parents' marriage was the first casualty. He is not an easy person, and their frustration ate away their relationship. My dad left first. My mother tried longer, but it was easier for her once she found a placement for my brother."

We walked as I weighed what to say.

"Don't say you're sorry. He is who he is."

I absorbed Remi's words. I had been about to apologize and wondered how many times people had apologized for something that could not be fixed. "They ran away, but you didn't."

"No. I cannot. I will not. I'm all he has left."

"Did he influence your decision to become a psychologist?"

"Yes. I wanted to understand him. I gained more than that, like a better understanding of my mother and my father."

I squeezed her hand. "Where do they live now?"

"My father is in Virginia, my mother Tel Aviv."

I don't know what I'd expected her to say, but her answer stopped me in my tracks. "How did you and your brother end up in Southern California?"

"We are here because of Legoland. Neil became more difficult when our father's diplomatic appointment took us to Greece. They hoped that returning to the States would 'fix' him. The permanence of our home helped. But it was not what my father wanted. His unhappiness affected us all."

"He missed being overseas?"

She nodded. "Everything about it, especially the prestige. When he left, he cashed in every favor owed to him in hopes of securing a professorship at Georgetown or Harvard. That would have at least maintained his sense of status. Instead, he is at a school without name recognition teaching students who could not care less about his experience."

"Being in the States was hard on your mom as well?"

"Yes. She is a news correspondent, so moving did not affect her career as much. She was freelancing when we were young, and when we moved to Virginia, she got picked up by Reuters. She easily transferred to LA when Neil fell in love with all things Lego. She was more patient with Neil than my father, but about a year after I finished my master's, a position overseas became available, and she took it."

"And you stayed."

"I stayed."

Remi stopped, and I turned to face her. "I like that. A lot. And if we're being truthful, I like you. A lot."

"Then it is settled," Remi said seriously, but the side of her mouth rose in a smile.

"What is?"

Remi took a step closer, and I felt a rush of anticipation for our first kiss zip from my belly button to my chest. Then I felt

Remi's soft lips on mine. I pressed closer, wrapping my arms around her to block out the world. Remi's tongue traced my bottom lip, and I answered her invitation with mine, shuddering as I tasted her and felt the catch of her breath. I had to pull away before I completely lost myself. "We are going to need to spend a lot more time together."

"Agreed."

Remi's lips found mine again, and I easily pushed where we were from my mind. I was imagining lowering Remi to the sand, knowing how good her body would feel with gravity pulling us closer.

Cold water crashed on our calves, pushing us apart with shrieks and wild-limbed running for dry ground. I looked down at my soaked pants trying to avoid the eyes of bystanders laughing at us for tuning out the ocean. We laughed at each other for the proper soaking we'd received.

"I guess someone is telling us to get a room," I said, tipping my eyes skyward.

"You surprise me. I expected the scientist to admonish herself for turning her back on the ocean."

"I was raised Catholic. They drum guilt in deep."

"I am hoping you don't feel guilty about that because I was looking forward to more."

"No guilt in what I want, only where it happens. I'm not usually a PDA kind of a girl."

Remi took my hand again and studied me. "No lies. What else do you have on your schedule today?"

I thought of my cells, glad I had asked a colleague to split and treat them. "Nothing. I am yours until you get tired of me."

"I don't see that happening. How about food, an early dinner to give you more time to study my linguistic patterns?"

"I wonder if linguistic patterns influence the way you kiss," I said, tapping my chin.

Remi pushed against my shoulder. "It is no wonder you are a scientist."

CHAPTER NINE

"I don't even know why I have to know this. It's stupid," Maricela said. She sat with me in my cubicle, worksheets from her General Biology class strewn across the desk.

I scanned the graded sheets and piled them together, quickly assessing what Maricela needed to do on the current worksheet.

"You have a basic understanding of photosynthesis, right? This is adding depth to what you should already have from high school."

"See? I already did this, so why aren't they teaching us something useful? I want to learn about diabetes. I don't care about plants."

"You don't have to care about plants, but you do have to care about how things work. Your class is about life. Plants are an intricate part of that, and you have to understand how they work. First, we figure out how things work, so that when they don't, we can try to figure out how to fix them."

I pushed the worksheet toward Maricela. I could have finished it in three minutes, but that wasn't the issue. Helping

Maricela see its significance was. Before I could speak, Judy appeared in the hallway. When it was clear that she was heading straight for my office, I leapt up to meet her at the door. Maricela remained seated, and I wished Judy had called me to her office instead of seeking me out.

Her eyes on Maricela, Judy said, "I saw Jim on Saturday doing the three o'clock cell treatment and sample collection."

It wasn't unusual for Judy to be on campus over the weekend, but I could not see a reason that she would be in the lab instead of in her office. "Yes," I answered, figuring the less I said the less she had to use against me. I'd often traded weekend cell treatments if I had to be away from the lab all day.

Finally turning her gaze to me, she said, "How soon will you be able to process the samples and have the analysis ready?"

"Done and emailed last night."

"Oh! Marvelous. Were you in the lab last night? I must have missed you."

"It was late."

"I should have checked my email. I was worried that the project did not have your full concentration." Again Judy glanced at Maricela, an obvious distraction.

"It does. It determines my future."

"Indeed. This project is the culmination of my entire career. I need my team working to the absolute best of their ability."

"I understand that completely. That's why I wanted you to have the figures first thing."

"I am anxious to see the results from last week. Thank you."

"Let me know if you have any questions. I'm in the lab all day." I groaned as I sat back down, realizing the promise I had made essentially glued me to my desk. It wouldn't look good if Judy sought me out and found my office empty. "I'm so sorry for the interruption, but I have to send a quick message."

Maricela nodded wordlessly.

No exercise for me today. Promised Judy I'd be here to review data, I typed in a text to Valerie.

"Okay. What were we talking about?" I said to Maricela. My phone had already pinged, keeping my attention.

I was hoping to hear about Saturday's exercise.

I blushed deeply and frowned. "Sorry," I said to Maricela, typing a quick, *Mind on work. Not in gutter.* I placed my phone facedown. "Okay. Photosynthesis. Why we care about plants."

"You have a sunburn," Maricela stated.

Before I could comprehend what Maricela was doing, she reached out and prodded my pink forearm. The memory of kissing Remi flooded through me and refused to retreat like the white circle did after Maricela poked me.

We had strolled inland lazily, window-shopping and learning about each other. When I paused at a surf shop, she shared that she had never tried surfing, boogie boarding, or kayaking, and I told her how much I enjoyed boogie boarding with my family. She had always thought kayaking sounded fun, and I easily imagined spending time on the water with her. She lingered at apparel stores, which gave me time to admire her figure and her sense of style. I heard Emma chastising me about my limited wardrobe and imagined letting Remi pull me into stores and suggest clothes for me. It was easy to picture trying on new outfits to present to Remi, to see her eyes roam my body.

I had a hard time keeping my mind from exploring how Remi had said that she had ideas for how to further my niece's sleep study. I wrestled with whether I could come right out with a question about what she had in mind. I held my question back. As eager as I was to share a bed with Remi, I didn't want to rush there. I was absolutely content to stand in front of the bookstore listening to her talk about books she had read and those on her to-read list.

I had more to say about karate when we passed a dojo. My brother had enrolled Beto in martial arts to help control his boundless energy. Remi laughed appreciatively at the antics of my hyperactive nephew and assured me that most boys his age had energy to spare. She rested her hand on my arm and startled when she saw how much sun I'd gotten. Equal parts sympathetic and chastising, she pulled me into the cool darkness of a pizza joint down the street from the bookstore.

Once we were seated, she ran her fingers over my forearm, her touch feather soft, as she listed remedies for sunburn. Aloe vera extracted from the plant. Black tea, cooled, applied with the teabag. Everything she had suggested ended up sounding far more erotic than medicinal, of course making me think about the sleep study again.

But Rosa had argued that what I really needed was a girlfriend. The tenderness in Remi's expression held the promise of something significant, and I was quite familiar with things of significance taking a long time. The retinal trial was the culmination of years and years of experimentation, grant applications, toxicity testing, stability studies, and ethics submissions.

Maricela touched my arm again, and the contact sent me reeling. It slammed me back into the harsh bright lab and my work. Work! I was supposed to be thinking about work. But I was also supposed to be tutoring Maricela about something... I could not remember what. Most embarrassingly, though, it ignited the desire I'd felt when Remi touched me, something I definitely wasn't supposed to be feeling in the lab. "I spent the day at the beach." I pored over the worksheets on my desk, hoping Maricela would accept the redirect to our lesson.

Maricela leaned forward and said softly, "With your girlfriend?"

"Girlfriend?" My mind tried to grasp how Maricela had made that leap.

"You were walking with her last week."

"Oh!" I laughed, relieved. "Valerie! We work here together. She's my pal."

"I'm so sorry!" Maricela looked mortified. "I thought the two of you..."

"No. She and her wife are very happily married." I couldn't figure out how this conversational track was still in motion.

"So she is...gay," Maricela all but whispered. "When my mom saw you and your...friend...she thought you two were a couple. She was very upset to find out that I have been spending time with a lesbian."

"I can see where she could get that impression. We're very close."

"You're not offended?"

"Why would I be offended?"

"That my mom thought you're gay."

I sat back remembering not only the way the elder Gonzales had scowled at us but the wide-eyed wonder in Maricela's eyes. I recalled thinking how difficult it would be to come out to that expression, and so much became clear. "Is she upset about gay people in general or about you?" I ventured.

Maricela reacted like she'd been struck by a bus and a flood of Spanish rushed from her mouth.

"What?" I was forced to ask.

Maricela's eyes darted around the lab as if she were worried about people eavesdropping. "Don't you speak Spanish?"

"Not that well."

Shaking her head, Maricela mumbled to herself in Spanish. Finally, she leaned closer. "My mother would kill me if I was gay."

She sounded as if she meant that literally. "I can't imagine that any mother could cut herself away from her daughter."

"You don't know my mother. She is very upset that you are gay. If she knew you're connected to the clinic, she would stop donating samples."

"Wait. What did you say?"

"My mother is so homophobic she wouldn't volunteer here if she knew you had something to do with the research."

My mind spun for so many reasons.

"Are you okay?" Maricela asked. "Should I not have said that?"

"I didn't know your mom was volunteering samples."

Everything that came from the clinic was de-identified and coded to protect confidentiality and blind the data. I had no idea what samples belonged to her mother. Still, knowing Maricela, talking to her, helping her... I took a deep breath trying to determine whether I had an ethical problem. "What did you tell her when she assumed Valerie and I were a couple?"

"I said I barely see you and that you work in a different lab. She has no idea your lab works with the samples from the clinic."

I nodded. That was good. The question was whether Judy should be made aware of Maricela's connection to my research.

"So who did you go to the beach with?" Maricela asked.

"Have you come out to your mom yet?"

The two questions hung in the air. She didn't answer, and I felt no need to break the silence.

"I can't talk to my mother," Maricela finally said.

"She supports your education. My mother is more understanding about me dating women than she is about my career."

"So you are gay!"

When I had decided to mentor Maricela, I'd pictured discussions about science and university applications. It never occurred to me that I would be talking about my personal life. "I am." Maricela reached out and touched my arm again. I scooted my chair back, out of Maricela's reach.

"And you were at the beach with your girlfriend."

Why wasn't she letting this go? If I didn't claim a girlfriend, was Maricela going to develop a crush? "If you don't have any other questions about your photosynthesis homework, I need to get back to my samples."

My words hurt her. Her whole expression shut down when I refused to talk about the beach. "No. I don't have questions. I can write whatever and get credit. It doesn't have to be right." She gathered her homework sheets.

"But you'll need to understand it for the exam."

"Fine. Whatever."

"Maricela?" I struggled with the dilemma of whether to stay professional or allow the personal and wished I had more time to plot out each decision. Pressed, I thought about what I would have wanted at twenty and relented. "It was a first date."

Interest sparked in Maricela's eyes. "And it went good. That's why you got sunburned?"

"It did. It was really good." I said this for the same reason I had told her not to drop out of school. I wanted Maricela to know I was not ashamed of being a lesbian.

Maricela nodded, satisfied.

"Do you have any more questions about your homework?"

"Nah, I'm good," she said and left me sitting alone trying to switch my brain back to work. I pulled out my phone and texted Remi. *Someone noticed my sunburn.*

Remi's reply pinged immediately. *Need aloe? Could help with application…*

I smiled. *Tempting, but stuck working late.*

Call me.

Later? Now? I took a chance and pushed the phone icon at the top of my screen.

"Hello?"

"It's not that I don't want to see you again. I had a really good time."

"So did I."

I could hear the smile in her voice, one that made her lips all the more tempting. I closed my eyes, wishing I could steal another kiss. Remi's velvety lips nestled so perfectly to mine, and I longed to continue the discussion we had started with our kisses.

Remi interrupted my daydream. "I've got an IEP meeting. I meant call me later, and we'll set up a date."

"IEP?"

"Individualized Educational Plan for a student. They're incredibly difficult to schedule."

"Got it. It might be late by the time I call. Is that okay?"

"I can handle it. Go do your work."

"Right. Have a good day." I tapped my phone against my thigh, smiling at her command. I wasn't used to being told to get back to work, and it felt nice. I finally understood what Emma meant about needing someone who had her own life. Free of guilt, I got back to work.

CHAPTER TEN

Shit, shit, shit, shit, shit, shit, shit I chanted, trying to pipette faster. My right hand cramping, I switched to the left. *Don't look at the clock again*, I snapped at myself. *It will not change the fact that you are running late.* I looked anyway. *Very late.*

I had hoped to be on my way out of the building by now to meet Remi in the parking lot. At least she hadn't texted yet. I should have texted her when I realized the patient samples were taking more time to process than I had anticipated. Maybe luck would be on my side and her last meeting would have run long, or maybe a traffic jam would buffer the time.

My phone buzzed. "Shitty shitsters!" I finished the tray, snapped off my gloves and pulled the phone out. *Tiny bit behind. Give me 5? Or you can run up to my lab?*

I kept an eye on the *Remi is typing* message that flashed on and off while I caught a bit of air in my gloves to pop the fingers out, so I could put them back on.

I'd love to see your lab!

Second floor, door on the right. Knock. I'll let you in. I worked as quickly as possible, painfully aware that the cushion of time we had to begin the date I had planned was slipping away. I could feel my whole family rolling their eyes at the hope I held for making it on time. "Almost done, almost done, almost done," I chanted, finishing as I heard a tap at the door. I held up a finger as I passed by the door to the hallway and carefully carried my trays to the incubator before I let her in.

"I'd hug you, but…" I held up my gloved hands. "I still need to clean up."

"I am fine admiring you in your lab coat."

I flushed under her admiration. "I'm sorry I wasn't ready when you got here. With cell culture, you never know if they're going to grow according to plan." She followed as I walked to the bench to clean the area. I was nervous with her in the lab and was babbling. I snapped off my gloves and tossed them in the trash. I turned to find Remi studying me. "Too much?" I bit my lip wishing I had listened to Emma about shoptalk. "Valerie's wife says I 'prattle on' when I talk about work."

"If I was not interested, I would have stopped you. I'm of the opinion that there is nothing sexier than an intelligent woman discussing her work."

Embarrassed, I searched for a diversion. "So this is the lab." I pointed out each area. "Benches, cell culture room, darkroom."

She stepped close enough that I smelled her faint lilac perfume and felt the heat of her body. "I would greatly enjoy a tour of the darkroom."

I consulted my watch and grimaced. "We'll be late. If you're not early, you're late."

Her eyebrows did a little dance and her gaze dropped to my lips. I imagined her weighing whether being on time was more important than kissing me hello. Was I reading too much? Would our appointment wait? I shoved the question aside and led the way to the darkroom. I knocked and, hearing nothing, opened the door. I was about to say there was not a whole lot to see once we'd stepped inside, but then Remi's hands slid inside my lab coat and around my waist. I leaned around her to engage the lock on the door, my body tingling at the contact with hers.

Remi leaned with me, whispering, "I could not wait another minute to kiss you."

Her lips met mine, sending a zing of electricity along my thighs. I longed to lose myself in the kiss, but I could not forget where we were.

"You are uncomfortable."

"A little."

"It does not excite you, thinking about what you could do in the dark?" She found the light switch and left us with the faint red glow of the darkroom's safety light. "I am guessing you have to be very adept with your hands in this light." As if she were the one instructing me, she reached under my shirt, sweeping her soft hands across my belly.

I hissed with pleasure, hoping her lips would return to mine. Instead, I felt her hot breath as she placed the most delicate of kisses on my neck, climbing from my collarbone up toward my ear. Slowly, deliciously, erotically, she traced my outer ear with her tongue. My entire body screamed the need to get naked with this woman. Her tongue traced my earlobe, and she paused suddenly.

"What's this? You have uneven earrings?" Again, she nipped below the lowest of the three hoops on my left ear. She returned to the right and circled the stud in the upper cartilage before slipping her tongue through the single hoop in the lobe.

Her tongue on my ears was doing magical things to my body. "I do."

"I like that."

I took advantage of the pause and peppered the gentle curve of her neck with my own kisses. "Why is that?" I whispered as I clasped her ear between my teeth, delighting in the way her fingers clutched at my hips.

"It makes me think you are edgier than I realized."

"What I do with my body is separate from what I do professionally."

She hmmmed at my response, her skin vibrating under my lips.

"What else have you done with your gorgeous body? Tattoos? Other piercings?" Her hands traveled up toward my breasts.

Muffled voices on the other side of the door made me grasp her wrists and step back. My face flushed hot and red, I waited for a knock at the door, my mind spinning on how I would explain Remi's presence. "Now isn't the time to find the others."

"Others. Plural."

Her voice rippled through me, and I wanted to lead her to every secret I had. "We have to go," I whispered. "Friday traffic is going to hold us up even more."

"That is a shame," Remi said. She tried to move her hands back to my hips and stomach. "Perhaps our date will provide a more private dark place?"

"Stop!" I said, laughing. "I'm trying to figure out how to get you out of here without having to explain why you were in the darkroom and get you to our date before they cancel our…" I almost let the destination slip. I flicked on the fluorescent lights, regretting that it made both of us flinch.

"Our what?"

"You'll see. If I can get us out of here. Let me peek and see if the lab is clear." I filled my lungs and let the breath out slowly, hoping that as the air left my lungs, the blood pounding through my veins would leave my face. A prayer on my lips, I eased the door open. Clear, thank goodness! I ducked back in. "I have to get my things from my office. You're going to head toward the back exit. Head left and wait for me in the hallway. I'll be right behind you."

"I will allow you to rush me out of here only because I am intrigued about this mystery destination. Are you going to tell me why I had to wear jeans and boots?" Remi asked.

"You'll see when we get there," I answered, trying not to look at her.

"What is it?"

"Nothing." I didn't want to tell her that I never in a hundred years thought she would wear white jeans. Who owned white jeans?

"It is not nothing. You are worried. Your eyes give it away."

"You'll find out soon enough! Keep your head down. We have to get out of here!" I squared my shoulders and pushed open the door, walking away from the darkroom without scanning the lab. Nothing to see here! Not a thing out of the ordinary! I rushed to my office and then back through the lab to where Remi was waiting at the end of the hallway. I grabbed her hand and ran down the stairs, bursting through the back door.

Laughing together, we ran to the parking lot where I had to stop, I was panting so hard. The way her eyes raked my body made me consider skipping our date and taking her home instead.

"Are you running because we are late or because I was so close to stripping you?"

She wasn't even out of breath and I had yet to catch mine. I squeezed her hand with equal parts terror and titillation. "That's where I work!"

"If you saw how you looked in that lab coat, you would understand my struggle…the contents of a girl's fantasies," she said with a grin.

I didn't quite know what to say, and then she stopped in front of the most magnificent car. "Look at those wheels!"

"You approve?"

Something in her voice made me drag my eyes away from the sleek black car with the rearing stallion logo. "This is your car?" I could not mask the envy in my voice.

"I didn't get it new."

"Still!" I openly admired the impeccable exterior of the Ferrari and imagined what the interior must feel like.

"It was a gift from my father."

"Damn! I can't imagine…" I awkwardly cut myself off when her bitter tone registered. It was clearly not a welcomed gift. I wanted to know what he hoped to convey with the gift. It had to be about impressing Remi. Making up for being an absent dad. I would much rather my father know me than be bought off with a luxury car.

"No. You don't want to," Remi said honestly. "So, this date?"

"For this date, we should take my car. But when you see my car, you might decide you're not on the right date, *Chica*."

"Nonsense. I am with you, and I sense an adventure is upon us!"

"I hope so." I led her to my old faithful Sentra trying not to worry about the difference between her ride and mine. Once we were on the road, I picked up a conversational thread from earlier in the week. We'd been talking each night while I threw my dinner together. I filled her in on the progress of my research, and the pressure I felt from Judy as we moved toward the clinical trial. Remi talked about a run of stressful meetings with parents and teachers.

Before Remi, Valerie was the only person I could talk to about my frustrations at work. It was such a relief that Remi understood the delicate balance of meeting someone's demands while maintaining one's own sanity. "What ended up happening with the hysterical mom you met with yesterday?"

Remi growled, and though it had no innuendo attached to it, my adrenaline surged, making me think again what it would be like to drive Remi to my house.

"She still doesn't get it. She insists that I didn't test her daughter properly. She probably spent five minutes on Google and now she's an expert."

"She doesn't agree with the tests? Or she doesn't agree with the results?"

"Such a nuance would be lost on her. She wants more support for her daughter. The real issue is that she wants to see her daughter's test scores come up. I get that. All parents want their children to succeed, but there are limits. This is a mother who would step in and take the tests for her daughter to see the scores improve."

"How would that help her daughter?" I asked.

"Precisely!" she said, her hands up as if to hold my sentence up as evidence. "Passing scores are most important to her, not figuring out how her child learns or what she needs."

"That's so frustrating. I've been fighting the same thing with a student working in the adjoining lab. She wants to know how I got good grades but doesn't want to hear that it took hard work and making a lot of mistakes, failing here and there. She thinks smart people get good grades. I tell her curious people do well, no-matter what their grades look like."

"Next time, I am calling you to talk to this mother."

I smiled at her. "And afterward, you would take me to…what do you have that's like my darkroom?"

She lightly smacked my thigh. "There are children where I work!"

Her touch sent a very disproportionate wave of desire up my leg. "It's good to know you have boundaries."

We drove in silence for several minutes, my mind traveling back to the darkroom, spinning on how far I would have let Remi take things had we not had to go. "Here's why we brought my car." I pulled off the paved road onto gravel. I slowed as the road took us closer to the coast. After five minutes of bouncing along the potholes, a small barn emerged. A dozen horses stood at a rail swishing their tails.

"Horseback riding?" Her voice rose with surprise.

"When I talked about racehorses, you said you'd rather ride, and you mentioned the burros being led to the beach. It seemed like a logical idea. Should I have warned you?" I eyed Remi's white jeans.

"No. It's a wonderful surprise! I haven't ridden in ages!" Remi leapt from the car and strode toward the horses unhesitatingly.

After we checked in and signed our waivers, we returned to the sleepy animals. Remi patted the horses' faces one by one. I walked beside her, my hands safely in my pockets.

"I want to take this one," Remi said, patting a small caramel-colored horse.

"How do you know which one to pick?"

"She speaks to me. None speak to you?"

"The shorter ones look a little more friendly."

Remi observed my pocketed hands. "Are you nervous?"

"No," I said quickly. "Maybe."

"Have you never ridden before?" Her eyes twinkled with all sorts of emotion, mostly excitement.

I looked away.

"This is true? You've never ridden before? Why in the world did you pick this as a date?"

"It seemed…" I wished I could hide the blush creeping up my neck.

Remi maneuvered herself to recapture my gaze. "Romantic?"

"Memorable." I smiled.

"You are going to be so sore," Remi laughed. "We'd better pick the smallest one for you."

A young man approached, wiry thin with body language more skater than cowboy. "Hi, I'm Alex," he said, his eyes still hidden behind his grubby baseball cap. "I'll be taking you guys…" He glanced up and corrected himself… "gals out today. You have any riding experience?"

"I do," Remi said. "I'd like this little mare."

"Sure. M&M is as sweet as her name. Let's get you in the saddle."

As he adjusted Remi's gear, my heart rate accelerated. Until now, the planning had all been to create a memory for Remi. I had not considered my part in it at all. Before I was anywhere near ready, Alex was leading a darker animal toward me. I followed his instructions and found myself astride the beast, trying to get comfortable. "Maybe this was a terrible idea," I said, gripping the knob in front of me with one hand and the tangle of leather Alex handed me in the other.

"It was a great idea. This is going to be fun. Relax." Remi held up her phone to take a picture.

"Shouldn't you keep your hands on these?" I held up the leather strips, worry in my voice.

"She's not going anywhere without you, is she?" Remi asked Alex.

"No ma'am. They follow along once we get going. Keeping them moving is the tricky part. I hope you two aren't afraid to kick 'em hard."

"I can," Remi replied. "Karla? Can you dig your heels in?"

Her words whipped me back to the darkroom, imagining Remi's hands beneath my shirt, in my pants, bracing myself to feel her inside. I gulped, surprised by where my mind had gone, more so because of how far my imagination was taking things. I barely knew this woman, and I wanted her. Fiercely. "I'll follow your lead," I rasped.

Remi's eyes traveled up and down my body, warming more than my face. I thought maybe she, too, was remembering the darkroom.

Alex swung aboard his own horse and gave a few more instructions before he directed us to the trail. As we departed, we passed a family of five on their way back. The mom and dad wore matching pinched expressions. The two boys were full of smiles, swinging their reins around, trying to hit each other's horse to make them go faster. Last in line was a princess. She wore pink pants beneath her ball gown. I recognized Belle's signature yellow dress, having watched *Beauty and the Beast* with Rosa many times.

I was so intent on the dressed-up little girl that I didn't even notice my horse turn to follow their crew, moving farther and farther away from Alex and Remi.

"Remi?" I called, worry in my voice.

Alex stopped his horse and turned in the saddle, his expression bored. "Bring Brownie this way," he instructed.

Remi trotted back and grabbed Brownie's reins.

"Do I have to worry about your eyes roaming?" she said with a grin.

"That little girl!" I could not keep the wonder from my voice. Even now, I turned for another peek.

"I agree. She has a certain *je ne sais quoi*." With ease, she swung both horses around and swatted Brownie into a teeth-jarring pace to catch up with Alex.

"Now that we're on the trail, Brownie should be fine. Long as you keep his head up when we're going through the brush."

I nodded.

We followed a narrow trail above the ocean, and though the shrubs looked coarse and unappealing, my stupid horse kept jerking the reins out of my hands to grab mouthfuls. I was grateful when we reached the barren beach and headed toward the ocean. Alex led the way down toward the waves.

"They have an easier time close to the water. You two have a half hour. You don't want to go into the water. Lots of the horses will paw and splash you or even lie down. You can trot or canter them."

"You're not going with us?" I asked.

"Can't get lost, and with the high tide, you can't go too far."

"I'm sure we'll be fine," Remi said. "Come on!"

Glad for Remi's confidence, I gave my horse a nudge with my legs.

"Is that all you've got?" Wind blew Remi's otherwise tamed hair, and her wide smile was childlike in delight. The expression was precisely what I'd hoped for, and I didn't want to disappoint her. I kicked harder and finally got Brownie moving. Not having Alex with us made it feel more intimate. The afternoon sun gave off little heat to counter the cool ocean breeze, so we had the beach practically to ourselves. The few people we passed admired the horses.

"It's okay I didn't tell you what we were going to do?" I asked.

"Not entirely."

"Are you mad about your jeans?"

"I was thinking that I could have dressed better, but having seen Belle, I still wouldn't have thought ball gown."

"She was lovely, but not my type."

"You're not over there wishing you were on a date with Emma Watson?" Remi teased.

"Hardly," I said. "She lacks a certain *je ne...*" my mind was working on the pronunciation and something hit me. "How did you say that again?"

"A certain something?"

"*Je ne sais quoi*," I said, hearing how dorky and strange I sounded. "You said it prettier. You speak French, don't you?"

Remi smiled. "What do I get if I tell you?"

"Depends on if I'm right or wrong."

"You divulge the answer to my question about your tattoos and piercings."

I pursed my lips. "That's a lot of information. I'll tell you the number but not location. How about that?"

"Deal."

"But I think I'm right. What does that get me?"

"Another date?"

I laughed. "I was kind of hoping I'd already earned another date."

"What would you like?"

"Details about your worst date."

"Deal."

"So, am I right?"

"Yes. Before Greece, we lived in France. That is where Neil was born." She looked past me and her thoughts drifted far away from our date. I wondered if things had been easier for her family when her brother was younger. Before I could ask, something caught her attention and she nodded. "Alex is waving us back."

I wanted her back on the date I was enjoying so much and prompted her back to my request. "Worst date! Out with it." I caught gratitude in her eyes when she turned back to me.

"High school. I went out with the boy who had a locker next to mine." She paused and turned to me.

"And?"

"The boy part does not worry you?"

"Not unless you're married to him and about to tell me that I only have the potential to be your mistress."

She laughed and the sea breeze tousling her hair carried the joyous sound. "We went to see a movie. When we came out, his car had a flat tire. He was going to call a company for help, which was unnecessary. My father had taught me how to take care of a car, how to change oil, change a tire."

"I'm guessing he didn't appreciate that."

"Correct again. The whole drive home, I was thinking about what to do when he tried to kiss me. But when he pulled up at my house, he said thank you for changing the tire. He didn't even put the car in park."

"Too bad you weren't out with a girl. I would've let you get to first base for changing my tire."

"I have met women, too, who did not like to be made to feel incompetent."

I considered her words, sifting through them because I could not see why a date changing a tire would make anyone feel incompetent. It was something learned, and diversified skills seemed like an asset, not a threat. "I would think it's on them if they felt incompetent around you. For me, that's hot. I know it's only one example, but..." We had met back up with Alex by this time, so I whispered the remainder of the sentence. "Hot."

Back on the trail from the beach, I fell behind Remi. I couldn't feel my hips anymore, and I was fairly certain I'd lost some skin on my knees, but I couldn't remember feeling more satisfied with how well a date had gone. At the top of the hill, Alex stopped to let the horses graze while we waited for the sunset.

"Could you take our picture?" Remi asked.

He took her phone and backed his horse away from us. Remi swung her horse around, trying to get next to me. "Give Brownie a kick. Bring him up next to me."

I tried tapping the horse with my heels. Brownie shifted his weight, pushing up into M&M's rump. The little mare raised her tail exposing the biggest vulva I had ever seen. The horse let loose a waterfall of urine before I could even comment. I tried to swing my leg away from the steady yellow stream, but Brownie refused to move, and I stared in dismay as the flood hit my ankle and foot. "Your horse is peeing on me!"

This was the image Alex captured. Two horses pushed together, Remi's head thrown back in laughter, and my face contorted in disgust. And in the background, a gorgeous sunset.

I stood barefoot in the parking lot of The Miracle Center next to Remi's car, my urine-soaked shoe and its mate in the trunk of my car.

"Can't I post this?" Remi asked, studying the photo Alex had taken.

"I'd rather not be introduced to your friends and family as the *pendeja* who let a horse piss on her foot."

Remi frowned, but her face was still full of mirth. "You did get what you wanted." She stepped forward and clasped my hand.

"How's that?" I could not take my eyes off Remi's mouth.

"That was the most memorable date I've ever been on," Remi said. She traced one finger from my ear down to my shoulder, awakening every nerve ending along the way. Sweeping her hand around the back of my neck, she pulled me into a kiss. I could have lost myself in the silky softness of Remi's lips had they not parted once again in laughter. "But you smell awful!"

I reached around and playfully swatted Remi's rear. "Well at least my ass isn't black."

Remi's eyes widened in surprise. "My ass is black?" She bent to examine her legs. Her knees and thighs were equally stained with oil and dirt from the saddle. "Oh! These pants are ruined!"

"I'd say I'm sorry, but my shoe is toast."

Remi kissed me again. "It was still a great date."

"I'm glad you enjoyed yourself."

"I more than enjoyed myself." Remi took my hand and squeezed it tightly. "I kind of like you, Karla Hernandez. *Tu me rends tellement heureuse.*"

"I have no idea what that means, but it sounded good."

"*Me kaneis charoumeno.*"

I hesitated, not understanding a word. "I still have no idea what you said."

"Same sentiment, different language."

"Greek?"

"Very good. You make me so happy."

"I thought you swore in Greek."

"Only when someone makes me mad."

"Then I'll do my best to stay on your good side," I said, sneaking one last quick kiss.

CHAPTER ELEVEN

I also had to stay on my family's good side, which meant going to mass on Sundays. Remi and I exchanged a few texts comparing how stiff the horseback riding had made us, but we hadn't talked about when we'd get together again. I had no doubt we would, but since I had chosen the last date, I would wait for Remi to make the next suggestion.

I would have obsessed about it, but Monday's routine was blessedly busy, helping me shelve the question. I'd barely finished and was ready to leave for the monthly seminar when Judy came into the lab anxious about the results from the latest batch of volunteer white blood cells.

My back pocket buzzed, and I glanced quickly at my watch. It would be Valerie waiting in line for the box lunches wondering where I was. Judy was still talking, and I couldn't find a logical spot to interrupt her. My phone buzzed again. It took all my self-control to nod politely and ignore the texts. Judy knew about the monthly seminars, and my stomach turned uncomfortably as the seconds ticked by.

"I just need to do the western blot analysis," I said, "but I'd better get to the seminar before the speaker starts."

"Who's talking today?"

"Someone from Coastal State University."

Judy shrugged. "Fill me in if you learn anything meaningful."

Typical Judy, wanting her lab to make an appearance but not worth her time. I ran down the stairs and sprinted across campus, grateful for the exercise I'd been doing with Valerie that made the run possible. Glancing at my watch, I hoped they had not started on time and that I would be able to slip in with other stragglers. Since Valerie always grabbed lunch for me, I could at least beeline for the auditorium, but I always felt better with a few people entering behind me.

When I whooshed open the door to the lecture hall, I could already hear someone from The Miracle Center introducing the speaker. Valerie sat where we usually did, a few rows in on the left. I bowed my head, trying to fold myself invisible as I scooted to my seat.

Valerie handed over my lunch with a dramatic eye roll.

I opened the box whispering my thanks. "Got caught up talking to Judy."

"Punctuality is important, mate. And I betcha she would've agreed if you worked up the balls to say something."

I shook off the familiar dig and focused my attention on the speaker. Though I was doing my best to focus on the talk, snippets of the hours I'd spent with Remi kept taking over. I shut my eyes and stopped chewing. Something in the speaker's cadence reminded me of Remi. "Where's she from?" I asked Valerie.

Valerie set aside her lunch and ruffled through some papers. "Lebanon."

"Let me see?" I took the flyer and studied the picture. I saw a resemblance to Remi in the rich skin tone and sculpted brows. I closed my eyes again and listened intently.

"Are you catching any of this, or are you napping?"

"It's her voice. It doesn't matter what she says. I could listen to her all day."

"Accent whore."

I swallowed a laugh, coughed and took a sip of water. All of this brought Remi to mind again. I pulled out my phone and found two messages from Valerie. One about lunch, the other about my "chronic problem with promptness." As I was about to text Remi, my phone buzzed. Angling the phone away from Valerie, I opened it.

Trying hard to think of a date to top horseback riding. Would very much like to see you again.

I smiled, and Valerie elbowed me and pointed to the screen.

I can swing that. I added a smiley emoji. *What do I get if I guess another language correctly?*

We could use rules for strip poker.

I couldn't quite stifle a snort. Valerie leaned into me and mimicked my voice, "It's rude to text during a talk." Caught by my own reprimand, I grimaced. Still, I couldn't resist answering. *I'm right, you lose an article of clothing. I'm wrong, you get one of mine?* I did feel guilty about how little attention I was paying the speaker. Plus, Judy would be quizzing me. Only one more text, I told myself.

Precisely. And then I can make a guess about your body adornments.

Several flirty replies flashed through my mind, but I had to tame them. Reluctantly, I tapped out. *Have to text later. At a seminar.*

I tucked the phone between my thighs and concentrated on the speaker. My phone buzzed. Valerie glanced at it, but I kept my attention glued to the speaker.

"Following the correlation between the integrated samples and the meta-analysis, we found a proportional…"

"Are you following this?" I whispered to Valerie, worried that my texting had cost me the ability to comprehend.

"Not a word. It's all English, but she lost me at the first slide."

After another five minutes of concentrated listening, I still could not make sense of the talk. Leaning toward Valerie, I whispered, "They're good slides."

"Agreed. Brilliant graphics."

"Yes," I echoed. "Very pretty." I tried as hard as I could to grab hold of the speaker's information. I thought back to last month's, a challenging talk on technological advances in bypass surgery. Even though I knew little about surgery, it had made more sense than this presentation. I was surprised by how easily I was distracted by Remi.

Heat and desire flashed through my belly as I imagined a game of strip poker. It was not difficult to think of Remi removing clothes, and I was grateful for the dimmed lights when my mind willingly switched gears to how Remi and I could make good use of a dark room.

Valerie and I carried our lunch boxes toward the exit. I dropped the box and sandwich wrapper in the trash can and held the cookie and chips I hadn't eaten.

"You going to eat those?" Valerie asked.

I brightened. "Are you eating for two?"

"Bit early to be thinking about that, mate. Sadly, I have to stay late tonight. I have an appointment at the mouse house at nine."

"What about that new intern you hired? Why can't he do it?"

"He quit already."

"Amazing! You go through interns faster than Judy goes through office administrators."

"Nobody can stand working for the sloth. If I didn't have two years invested in this project, I'd leave as well. I can't blame people for bailing so quickly when they don't have a whole lot invested."

I had grown used to Valerie referring to her boss by the animal she claimed he resembled. The description went beyond his eyes, which he barely opened, and his swept back hair. More of a problem for Valerie was his laziness. I often thought of our PIs as at different ends of the scale. Sometimes I wished Judy would ease off the gas pedal, but I knew that Valerie wished Dr. Seonwoo was more active in driving his lab.

"Sorry to be such a downer."

"You're not a downer."

"What were you and your hottie texting about?"

"What I get if I guess the next language she speaks correctly."

"That sounds a lot more interesting than our speaker. Have fun with it!"

As soon as we parted ways, I pulled out my phone. I texted *Can u talk?* A moment later, my phone rang.

"I guess the answer is yes," I said, not bothering to suppress the smile that blossomed when I heard her voice.

"You had a seminar?"

"The monthly speaker at The Miracle Center. Valerie and I attend as often as we can. She pestered me about how rude it was to text even though we didn't understand the speaker at all."

"Still, I imagine your being there makes a good impression. As long as you're not on your phone."

"Thanks for understanding. The only thing I got from the presentation was that you must speak Lebanese."

"Very good. I do speak Lebanese Arabic. How in the world did the talk help you establish that?"

"The speaker was from Lebanon. Looked a smidge like you, too."

"My mother is from Lebanon."

"Ha! Knew it!" I punched my fist in the air victoriously. "Is that where you lived before Greece?"

"No. My parents met there when my father was an aide to the ambassador. It is my birthplace and where all of her family remains. I try to visit every other year."

I stopped outside my building, reluctant to end the conversation, especially as I had won with my guess. I said as much and added, "I cannot wait to pick the article of clothing for you to shed."

"What makes you think you get to pick? You said nothing about selecting the garment."

"Damn," I said with mock disappointment. "Probably better for me not to give it more thought right now since I have to get back to work."

"Too bad I am not waiting in the darkroom for you. I have some ideas of where I might find other piercings."

"You're cheating."

"Or tattoos."

"You'll have to earn that information fair and square."

"You could make a wrong guess about the last language on purpose."

"What's the fun in that?"

"I could make it very fun." The richness in her voice gave me no doubt to her sincerity.

"You are not making this easy."

"Make the most of the time you have to make your selection. How about that?"

"And when do I get to make my request?" Was it too soon for me to ask about tonight? Before I could overthink it, I said, "Are you free tonight?" The drawn out silence between us made me kick myself. It was too early. I sounded desperate. "That was stupid…"

"Don't," she interrupted. "I would have suggested the same except…I am otherwise committed."

Silence again. And I needed to work. But I didn't want to hang up, not when the conversation was going like this. *Fix this! Fix this!* I mentally admonished myself. "Tomorrow it goes up to two articles of clothing."

"Thank you for understanding." Her voice softened. "Dinner?"

"Absolutely."

"On a weeknight I won't be able to plan something to top our last date."

"Maybe there are other ways to make it memorable," I suggested.

"Unquestionably, there are," she answered. "And now I have to do my best not to let my thoughts linger on that. *MneHkeh areeban*, Karla."

"Showing off your Arabic?"

"It seemed appropriate. We will talk soon, Karla."

"I look forward to it. Bye."

Floating from the brief exchange, I continued with a spring in my step. Someone was standing outside the clinic, and I started to smile in passing. Then I recognized the figure. I stopped in my tracks. Maricela's mother. We stared at each other. Had I been in motion, I could have kept walking. I had to say something despite the hostility she radiated. In my rudimentary Spanish, I tried to share that Maricela was working very hard and had a lot of potential in science. I was trying to think of the word for "proud," but her expression cut me off.

Her eyes narrowed and I could feel her disgust. She stood fortress-like, her arms folded. Her flowing black skirt and long-sleeved black tunic made her look funeral-bound. A flood of Spanish invective erupted, and I scrambled to translate. My skin flashed hot when I realized I didn't need to understand what she was saying to capture her point. There was no misunderstanding "dyke," "bad influence" and "disgraceful." Her words pierced me, yet I did not move. I couldn't until others started heading down the sidewalk. I tried to direct Maricela's mother to a bench, but she swatted me away and stood her ground, her color and voice rising.

I held up my hand and shut my eyes in an effort to block out her words, which seemed to ruffle her further. My body screamed at me to run, but I couldn't. I refused to walk away from this woman and make her think that she had won.

After what felt like an eternity, Maricela appeared. "*Mamà!*" she cried, wrapping her arms around the shorter woman's shoulders.

She pushed her daughter aside and turned her venom back on me. More "dyke" arrows flew and Maricela winced.

"*Mamà*, calm down. Please, *Mamà*." The look she shot me was mixed with apology and something else. Shame? Or Blame?

Anger bubbled up in me. I had done nothing to invite this woman's ire, yet I was somehow being held accountable. Maricela wrapped one arm around her mother and guided her to a bench, murmuring in Spanish.

Crossing my arms, I waited while Maricela spoke to the irate woman. I hoped for an apology. I had done nothing more than help Maricela stay on track in both her service project and semester.

With averted eyes, Maricela finally approached me. "Dr. Hernandez, I am sorry."

"You are, but not your mother." Mrs. Gonzales and I continued to stare at each other angrily.

"Please take my apology. I told you about my mother. I am sorry because I did this. I should have told her that you and your friend are not a couple. But I didn't because I thought that maybe thinking you were gay would make her see that gay people aren't bad. You and your friend are successful and trying to help people. I'm sorry. I shouldn't have tried to use you to change her."

I finally blinked away from Maricela's mother. "I accept your apology. But your mother's outburst was unacceptable."

Maricela nodded miserably, and I finally let go of some of my anger. She was not going to agree with me in front of her mother.

Without another look at either woman, I stormed toward my building with an internal monologue of the things I would say to Mrs. Gonzales if I spoke better Spanish. The woman should be grateful for the hours and hours scientists, myself included, had invested in the drug that might save her sight. Yet she couldn't see past the fact that I loved women. If I'd been interested in her daughter, I could maybe understand her emotional reaction, but I wasn't. I wanted Remi.

A shiver of anticipation washed over my hot anger. Remi promised that we would talk soon, and that promise allowed me to set aside my hurt and return to work clear-headed.

CHAPTER TWELVE

I thought I had put the incident with Maricela's mother behind me, but by Thursday, my mood was seriously dragging. I had managed to distract myself on Tuesday by imagining what two articles of clothing I could ask for in our game. Could I skip the shirt and ask for her bra? All anticipation fell flat when Remi canceled. I teased that Wednesday earned me three articles of clothing, but her *Not free Weds* reply extinguished my flirtation. That at least saved me from a day of distraction. I responded with *Let me know when you're free* and was still waiting to hear from her.

I wasn't used to that. I was the one who messed up plans, whose work got in the way of dating. If indeed it was her work and not something personal. My own work had offered no refuge, and I was past ready for the week to be over.

I rested my spoon next to my bowl of soup, aware that my mother would not be pleased with how little of the *caldo de res* I had eaten. As much as I loved my mother's beef soup, I simply had no appetite tonight.

Snapping fingers brought my attention back to the table. "Ah! There you are," my mother chided. "Clear the table, *mi hija*."

She gave me the task not as punishment but to get me into the kitchen.

"I'm sorry," I said before my mother could question me. "I got hammered today."

"I can see that."

"I said I was sorry."

My mother hmphed as she sorted the dishes, waiting for me to talk.

"You know that college student that I've been working with, Maricela?"

"Yes."

"Sometimes I see her waiting for her mother, and usually I stop and check in with her about how her class is going. Make sure she's still going and everything." I stepped to the sink and filled it with soapy water for the handwashing. "Earlier this week, her mother was there, and I shared with her how impressed I am by her daughter."

"That was nice of you. What did she say?"

"Not 'thank you.'"

"Maybe she didn't understand you?"

"I told her in Spanish."

"Your Spanish isn't very good. Maybe you didn't say what you meant to?"

"My Spanish is good enough to understand that she thinks I'm a bad influence."

"Haven't you helped her with her grades?"

"That doesn't matter if you're a dyke."

"Is that what she said to you?"

"It's pretty hard to misunderstand that word."

"Does Maricela know you're gay?"

"Yes."

"Does it bother her?"

"No."

"Then why does her mother's opinion matter to you?" She crossed her arms across her chest. I scrubbed the cutting board and the knives. It didn't make sense to be upset about what Maricela's mother thought of me. So why *did* it matter? I rinsed the dishes and handed them to my mother to dry.

"I think she should be more appreciative. Maricela's education is important to her, and I'm the one who got her back on track. I thought that would count for something. Instead, she hates me." I held out one soapy hand and then the other. "Effort, return. That's what it is. The effort I put in doesn't match the return."

I was surprised to feel my eyes burning and quickly turned away from my mother to load plates into the dishwasher. I hoped she wouldn't see me swipe my wrist over my eye. Her hands closed around my arms, and she turned me toward her where I was forced to look at her and see how worried she was.

"Your research, is it not going well?"

"No, my research is fine." I cleared my throat and tried to turn.

She held me firmly. "Then what is this? This isn't your student's mother being impolite."

"Remi canceled on me again." I tried to hide from my mother's scrutiny by turning back to the sink.

She let me go with her hands but not her words. "The one you took horseback riding last weekend."

"Yes."

"Rosa's judge."

"Same Remi, yes."

"So you like this Remi. Why is she canceling dates with you? What did you do wrong?"

"I didn't do anything wrong! Why do you think it's me?"

My mother pursed her lips. "You don't make time for people."

"She's the one who canceled on me." I was making time for Remi, and it stung to push myself to wrap up work when I said I would and to go home just to get a text from Remi saying how sorry she was to have to cancel. "She didn't even say why." Even I could hear the petulance in my voice.

"It must be important, no? And if it is important, does the reason matter? She is probably as disappointed as you are."

"You're right," I said.

"Don't sound so surprised. I don't understand everything you say, but I am no idiot. I listen. I learn."

My mother's words surprised me. Did my mother feel that I lorded my education over her? "I know you listen, Ma."

"I am proud of you. It is such a good thing, you helping this young woman. You are a very good role model, and it is very sad her mother was rude to you."

My eyes stung at my mother's kind words. I felt bad for Maricela and then remembered something Remi had said at the beach. You don't get to choose your family. I paused midway to the dishwasher holding a dripping glass. How had I gotten so lucky? The question reminded me of all the luck-themed conversations I'd had with Valerie where I had always insisted that my brother was the lucky one. I turned to my mother and wrapped my arms around her soft frame. My mother's hug supported me in a way that made me aware of how exhausted I was.

"You are so tired," my mother said, petting my hair. "Are you not sleeping any better?"

"Some nights."

"But not the last few. Not with all this worry."

"No."

"Take Rosa home with you. You could use the sleep, and she could use some time with her favorite *tía*."

I thanked my mother for the pep talk and went to pitch the sleepover idea to Rosa.

"That was fast," I said when Rosa returned with a small bag slung over her shoulder.

"All I needed was my toothbrush. Everything else I have packed just in case." She turned to kiss her mother goodnight. Antonia shrugged her *Don't ask me, I've never gotten this kid* shrug.

The setting sun backlit the trees lining the street, making them glow. My conversation with my mother continued to tumble around in my thoughts. I had never questioned the stability in my life. Even when they didn't understand me, my parents, and in their own way, my siblings, always supported me. I had also been supported by scholarships. The only drag I could identify was the brief time I'd dated Ann who had made me feel guilty for the time I dedicated to my work.

Remi understood my hours far better than Ann ever had, being a committed professional herself. Maybe things were crazy at her work, and I needed to take her cancellations less personally.

"What happens when your project is finished, *Tía?*" Rosa asked out of the blue.

"I'll continue with other projects that have been on hold."

"When your boss retires, will you have her job?"

I laughed. "No. I'm a relatively new research scientist. There are others who have more experience writing grants. You have to be good at getting money to be the one running the lab."

"You're not good at that?"

"I don't have a lot of experience with it, and it's not something I'm interested in."

"You like working in the lab better?"

"I do," I said, thinking about how my research had once been all-consuming, but Rosa's question made me realize I had not been anticipating my next project. I had only been thinking about getting this drug into a clinical trial.

"Because you want to help people stay healthy," Rosa said.

"Exactly."

"Me too. *Abuela* says you need more sleep to stay healthy."

"*Abuela* is right about that. Thanks for helping me out." I swung my arm around Rosa as we crossed the wide street.

"You still have to do your stretches."

"Sure thing, kiddo. I'm not going to mess with a protocol that works!"

From her perch on the couch, Petri twitched her tail and allowed Rosa to pet her. I dropped my keys on the counter and took my phone from my pocket. Leaving my phone in another room was part of my winding-down ritual. Out of habit, I checked for messages and found nothing new. It would look bad to text her again when I'd said to let me know when she was free, wouldn't it? I set my phone on the counter. Picked it up again. What was the right thing to say?

That I wished I had been able to see her tonight?

Too needy.

Rosa threw me a smile. "We'd better get ready for bed," she said. I could hear Antonia's argument that Rosa made a better parent than she did.

Man, had I been looking forward to sharing my bed with Remi. "I have one message I want to send." I frowned at the thought of texting Remi how very much I would like to have her in my bed, hearing a tone somewhere between guilt and blame.

Rosa held my gaze. "Just one."

"Yes, Mom."

Rosa laughed and took her things to the bedroom.

My thumbs hovered over the screen. *I hope everything is okay.* That was the right sentiment, wasn't it? I hit send and silenced the phone, placing it facedown on the counter.

Rosa and I got ready for bed. Rosa crawled under the covers to read while I did my stretches. *Be Well.* Tonight, Remi was on my mind. I genuinely hoped she was well.

My phone buzzed on the kitchen counter.

Deep breath. *Be content.* I'd been disappointed when Remi canceled, but that was a small thing. In the larger scheme of things, I'd found her, and we had had a really good time together. That was something to be content about.

Be at peace. I tried to settle into my third meditation phrase, but I couldn't help wondering what Remi said. There would be no peace until I knew. I hopped up.

"You're finished?" Rosa asked dubiously.

"Be right back." How was it that a kid could make me feel so guilty?

I tiptoed to my phone and checked the message. *I owe you an explanation.*

The phone buzzed in my hands as another text came in. *If you're not fed up with me.*

Not at all. I typed before thinking.
Liar. At least I hope you are lying.
Disappointed, sure. Not fed up. I typed.
I'd like to see you tomorrow.
I'd like that. Can't say when I'll wrap up.
Maybe dinner if it's not too late?
I sent a thumbs-up and a sleep emoji.
"*Tia!*"
"Promise I'm almost done."
Remi returned the sleep emoji.

I returned the phone to the counter and jogged back to my room to settle back into my stretch, feet on the wall, arms out to my side. I buzzed through the first three phrases to get my breath evened out. *Be well. Be content. Be at peace…* I tried to keep my mind from whirling on what had happened with Remi this week that she would want to talk about but not text.

Be calm. I let the words flood through my body. Calm. Nothing to be done about it tonight.

CHAPTER THIRTEEN

On Friday, I finished my lab notes and shelved them, finally ready to head home. I'd been waiting all day for Remi to cancel but when I texted to say I'd be home by six, she replied to ask what she could bring. We were still on! I had given myself an hour of wiggle room to make sure I beat Remi there, and I had needed it.

Nervous about her seeing my condo for the first time, I spent a few minutes tidying. I surveyed the place objectively and scrunched my nose. Everything in my house looked so practical. There was art on the wall that my mother had pulled out of their garage to brighten up my bare walls after Ann had moved out. I'd put a few family pictures in frames, but my bookshelves were dominated by textbooks.

It was clearly a space I spent time in, but nothing in my house matched. The coordinated furniture had left with Ann, and I was happy to accept what my family no longer needed or what I could find at thrift stores. I wondered what impression it would make on someone who drove a Ferrari.

A knock at the door announced that it was a moot point. It was too late to change who I was. Remi stood on my doorstep, but not the Remi who had rendered me breathless at the science fair, nor the flirtatious one I had been getting to know on our dates. This Remi was off somehow. Not in her presentation. Her flowing black pants and a red wraparound blouse hugging her beautiful curves were stylish as usual. But her mouth was tight and her impeccable makeup did not quite hide the dark circles under her eyes. She had the look I'd had last night when my mother sent Rosa home with me.

Something was obviously worrying her. I almost didn't want to let her in, didn't want to know what had diverted her attention and made her so solemn.

"Come in," I said. We hugged, only our shoulders touching, and she stood in my living room, her eyes on the layout instead of me.

"How long have you been here?"

"Three years. I moved in when I started at The Miracle Center."

Remi's gaze settled on the family pictures on the bookshelf. She crossed the room and picked up a frame that held a picture of me holding Rosa in a baptism gown. She raised her eyebrows.

"I'm her godmother," I said.

"How seriously do you take your duties?"

I laughed. "You have to ask? You saw what I did to help with her science project. I'd do anything for that kid. Including swallowing embarrassment."

"I don't remember her embarrassing you."

I, on the other hand, easily recalled all the things my niece had said about me needing someone to sleep with and how suggestive her wording was when she talked about my lab. Just remembering brought color to my cheeks.

"There's no shame in sleeping better with a companion."

"No, but there is embarrassment when you feel like your goddaughter is pimping you to the cute judge."

Now Remi laughed. "I did not take it that way. How *are* you sleeping these days?"

I could let us keep exploring the tangent or steer us back to why Remi was here. I chose the latter. "Better than you seem to be."

Remi replaced the picture and gestured to the couch. "May I?"

"Of course. Do you want something to drink? Water? Something stronger?"

"No, thank you." She smiled, but only to acknowledge my attempt at humor, not because my words lightened her mood. "You said before that you and your siblings are close."

I sat on the couch careful to give Remi room. "Most of the time. As much as possible with four years between each of us."

"You're the baby."

I grimaced, hearing the way Luis teased me. "You're not the big sister who feels like her life was ruined by the kids who came along and stole all your parents' attention, are you?"

"No. Quite the opposite. Neil and I have always been very close. Perhaps growing up in other countries made us allies. I was six when he was born, old enough to appreciate having a companion."

I chuckled. "It takes a while until a younger sibling can be any fun, though. At least my brother told me plenty of times how boring a baby is."

"I enjoyed mothering him, and perhaps those preverbal years made it easier to navigate his lack of communication skills as he got older. I did not have my parents' expectations."

Something Remi had said at the beach flashed through my mind. When I had shared that Valerie thought I had some competition, Remi had said that could describe her brother. "He is why you canceled?"

Remi studied her hands. "Neil does best on a schedule, and Monday we were supposed to have dinner and watch his movie. I stopped by on my way here and thought I had smoothed it over to move our routine to Tuesday. On my way over here, the caregiver called me…" She interrupted herself. "He is not entirely self-sufficient. Even though he is twenty-four, he lives in a house with four roommates and on-site staff."

I nodded to show that I was still with her, that I understood.

"I should have known how this would impact his life. I work with this population all the time and tell parents how important it is to not disrupt routine. After my mother took a job overseas, I moved here to keep his routine intact. He needs the consistency of a family member visiting him. And here I am…" Remi looked up, revealing raw pain. I scooted up beside her on the couch and put my arm around her.

"And you said before that you're all he has."

She sighed deeply. "I am having difficulty explaining this new part of my life to him. Until I met you, I spent most of my free time with him. Now I would like to reallocate that time, but it is difficult. He doesn't have a whole lot of language."

"What movie do you watch? You watch the same one every week?"

"Yes, these days it is *The Lego Batman Movie*. Lego is his language. Building Lego, working at Legoland, playing the Lego videogame at Sloan's. It has made communicating with him easier than when we were children, but it still has limitations. How do I explain wanting to spend time with you? I thought I could use Lego figures, and he would get the transference." She frowned. "Apparently not."

I had no idea how to respond. I felt terrible for the weight Remi had to carry, and I felt even more terrible for wondering how Neil's meltdown about his routine affected the possibility of a relationship with Remi. It couldn't really count as a negative that she cared too much for her brother. That would be pretty low. "What if he met me?" I offered.

Remi quirked her head. "You want to meet him?"

"Is that a terrible idea? I'm sorry. I don't know anything. Don't listen to me."

"Don't say that. I have known Neil my whole life, and I still don't always get him, but I do know that he is more than most people can handle. I was thinking that when I told you about the trouble he was having adjusting, you'd…"

"Pack you out the door?" I said, surprise in my voice.

"I wouldn't blame you."

"But…" I remembered the hurt I had felt worrying that Remi might not have read our first dates as I had. It must have taken a lot of courage for Remi to come and talk about her brother. If she could be honest and upfront, I should meet her there. "This doesn't feel the same as anything I have ever done before."

"How's that?" Remi held me with her seductive brown eyes, brown like rich chocolate cake, and I wanted nothing more than to stay there.

"I don't know. This feels more…Does it sound weird to say more grown up? I'm not in school anymore. I'm becoming who I am, and you," I bit my lip, "are so together and driven and gorgeous and more than I ever thought I could ask for."

Remi's face finally relaxed. Her gaze drifted to my lips before meeting my eyes again. "That doesn't sound weird at all. It sounds a lot like how I feel about you."

I blinked. "Me?"

"You have a PhD, and a paper in a major journal that even I've heard of. You have your own place and don't go glassy-eyed when I talk about the tests and results I go over with my students. It's quite appealing to spend time with someone your equal."

"Spend time? That's all we're doing? I thought…"

"That I would be helping with your sleep study." Some of the shadow that had hung about Remi returned. "As appealing as that sounds, I worry my commitment to Neil would make that…difficult."

A lump formed in my throat. "Weren't we talking about how nice it is to be with someone who feels like an equal?"

"We were, and it's so easy when I'm sitting here talking to you to picture something fantastic with you."

"But there's your brother," I said.

"Always will be."

"Yeah."

Remi looked away, the first action that would take her away from me. I cupped Remi's chin, bringing her back to me. I kissed her softly, asking for permission. Remi kissed me tentatively, and

I closed my eyes, warmth spreading through my whole body. No one else's mouth had ever done this to me. No one had ever fit so perfectly, meeting me with exactly the right pressure, leaning in to chase the tail end of the kiss with the same reluctance to pull away. Out of breath, I broke from the kiss, pressing my forehead to Remi's. I breathed in her lilac sweetness. "Then it makes sense for me to meet him, doesn't it?"

"It could make things worse," Remi whispered.

"It can't be worse forever. You haven't gotten good results changing his schedule. So the next experiment is for me to go with you. I take good notes. I could make a spreadsheet. Graph something."

"I don't doubt it," Remi said. She leaned forward to kiss me again.

I wove both hands into Remi's thick, silky hair. A kiss like this made me forget feeling sidelined, made any time with Remi worth negotiating with Neil's schedule. I put how sorry I was that Remi had so much to carry into the kiss. I added my admiration for her, and from Remi's reaction, it seemed like she understood. My heart hammered like a fist on a door. I felt completely connected to Remi, our kiss a promise not to run from the complications of her life.

Remi pulled away. "I think someone's at your door."

"No," I panted. "It's my heart." I placed Remi's hand on my chest.

"Impressive," Remi smiled. "But there is literally someone knocking at the door."

"*Tía!*" Rosa's voice called.

I glanced at my watch. "What day is it?" I asked, wondering if I had somehow missed a dinner my mother expected me to attend.

"Friday."

"Weird." I stood on wobbly knees and stumbled to the door. I stared at Remi as the knocking continued.

"Don't you think you should open it?"

"Not until I'm not panting!" I said, making Remi laugh. That stilled the knocking, so I opened the door.

Instead of entering, Rosa leaned her head in the door and located the source of the laughter. "Sorry!" she exclaimed and backed away.

"No, no. Come back here. What's up?"

Rosa stopped at the sidewalk. "Homework. Mom was pulling her hair, and you said that I could ask you questions."

I closed my eyes, remembering very well what I had said and feeling very frustrated that she needed help on a rare evening Remi had away from Neil. Even as well-adjusted as she was, like Neil, Rosa depended on the grownups in her life, including her aunt. "Yes, I said anytime. Come in."

"But…"

"Come on. If I don't understand, maybe Remi can help. You remember Remi?"

"Hi," Rosa said shyly.

"Good to see you again. Congratulations on your second-place award. There was steep competition in that category, and you had a wonderful project."

They both looked at me, ratcheting up my embarrassment. To redirect their thoughts away from my insomnia, I pointed to Rosa's book. "What's got you stumped?"

"Math."

"Let's take a look." Over Rosa's head, I mouthed, "I'm sorry."

Remi dismissed my worry with the wave of her hand, and I followed Rosa to the small table between the living room and kitchen. Rosa set out her workbook and pointed to the problem. I read the question. It made no sense. Maybe because I could feel Remi staring at me. I read it again. "I think I remember how to solve this."

Before I'd gotten very far at all, Rosa interrupted me. "No. That's what my mom did. That's not what my teacher taught us." Rosa groaned.

"May I try?" Remi asked. She took the pencil and started drawing boxes that Rosa recognized immediately.

"Looks like I'm no help here. Dinner?"

"I'd love something if you've got enough," Remi said, only briefly glancing up.

"Absolutely," I said.

When Remi had returned her focus to the workbook, Rosa caught my eye and grinned like a fool. She pointed to Remi. Her jaw dropped open wide, and her eyebrows arched.

I gave a thumb's-up and mouthed, "Right?"

While I sliced onion and green peppers, I listened to Remi explain the math concept in a way I'd never heard before. I was impressed, not only by Remi's intellect but also her ability to make it understandable. I sliced some grilled chicken I had brought home from my mother's leftovers and added it to the pan with the sautéed vegetables. I seasoned the pan and turned my attention to making guacamole with fresh tomato and cilantro.

Rosa kept glancing between me and Remi as she ran through a second problem. "I think I've got it," she said when I turned off the burner.

"Are you sure?" Remi asked. "I don't mind spotting you through the next one."

"It's okay. It was the setup I had trouble with. Now that you showed me how, I think I'll be okay."

"Did you eat, kiddo?" I asked as I dragged a flour tortilla over a lit burner.

"We already ate dinner," she said, gathering her things. She sneaked another peek at Remi. "It was nice to see you again. I'm sorry to interrupt."

"Don't be. I was very happy to see you again." Remi waved to her.

"Thank you again for your help."

I followed Rosa to the door and gave her a big hug. "You need me to walk to the corner?"

Rosa's withering expression was answer enough.

"Give *Abuela* a hug from me." I squeezed her again.

Rosa waved over her shoulder and trotted down the sidewalk. I shut the door and returned to the stove, piling the fajita fixings on top. "Someone was pretty excited to see you here. In approximately three minutes, she will be telling my mother and sister."

"Your family is wonderful," Remi said.

I handed her a plate and the bowl of guacamole, reflecting on how she had not been as lucky in the family department.

"This smells delicious."

"I am sorry for the interruption." Thinking of all I had been trying to communicate with my kiss, I said, "I had more to say."

"At least you have a good apology," Remi said, holding up the food.

"This is just leftovers."

"Still, on a work night? I'm impressed already." She leaned in and kissed me long enough that I had to turn off the stove for fear of burning my tortilla. "Impressed again, I should say. Over and over."

"Even though I didn't get her math problem?"

"You remember the way you were taught. The only reason I knew was because I'm around the teachers complaining about the latest version of the curriculum. That you gave your time and that your niece can approach you like that, it says a lot. It makes it a little easier to imagine introducing you to Neil."

We carried our food to the table. "Whenever you're ready," I said, glad my mother had so recently refreshed my memory on the importance of patience.

CHAPTER FOURTEEN

In my exercise leggings and top, I jogged down the stairs and was about to push through the doors when a familiar shape caught my eye.

"Maricela?"

The young woman lifted her head and guiltily swept her phone into her pocket.

"You're here early," I observed. Maricela had persevered to the end of her semester, and though her service-learning project had ended, she'd asked me if I would help her study for her biology final.

Maricela lifted her shoulder. "My mom's appointment time changed."

I pointed at the bag from the local fast-food joint on the table. "That was lunch?"

"Sure," Maricela said. She lifted the soda and wrapped her red, red lips around the straw.

"Come on." I sent a message to Valerie. I hated to miss our intense workout, but I would not be able to concentrate at all if I left Maricela sitting with her soda.

"What?"

"I said, come on. You're with me today."

Discomfort swept over Maricela's face. "Exercise?"

I read Valerie's reply and furrowed my brow. Even though I'd told her to go on without me, Valerie surprised me by replying that she'd find me. I texted that we'd be stretching outside my building. "You've got to pay for that." I pointed to the cup in Maricela's hand.

"I already did."

I hung my head. "You bought it. Now you've got to burn it off before your body stores it away."

Maricela remained seated.

"Get up. Go put your bag in the lab. I'm not leaving you here. I can't even believe you brought this crap on campus. You do realize why your mother is here, don't you?"

"Yeah," Maricela bristled.

I peeked inside Maricela's bag. "Burger and fries?" I said flatly.

"Yeah."

I wrinkled my nose. "You kill me, you know that?"

"You're saying I'm fat? This is beautiful." She gestured to her curves. "These are the hips of my culture, my heritage. I am beautiful."

"You are very beautiful," I agreed. "You don't need to change your body, just what you put in it or else you're diabetes waiting to happen."

"I'm not diabetic."

"Not yet. I'm not, either, but I bet your family tree looks a lot like mine. Diabetic grandmother, aunt, cousins. I don't even have it in my immediate family, and I'm making choices to avoid it. Go put your stuff away. I'll wait for you outside." I pushed her through the door and searched for Valerie.

Maricela returned without her backpack. "It was just a lunch," she pouted.

I was pleased that Maricela had followed my instructions, but I was still pissed by her attitude. It was all I could do to keep myself from exploding at the young woman. "Do you know what your mom is supposed to eat each day? Do you know how many calories she gets? And don't you dare shrug as if you don't."

Maricela stared at me.

"Your lunch had more calories than she's supposed to consume in a day. Is that what she's eating? Because that will kill her."

"No. I just got something for myself. She doesn't eat like that anymore."

"Maybe try to be supportive. Eat what she's eating. It's good to support her, and it certainly won't hurt you."

"Okay. I'll try," she said.

Better answer. I scanned for Valerie and still didn't see her. Brows furrowed in concern, I tugged on Maricela's sleeve. "Come on. We need to find my friend."

We walked through campus past the creepy statue and found Valerie doubled over by a trash can, her hands on her knees. I rushed to her side. "Are you okay?"

"I'm fine. Except for the fact that I hurled out my guts on the way over."

"Maybe you're pregnant," I said without thinking.

She straightened and froze.

I opened my mouth, glanced at Maricela, and snapped it back shut. I looked back to Valerie. "You think…"

Valerie raised her fingers counting. When she had four extended, she said, "Isn't it too early to know?"

"How would I know? Want me to Google it?"

"No. That's it." She shook her head slowly. "Oh, shit."

Maricela stepped back as if Valerie was going to spew again, but I stepped forward to rub her back. "You think you're pregnant?" I whispered, now that Maricela had put some distance between us. My stomach tightened with anticipation.

"I only missed my period yesterday. I haven't even peed on a stick."

Maricela took another step back, capturing Valerie's attention. "G'day. Nice to see you again. I'm Valerie."

Maricela introduced herself from a distance.

"Sorry to be gross. I think it's passed. I wasn't feeling top notch. It's why I said I'd walk with you when you said you were taking it easier."

"You up for walking the perimeter?" I asked.

"Let's give it a go," Valerie said. We set out, and Valerie called back to Maricela who stayed behind us.

"You're not thinking of dropping out again, are you?"

"No."

"Studying for a test?" Valerie asked. "You have some flashcards, Dr. Hernandez?"

"Funny, but no," I answered. "She decided to walk off the shitload of carbs she just consumed."

Valerie gave Maricela an obvious once-over.

"I already got the lecture."

Valerie lifted her hands in surrender. "Half of it she probably stole from me. I hope she gave me credit."

"What are you going to tell Emma?"

"Emma's my wife," Valerie tossed over her shoulder to Maricela. Her head snapped up like she'd been hit by a water balloon. To me, she said, "How should I know? First try and all, I was sure it wouldn't work. After how hard we tried with her, I'm going to look like an asshole if it worked the first time."

"She'll be thrilled," I said.

"Unless she's not. She wanted to be pregnant so badly."

"And lucky her, she had a backup uterus."

"That's true."

"She's going to be a parent. Think of all the dads out there who can't pinch hit if their wives can't carry. Carrying the baby is just the first step, and she still gets to experience it with you. You guys are going to be fine. You're the oven, and she's the ladydad."

Valerie laughed. "Ladydad. I love that. It sounds like katydid."

"Have you two talked about what the little cricket is going to call you? Are you going to do the whole Mama V and Mama E thing?"

"I'll be Mum, of course. I don't know if she wants to be Mommy."

"Or Ladydad."

"No way is she going for Ladydad."

"I like it. One of you should be Ladydad."

"Save it for your own kids. You and Remi have been dating long enough to talk about kids, haven't ya?"

I peered over my shoulder to find that Maricela, though breathing heavily, was keeping up with us. "We've only been on a few dates."

"Right, so you should be living together by now. Stereotypes to uphold, mate!"

We reached a corner where we could either loop back around to my building or continue to circle the entire campus. "Tired? Straight or left?"

"Gayly forward!" With a finger thrust in the air, Valerie punctuated the expression she'd picked up from Emma.

"Gayly forward it is," I consulted Maricela, "unless you're tired?"

Breathing heavily, Maricela said, "Forward."

Valerie met my eyes, and we shared the observation of the dropped adjective. She leaned over and whispered, "Are we all gay here?"

I turned to Maricela. "She hasn't said anything out loud, but her mother was very upset when she thought we were a couple."

That made Valerie laugh. "Oh, Emma will love that. You're my work wife!"

Redirecting to Maricela she asked, "So are you?"

"What?" Maricela asked.

Valerie and I rolled our eyes.

"Gay," Valerie said. "I'm pretty sure it's a requirement for joining our workout program."

"I'm not."

"Not gay or not joining our workouts?" Valerie asked.

"I don't have a girlfriend."

Valerie pulled her eyebrows together, confused. "You have to have a girlfriend to be gay?"

"That follows the principle of not caring what you eat until someone formally tags you with the word diabetic." Maricela didn't meet my gaze. "Forward it is," I said, leading the group.

Valerie returned her attention to my dating life. "So you haven't gotten any clothes off your hottie yet?"

I glared at her, not wanting to discuss my dating life in front of Maricela. I thought back to the way Maricela had prodded my sunburn and the interest she'd had in what had kept me out in the sun. But Valerie had openly discussed the likelihood of being pregnant, and the conversation was certainly motivating Maricela to keep up a good pace.

"She came over last night," I finally answered.

Valerie rubbed her hands together. "Annnnnnd?"

"And said that her brother makes dating very complicated."

"Sexy," Valerie said, disappointment weighing the word.

"And then Rosa came over needing help with math."

Valerie smacked her palm to her forehead. "I'm never having sex again."

"That's a little dramatic, don't you think?" I asked.

"Once the cricket is born, my sex life is toast. Rosa doesn't even live with you, and she is ruining your sex life. There's no getting away from your own kid."

"I'm sure you and Emma will find ways. You've got time."

"Doesn't feel like it."

"Start with telling her you're pregnant."

"You think I pee on the stick with her or without her?"

"How did you do it when it was her?"

"She waited until I was home, and we read it together."

"Then that's what you do."

We walked in silence, the three of us were in such different stages. Single. At the beginning of a relationship. Married and about to start a family. Valerie's head had to be spinning with the way her life was about to change. What was Maricela thinking about? Was there someone she had her eye on? Butterflies flittered in my stomach as Remi entered my thoughts. As we walked, I allowed myself to think about what was growing between Remi and me. For so long all I envisioned was professional success. Now I pictured Remi's hand in mine, heard us sharing our days. I wanted to tell Remi about Valerie and Emma. Did Remi think about having her own children? A smile crept to my lips at the new possibilities.

Valerie stopped at her building.

"Call me when you know for sure," I said.

Valerie's "Okay" lacked the volume and confidence she usually radiated.

"You can do this."

"Thanks. Hope I see you again, Maricela. You don't have to be gay to walk with us. Or pregnant." She looked like she might be sick again as she said it.

Maricela responded with a wide-eyed nod.

I gave her a hug before heading back with Maricela. Though my own heart rate had barely climbed, sweat darkened the pits and spine of Maricela's shirt.

With great difficulty, I turned my thoughts from Valerie's physical state to Maricela's final. "How do you feel about your exam coming up?"

"Good. I think I've got this. My teacher said she's never seen such a comeback."

"Your professor," I corrected. "Earned titles are important."

"Okay." Maricela nodded. "My professor. She said all I need is a C on this last test, and I pass. But I been getting Cs and Bs on my quizzes, so I'm thinkin' I can score at least a B."

I marveled at the turnaround in attitude. I was even more proud of the fact that Maricela was striving for a higher grade than she needed than the fact she would pass. "Proud of yourself?"

"Yeah. I know I messed up other stuff, but at least I got the class right." Her voice cracked.

"You did. You really did."

"So after this week, I don't have class. Not until the fall semester."

"If you need help, with anything, let me know. I mean that."

Maricela smiled shyly. "I was wondering, though, if maybe I could walk with you and your friend again."

"We walk Tuesdays and Fridays. Same time. You're always welcome." I linked arms with Maricela, and we walked up to the lab together.

CHAPTER FIFTEEN

"Are you available to drive me to work every day for the rest of my life?" I asked, melting into the tan leather upholstery of Remi's Ferrari.

"I might start to think you are dating me for my car."

I sat up, surprised. "Are we dating?"

"I am taking you to meet my brother. I am pretty sure that means we are dating."

"All right," I drew out the word as I settled back into luxury. "I'm dating a hottie in a Ferrari!"

"I will accept the compliment about me, but please do not let the insignia of the car fool you."

"You weren't happy with your father's gift." I remembered the bitterness in her voice when she'd told me how she'd gotten it.

"A used Italian car can hardly be considered a gift. It is unreliable and nearly impossible to maintain, but because of the sentimental gesture, I cannot get rid of it." She laughed softly. "Much like my father himself."

I was still trying to think of a response when she changed the subject. "Are you nervous?"

It was Saturday and we were on our way to Neil's group home. She had described their typical routine, which, until we had met, had mostly included her listening to Lego facts on days he didn't work and a catalog of what he had stocked at Legoland on days that he did.

That she had never brought anyone along with her worried me. I had no way of knowing how Neil would react to my being there. "There are so many unknowns for me. Google gave me an idea of the whole autism spectrum, but a spectrum is intimidating. Even based on what you've told me about him, it's hard to predict what meeting him will be like."

"Hence the bag."

I had tossed a large backpack on the backseat.

"Still not telling me what's inside?"

"What I hope is some Lego magic."

"The most important thing for you to know is how much I love him." She glanced at me and smiled warmly. "And I know you know that. But you go further than that. Spending time researching autism? You're amazing."

"Research is what I do. I want to understand."

"Knowing that's who you are is what makes me think this is going to be fine. You've already shown more interest than my ex ever did."

I remembered that "the ex," as Remi always referred to her, had simply acted like Neil did not exist. She interpreted Remi's decision to move closer to Neil as putting him first instead of their relationship. I sympathized with both. I couldn't imagine living far away from my siblings, but I could also understand how the ex had felt like she wasn't a priority in Remi's life.

Remi parked in a lot behind a large stone home set far back from the street. An immaculate green hedge lined the perimeter, and the lawn was perfectly tended.

"This place looks super nice."

"I think the same thing every time I come to visit. I should admit now that it's much nicer than my place."

"Oh, will I be seeing this subpar housing?"

"It's entirely possible that's in your future." Remi leaned across the console to give me a kiss that previewed her plans after visiting her brother.

"It might not have been the best idea to do that right before I meet Neil."

"Rosa would notice," Remi said, "but Neil will not."

I followed Remi inside. Remi greeted and introduced me to Adam. He was short and balding early, but everything else about him was large, eyeglasses, nose, and smile. He acknowledged me and then told Remi that Neil was in his room.

Remi led me down the hall, knocked lightly and opened the door. I stood at the doorway as Remi entered. Neil was seated on the floor, one leg folded underneath him and the other leg in front, his chin resting on his knee. He had to have a slight frame to be able to fold himself into such a position. In front of him was an elaborate Lego building. He looked up when Remi ruffled his close-cropped dark hair. "Hey, Neil! Anything exciting happen today?"

"I saved the city again." His coloring matched his sister's, but his expression was unquestionably open. He lacked Remi's guardedness, the reserve that came with maturity. Though his size made him look like an adult admiring a child's toy, his devoted attention to it made him seem younger.

Remi gave me a thumbs-up. She had explained that Neil often communicated in movie dialogue, and if he responded to her prompt, it was good sign for my visit. "I brought my friend Karla to see you. Do you remember me telling you about her?"

He raised his eyes so briefly that I would have missed it had I blinked. "Did you tell her about me?"

"She did," I said, entering and sitting some distance away from him. I pulled from my backpack a large book and a baggie of Lego. "She said you might be able to help me put this back together."

He glanced at Remi, but she was staring at me, her eyes twinkling. I could tell I'd done well and loved her eyes on me, but Neil was still waiting. I inclined my head in his direction to redirect her attention.

Blinking rapidly, she said, "I told her you were kind of a Lego expert."

He put his hand out for the baggie. "You don't have the box," he scolded.

"But I found some instructions on the Internet. It's Batman's Dragster."

He read from the pages I had printed. "Two-thousand and six. Catwoman Pursuit. Catwoman and her motorcycle should be in here, too." He stood and took the baggie to his desk, which was clear of clutter, and gently poured out the contents. He quickly sorted them into piles and held up two figures. "Batman and Catwoman!" He turned to Remi. "Both figures!"

"How about the rest of the pieces?" When he turned back to the pile, she whispered, "Where did you get this?"

"eBay! I found it when I was researching," I said. Hearing the wonder in her voice made me bubble with pride. I pulled the large book toward me and thumbed through it.

"Yours is this two-thousand sixteen Batcave, right?" I asked, pointing to the picture I found.

"Classic TV series," Neil added. "I put it together myself. I am very good with Lego. I am better at Lego than cooking, but my sister says I should learn to cook."

"Did you help with lunch today?" Remi asked.

Neil's focus stayed on the Lego in front of him when he answered. "Gerald made lunch. I live here because I can't live in a house without help. My sister can cook for herself, but she is not very good at making Lego."

"I can usually get the first five pages."

"You are missing seven bricks." Along his desk, he had arranged the bricks to match the inventory I had printed out. Beside his desk was a plastic set of drawers. When he pulled out a drawer, I saw that it had only one color, and the different shapes were housed in storage containers with the information written on the top. Red 1x2. Red 2x2 corner and so on. He frowned. "I do not have a dark red 2x2 with a groove." He began to tap his left elbow with his fisted right hand.

"They would have it at Legoland, wouldn't they?" Remi said in a soothing voice.

"I go to work on Monday. That is two days away." He started to gather the pieces on the desk.

"Do you think it could stay here? If I take it home, I'm afraid my cat will knock it off the bookcase again."

His brows knitted together, and he seemed to be searching inside his head for an answer. "I am not good with animals. I do not know how to train a cat not to break toys. Temple Grandin is good with animals. She might know. She is good that way. I am good with Lego."

"So maybe it could live here in your room," I suggested.

"I am very careful with toys. I am like a grownup and a child. I like toys, and I take good care of toys. I have a job because it is important to be responsible, but I mostly like to play with Lego."

"My sister has an eleven-year-old daughter. She likes Lego. She stays with me sometimes, and we like to go to the beach. Do you ever go to the beach?"

It was Remi he looked at, not me. Remi said, "Neil doesn't like the water or sand. We go once in a while to listen to the waves."

"The sound is nice. From the sidewalk," Neil said.

"I like the sound too," I said. "Way more than toys that make sound. Neil, do Lego toys ever make noise?"

He looked at the carpet. "There are some lasers that make noise and light up. I don't have any of those."

"What cool things does the Batcave do?"

He revealed a hint of his sister in the way his eyebrows lifted. "The study is the best part. It has the Batphone, and you can move the bookcase to get to the secret entrance to the Batcave. I could show you."

"I'd like to see," I said. Remi and I joined Neil on the floor and listened intently as Neil pointed out his favorite features of the Batcave. When he asked if I wanted one of the figurines to play, I picked The Penguin. I couldn't help smiling when Remi picked the sexy Catwoman.

The afternoon with Remi's brother sped by, and I was genuinely surprised when she pointed to her watch and then to the door. I thanked Neil for his help with Batman's Dragster. He nodded without looking at me.

"Fist bump?" Remi asked.

He held out his fist and let his fingers burst out after they'd touched knuckles.

"I love you."

"Love you," he responded, still absorbed with his Lego.

Remi led me from the room. At the end of the hall, she let out a long breath. "You were perfect with him. Was that hard?"

"Not hard at all. Honestly, I had fun. Is that weird?"

"No, not weird. When he said that he's a grownup and a child, that's him exactly. That's the part my parents have a hard time with. They do better with adults. Our childhood wasn't fun for them. They put up with it as a necessity to having adult children. Neither one of them could adjust to the idea of Neil never being able to be fully independent."

I didn't know what to say about the family conflict that was part of Remi's life. We walked to the car in silence, and before I got in, I wrapped my arms around Remi. "Thank you for introducing me."

"I can't believe you brought Lego." She kissed me warmly, if chastely. "That's not true. It was the conclusion of the research you were telling me about, wasn't it?"

I was glad Remi wasn't teasing me about my need to find answers and the time I took to look things up. "The stuff I read on the Internet said to communicate in the language they're comfortable with. You already told me that was Lego, so it was a pretty logical conclusion."

"Not one that many would bother thinking about. I love that you had a plan for how to get to know him. It means the world to me." She wrapped her arms around me, and I felt the depth of her appreciation. I held on tightly, tightly enough to convey how much I liked Remi and all she came with. I didn't move until I felt Remi's arms soften.

When we stepped apart, I melted once again into the passenger seat of the Ferrari and said, "What happens after you see your brother? You meet up with your girlfriend for a nice dinner?"

"A nice dinner could be arranged. And perhaps even some dessert."

I reached across the console to rest my hand on Remi's thigh. "Dessert sounds good."

"There is also the issue of the articles of clothing I owe you," she said with her eyes fixed behind the car as she backed up. When she turned back, her chocolate eyes locked with mine. I swallowed, nervousness mixing with desire. "We didn't get around to that last time, did we?"

"Indeed, we did not."

"And now it's Saturday." Three items Wednesday. Going by the penalty I imposed on Monday, she owed me six articles of clothing. I openly appraised her outfit: the elegant cut of Remi's charcoal coat which hid nothing of her figure, silky black shirt with veins of gold running through it. What kind of bra would she wear? Lacy? Silky? Either way, I was certain she would match her bra to the panties under her flowing black pants. The thought of her in nothing but panties and bra left me speechless, aching to run my hands along her perfect skin.

Remi's voice, low and sexy, interrupted my thoughts. "You are undressing me now, aren't you?"

I blushed, surprised my body was able to do so with how much blood was pumping through my groin. If there was any hope on making it through dinner, I was going to have to backtrack. I needed something safer. Something less erogenous that would help her cool down. "Are shoes one item or two?"

"That is not what I was expecting!" Remi's laughter filled the car. "What are your thoughts, Dr. Hernandez?"

"I think that even if they count as two items, you are going to be wearing far less than I will."

"With six choices, I thought some of your own might be in play."

I rubbed my chin as I considered her suggestion. "I don't know. That doesn't get me enough of your skin."

Remi laughed again mirthfully, making me smile. "Maybe I could win some of your articles of clothing by guessing about your body adornments."

"That could get you a few articles of clothing."

"How many is a few? Two? Three?"

"You're trying to cheat."

"If you have more than two, wouldn't you have said 'several items'?"

"You'll have to find out later."

"After dinner."

"Yes, you promised dinner." I rested my elbow where the door met the window and my head on my hand, studying Remi as she drove, thinking about how fun it was to banter. It was hard to keep my mind on the present instead of anticipating the removal of this woman's clothes.

CHAPTER SIXTEEN

We had dinner. At a restaurant. I cannot tell you which one or what I ordered or even what we talked about after Remi had given up on her guessing. No nipple or belly-button piercing. No unicorn—that had given me a good laugh—on my ankle or rose on my lower back. Though she admitted defeat and stopped guessing, she didn't stop picturing me naked, seeking my secrets.

I knew because that was what I was thinking about. We were going to have sex. The gorgeous woman sitting across from me had already agreed that I would be removing just about all her clothes, and I didn't see us watching a movie or kicking back on the couch with a beer, her naked and me fully clothed, my tattoos and piercing hidden from her. Her slender fingers twisting the stem of her wineglass tightened my nipples. When her lips closed over her fork, my clit pulsed to the beat of my racing heart.

We held hands on the way back to my place. My mind raced. I had engaged in so much mental foreplay that I was ready to rip off Remi's clothes the second we got in. But this would be our first time. The first time to touch her skin, first time to taste her. What we were about to do was in no way giving in to our impulses. We were starting *something*. I felt the weight of it.

I slipped out of my jacket and held out my hand for Remi's. Her eyes never leaving mine, she set her purse on my counter and slowly removed her coat. "One."

I pointed to her feet.

"Two," Remi said as she slipped off both shoes and arranged them neatly by my kitchen counter.

"That's kind of you."

She tipped her head slightly in acknowledgment of my words and silently stepped closer, our hips almost touching. When she leaned forward, I expected to feel Remi's lips on mine. Instead, Remi gathered my hair away from my neck and traced my ear with the tip of her tongue before gently biting the lobe.

I shivered and tilted my head to reveal the canvas of my neck.

"Oh," she said breathily before kissing each of the small stars behind my left ear.

"I'll give you those since you counted the shoes as one item."

"Significance?" Remi placed her hands on my hips and continued kissing her way down my neck, across each clavicle and up to the other ear. The feathery touch of her lips and tongue made it almost impossible to speak.

"One for each niece and my nephew."

"I am fortunate you are such a dedicated auntie." Her lips finally found mine. Soft, so soft, yet so clearly expressing her appreciation and attraction.

I stepped closer, very aware that without her heels, her hips were now parallel to mine. I kicked off my flats and ran my hands from her hips to her shoulders, pulling her closer. I savored the light brush of her body against mine and shuddered as she ran her hands up my front. Her eyebrows rose in question, and I smiled shyly. She paused below my breasts and traced her fingers across them causing the already peaked nipples to harden underneath the fabric. Remi took each peak between thumb and forefinger. "You said no piercings here."

The pressure and the huskiness in Remi's voice made me dizzy with desire.

"Correct," I whispered.

"I hope you do not mind my double-checking."

All I could manage was to shake my head. I could not form words when Remi's hands returned to my waist to explore the smooth expanse of my belly. My heart raced, and I opened my eyes to find Remi studying me. "What?" I asked. Self-conscious heat crept up my neck.

"You said no belly button piercing when I was guessing at the restaurant, yet you did not correct me when I said I was looking for another piercing, not another tattoo."

"Correct again. The change in environment has improved your game."

Her eyes still locked on mine, she pulled against my hips, grinding against my center. I had to break away from the kiss when she engaged my piercing. "Getting closer, I see," Remi said, continuing to grind.

"If we don't move," I groaned.

"Yes?"

"I might…" Remi felt so good against me that, again, words abandoned me.

"As good as this feels, I imagine it would feel even better without any clothes," Remi said, loosening her hold on me.

In total agreement, I led Remi to my bedroom. Walking cleared my head enough to see that Remi had only given me two of my allotted six items of clothing. I kept my eyes locked on hers as I slipped the thin buttons from the delicate fabric of her shirt. "Three," I said, pushing it from her shoulders to reveal a whole landscape I wanted to explore. I swept my hands over her contours, my hands gathering information that I could only discover through touch. Moving from hips to the small of her back, up to her shoulders… Her bra impeded my progress.

"Four." She wore a black silky bra fastened in the front. Before I released the clasp between her breasts, I studied her eyes again. I could feel how quickly her breath came and smiled at the hitch when I freed her breasts, but her eyes remained steady on me, fairly melting my insides.

Her eyes closed only when I grazed her nipples with the palms of my hands, giving me permission to explore with my eyes as well as my hands. The contrast between her skin and nipple pinpointed exactly where my mouth belonged. I bent to wet one nipple with the tip of my tongue as I applied more pressure to both breasts with my hands, again trusting the communication between her skin and mine to tell me what she liked best.

I lowered my hands to the waistband of her slacks and whispered, "Five and six separately or together?"

She answered my question by unfastening her pants herself and pushing both items from her hips. She stepped from the puddle of her pants and underwear, unveiling a body more beautiful than any artwork I had ever admired. "You are absolutely gorgeous."

The way she did not deflect my compliment made her even sexier.

"I need to see you." She tugged my shirt free from my pants. "I have not found what I am looking for."

I sucked in my breath when she unbuttoned my shirt. Warm, sure hands wrapped around my back to liberate my breasts. "You think I'm going to let you take those for free?" I asked. With my body, I guided us to my bed and pulled down the covers, thinking I was in total control. Instead of climbing onto the bed, she remained standing.

"Yes, I do." Her words surprised me, and I chuckled, but what she said next turned up the burner on my desire yet again. "You sounded like you were going to climax on your feet. I think you want to give these to me. You have wanted me to take them off you since you first saw me at the science fair."

"Not at the fair! There were children everywhere!"

She eased my shirt from my shoulders and flicked away bra straps to expose my breasts. I shivered underneath her careful study of my body. "You are a puzzle, Karla Hernandez."

I loved the way she said my name. "Puzzle?" I asked, leaning into her in case she had forgotten that I was still clothed from the waist down.

"I have conducted a thorough search above the waist…" She paused here to kiss my earlobes again, engage my tongue in a passionate dance, brush her lips over each of my nipples and kiss my stomach. Each place she touched made me pulse with desire. "I can think of only one other area suitable for piercing, and I would think that someone brave enough to pierce below the waist would be titillated at the idea of being seduced in a place that risked discovery."

"Is that something that you're into?" I asked, feeling uneasy.

"No. This temptation is unique to you. When I saw you at Sloan's, I suddenly understood how people find themselves making out in bathrooms. Although in a bathroom, one's access would be limited." She unbuttoned my pants and hooked her finger at the waist of my underwear, slowly drawing her finger from one hip to the other. "If I had you pressed to a stall door, these would have stayed in my way."

With my eyes closed, she had me in that stall, the imagined restaurant noise ratcheting up anticipation that was already almost more than I could bear.

"Believe me, I could make do, but tonight, I must see all of you" She lowered me to my bed and coaxed my slacks and underwear off. I felt faint with want, waiting on my bed completely exposed. "That's better," she whispered. "You are a work of art."

She joined me on the bed, then, placing a knee between my legs and crawling above me, peppering my body with warm kisses. "I plan to appreciate you accordingly, but I cannot do so properly until I confirm whether my guess about your piercing is correct." Remi traced my naked belly button with her tongue, picking up where she had left off when she began to remove my clothes. She moved lower and ran her hands up my bare legs, her breath warm on my thighs. I gripped the sheets in both hands, panting. Finally, finally Remi wrapped her lips around my piercing. Already on the edge of tipping over, the tiny vibration of Remi's moan against the ring above my clit was all it took to catapult me into spasms of delight.

Remi stroked my sides as my body rode the waves of pleasure from the pressure of her tongue. When I finally lay quietly, Remi rose to mirror my body. "I'm sorry. I did not realize you were so close."

"I told you I was close in the hallway," I reminded her.

"That was too fast," she said, her smoldering eyes on mine. She watched me as she traced sensual circles around but not on my piercing. My insides began to gather again.

"Not yet." I pulled Remi to me, our legs scissored so our centers met. "I have to feel you."

Remi gasped against my neck. "Oh! That. Feels. So. Amazing."

I held her hips as she rocked against me. Her eyes closed, her lips parted and she began to grind with more purpose. She was going to finish before I could even begin my exploration. I exploited her distraction, scooting to my side in order to reverse our positions.

"You said I came too fast." I hovered above her and kissed her deeply.

She pulled at my hips.

"What about slow?"

"Next time. I am too close. I want you on me."

How could I refuse? "Here?" I asked, slowly lowering myself until I felt the pressure of my piercing against her. My whole attention was captured by Remi's body and the way we fit. I thought exclusively about how to coax the same rapture from Remi's body as she had from mine.

Remi tightened her hold, pulling me closer. Her breath quickened. "There. Yes. Don't move. Please."

It was the please that did me in. I wrapped my arms around Remi, wove my hands through her hair and thrust until I felt Remi quake underneath me. The groan that accompanied Remi's climax lit another explosion inside me, and we cried out together as a second climax ripped through me. I continued rocking gently until Remi's hold on my ass relaxed enough that I could move next to her.

"That thing," she panted. "Is so hot. You are so hot."

"No, that's you," I argued.

"Are you always that sensitive? Is that why you got pierced?"

"Yes to the sensitive, but it's a lucky byproduct, not why I got pierced."

Remi propped herself up on her elbow, stroking my belly and hips. "And that was because?"

"My twenty-first birthday, my sister felt sorry for me because I didn't have any friends or plans. She drove me over to Vegas to party. We had drinks, and she got to teasing me for saying I was done in after two. She said I needed to loosen up and confessed that she was going to get her hood pierced. I was like, fine, do what you want to do. I went with her to the shop and waited as she made sure it was all legit. And waited for her to work up the nerve. And waited. Finally, I said that she was making it worse by not just doing it. She dared me to go first, so I did."

"And your sister?"

"Chickened out."

Remi gasped. "Did she feel so bad?"

"No. She told me I could take it out, but it made me feel invincible."

"Do you do everything your siblings dare you to do?"

"I didn't go bungee jumping with my brother."

"Limits are good. But I will say that I'm glad you took this risk." The playfulness in her eyes and the tilt of her smile made me think she was thinking about public places and the risk of getting caught again.

"I have a feeling you are going to push for more risks," I said, searching her eyes for her own limits. I thrilled inwardly at the discoveries in our future. We were going to have a lot of fun.

"Absolutely, I will." Her hand glided down to my piercing. "But not tonight. Tonight it is enough to appreciate the lucky byproduct of your previous risk-taking."

"So glad you approve," I said, surrendering, once again, to Remi's touch.

CHAPTER SEVENTEEN

Music drifted into my dreams, dreams I had not even had to work for. Dreams that had come to me after Remi and I dropped into exhausted sleep sometime in the wee hours of the morning. Remi. I opened my eyes and found my beautiful, sleep-rumpled lover staring back at me.

"Are you going to answer that?" she whispered.

I grimaced. "It's my mother. Oh, shit! It's Sunday, and it's my mother. I have to answer." I mouthed *sorry* as I swiped the screen. Remi waved off the apology and tipped her head toward the bathroom before scooting out of bed.

"Hi Ma." I shut my eyes to keep myself focused on my mother instead of the tempting view of Remi's naked body.

"What's wrong?"

I tried to clear the sleep from my voice. "Nothing's wrong."

"It sounds like I woke you! You never sleep this late. You'll be late for mass!"

"Mass?" I smacked my palm against my forehead.

"You're still in bed, aren't you? Are you sick?"

"I'm not sick. I promise."

"Is it about the woman Rosa saw at your house?"

"Ma!"

"So you are missing mass for a woman. Are you going to miss dinner as well?"

"I don't know, Ma. I'll call you later."

"Karla…"

"Go! Mass is going to start! I'll talk to you later," I promised before discarding my phone on the bedside table.

Remi eased back into the room. She bent to retrieve her clothes, and I reached over to pull her back to bed.

"I am not sure if I should get back in bed with you. It sounds like you are in trouble."

"I don't want to talk about my mom," I said, resting my hands on Remi's hips. "Now that I've seen you like this, I don't think I can ever let you put clothes on again."

"That's going to make my errands difficult."

"You'd pick errands over being naked in bed?"

"You can't spend the whole day in bed. What about food?"

"At least let me say good morning." I walked my fingers up Remi's sides until I reached her shoulders and gently pulled her close enough to kiss. I ran my hands all over Remi's beautiful skin. Touching her made my entire body sing. Everything else in my life dropped away.

"It is a lovely morning." Remi combed my dark hair back from my face with her fingers. "I enjoyed myself last night. I enjoyed you."

"Me too." I leaned in to kiss her, but she dodged me.

"But you made me very, very hungry."

"Food it is," I growled, swinging my legs off the bed. I grabbed a pair of sweats and a T-shirt on the way to the bathroom and came out ready to cook breakfast. Remi had dressed as well and was commiserating with Petri about the lack of good service.

"Waffles or pancakes?" I asked, collecting my hair in a tie.

"Waffles with a side of why you're in trouble for skipping mass. Do you go every week?"

I gathered the ingredients. "Usually. If I'm not going, I tell my mom. That's why she called."

"How much trouble are you in?"

"I'll fix it tonight, but right now, I've promised someone breakfast. Coffee or tea?"

"Coffee. Point out where you keep everything, and I'll make it."

We worked in silence while I thought of what to say about my mother's call. Steam from the waffle iron and coffeemaker filled the kitchen making my stomach rumble. I pulled out some butter and maple as well as strawberry syrup. Remi squinted at the bottle of red liquid. "Rosa loves strawberry."

"She stays with you often?"

The waffle iron beeped, and I pulled out the golden waffle and handed it on a plate to Remi. "Sometimes her house is full of crazy, so she stays here. And sometimes she comes to help her *tìa* get a night of good sleep."

"How did you sleep last night?" Remi slipped her arm around my middle.

"I slept so well. All two hours you let me."

Remi beamed at me. "Are you saying I didn't cure your insomnia?"

"In my scientific opinion, one night of a few hours' worth of sleep is inconclusive evidence."

The waffle iron beeped again, and I grabbed a plate for myself.

"Then I will have to stay again."

"Can you stay and keep your hands to yourself?" I asked.

She feigned a pout. "Probably not."

We fixed our waffles and sat next to each other on barstools on the living room side of my counter, quiet while we ate. She interrupted the silence to say, "You can't tell your mother I'm why you missed mass. I don't want to be seen as a bad influence."

I tried to hide how the phrase "bad influence" hit me but wasn't successful.

Remi reached across the bar to take my hand. "Have I already caused some question about influence?"

"No, not you. Not you at all. It's nothing."

"It's not nothing. All the wind went out of your sails when I said that. Who has accused you of being a bad influence?"

"Maricela's mother cornered me at work the other day."

"Who?"

"The college student I've been helping with her biology class. Her mother has a problem with my being gay and being around her daughter."

"That's ludicrous."

I shrugged.

"No, it is. You went out of your way to help this student."

"Her mother would rather I didn't." I described my unpleasant encounter with her at the Miracle Center. "She didn't look or sound happy, and I keep hearing '*dique*' and '*mala influencia.*'"

Remi abandoned her waffle and stood to wrap her arms around me. "What an awful thing for her mother to say!" I buried my face in Remi's neck and wrapped my arms tightly around her.

The waffle iron beeped, and I left Remi's arms to take out the next waffle. "More?"

"No, this is more than sufficient." When I sat next to her again, Remi rubbed my back with one hand and reached for her coffee with the other.

I took a bite of my waffle and glanced at Remi. I felt so relaxed in her presence, I didn't want to spend a moment without her. "I didn't ask about your day. You said you had errands, and I need to spend some time at the lab today, but do you think I could still see you tonight?"

"You might get tired of me."

"Believe me. I am not getting tired of you, not for a long, really long, time. My family is going to be all over me for why I missed mass this morning. If you came with me…" I glanced at Remi.

"They do not know why you missed mass."

"Oh, they do."

"How can you be sure about that?"

"They live a block away. Your car is parked next to mine. They know."

"And you want me to have dinner with them after they all know I spent the night?" Remi set down her cup.

"They'll have to behave, somewhat, if you're there. Rosa already told everyone about you, so they want to meet you. If you're game. It would make my mother happy."

"Well…if it would make your *mother* happy." Remi smiled.

I waggled my eyebrows. "I'll make it worth your while."

"When you put it that way, however can I say no?"

Later, seated next to each other at my parents' table, Remi leaned against me and whispered, "I thought you said they would behave if I was here."

Rosa's question had silenced the table. My mother picked up her glass, hiding a wide smile in her sip of water. "Yes, Karla. Why *do* you look so tired if Remi spent the whole night with you?"

My siblings stifled their laughter, but only to avoid hurting Rosa's feelings.

"She doesn't know my nighttime routine like you do, kiddo. You're a lot better at helping me remember not to let my brain wake up too much before bedtime."

"You didn't do your meditation, did you?" Rosa asked, perfecting the tone of a chastising professional.

"Guilty," I said.

Rosa shook her head and leveled her gaze at Remi. "Once she's finished with her stretching and meditation, there's no more talking."

Luis mumbled, "Oh, I'm sure that wasn't the problem" and received a jab from Antonia.

"I'll remember that," Remi said. "I can see that you still take your project very seriously. You have the makings of a dedicated scientist."

"I still don't know about my conclusion, though," Rosa said. "I told Aunt Karla that you could help her sleep. Now that you know her routine, it should go better. Aunt Karla always looks way better when I stay over."

"Training people to conduct your experiments just like you would is super tricky. My boss complains about that all the time.

You'll be a tough Principal Investigator like her. We'll do better to follow your protocol," I said.

My mother's gaze zeroed in on me. "Tired or no, I am so happy to see you with a smile on your face. We are so happy to meet the person who can get Karla away from her work. You do not know the number of times she has skipped dinner because she got stuck at her lab."

My face burned with embarrassment, and it was my turn to lean into Remi and whisper apologies for my family keeping us under the microscope.

Remi's hand found mine under the table, and she squeezed. Her complexion either hid the effect of their scrutiny better, or she was utterly comfortable with the turn of the conversation. Her eyes made me fairly certain it was the latter. "I admire Karla's work ethic, but I am very happy to get to spend this time with her family. My family hasn't gathered around a table like this in a long time. It is an honor to be here with you."

My parents exchanged a look. They were falling for Remi just as hard as I was. I stowed the older couple's expression away to explore later. The evening passed quickly with my family's natural boisterousness widening to include Remi. I did not mind Luis's teasing about the fart study when it meant that Remi got to imagine how she might have judged such a project.

When we walked hand in hand back to my place, Remi sighed deeply.

"What was that for?"

"You are very lucky. When I met Rosa at the science fair, I thought about how lucky she was to have an aunt like you, how lucky Antonia is to have a sister like you. Now I can see how that comes from your whole family."

"It's weird," I said, replaying my parents' expression. "Having you there with me tonight is the first time I felt like my parents are proud of me."

We stopped at the corner under the streetlight and waited for the traffic to clear. Remi looked confused. "How can that be? Certainly they were proud of you when you got your degree?"

The traffic cleared and we crossed the street. "Pride, I think, is a reflection of them. They didn't feel like that accomplishment had anything to do with them. They acknowledged that it was an accomplishment, but I could see how getting a PhD baffled them."

"They were impressed."

"Yes. Impressed. But tonight they were proud of me. I could feel it when you said that you were honored to be there. The way they looked at us after you said that, I could tell how much they like you."

"And they're proud of you for catching me?"

"You *are* a catch."

"As are you, Dr. Hernandez."

"Say you're coming in to continue helping out with my sleep study," I said, leaning in for a kiss when we reached my condo.

"You know very well that we will not get any sleep if I stay tonight," Remi answered. "We both have work in the morning."

"Didn't you hear my mother saying it's good for you to pull me away from my work?" I argued, "I have the whole week to be the dedicated professional you admire." I stepped close enough to feel the heat of her body and pressed my hips ever so slightly into hers. I kissed her so deeply I felt my desire pooling between my legs. I told her as much, and she sank back against her car.

"You make me weak in the knees," she said.

"I don't think you should drive in that condition."

She clicked the fob in her hand, illuminating the interior of the car. A small duffel sat in the backseat, and a fresh outfit hung from the headrest. I opened the door, removing both. "You happen to have a change of clothes?"

"I didn't want to presume. What if your family had hated me?"

"Silly, silly woman," I said, carrying her things inside. "I should have warned you that my family falls even faster than I do."

CHAPTER EIGHTEEN

Maricela and I stopped with Valerie at the door of her building. "You sure you don't want to join us for a smoothie?" I asked.

"Sure I'd love to, but this blasted morning sickness has compromised my schedule to the point that I barely felt like I could get away to walk. I need for my boss to see me in the lab. I've seriously got to make up for all the time I'm spending in the lav."

"We don't have to get anything," Maricela said after the door to Valerie's building shut behind her.

"We're going. You deserve a reward for coming back and keeping up," I said.

During our walk, Valerie had been the director of topics. She gave a graphic update on the nature of her morning sickness before launching into an inquisition of my new sexual activity interspersed with stretches she was sure would be helpful to me now that I was working out a set of muscles that I had "probably forgotten I had." I'd elbowed her for the slight but honestly, I didn't care, and watching Maricela trying to pretend she didn't know what we were talking about was hilarious.

"I wasn't sure if you'd be joining us after what happened with your mom," I said once we had our smoothies.

Maricela poked her frozen drink with the straw and apologized again for her mother's behavior.

"I didn't understand most of what she said. All I know is that she thinks I'm a bad influence which makes no sense when your grades have improved so much."

Maricela didn't look up.

"Did something happen?"

She punched the icy drink with her straw before taking a deep breath and meeting my eyes. "Last week she maybe caught me flirting with the nurse at the clinic?"

"You're not sure if she caught you or you're not sure if you were flirting?"

"Oh, I was flirting!" Maricela's eyes sparkled for a moment as her thoughts shifted away from her mother. "You remember how I told you about my mom feeling so tired, and you told me I should be going to the appointments?"

"Sure."

"So I listened, and there was this nurse." She blushed hard. "First, I couldn't tell if she was, you know, into me. I mean, they have to look interested when you're talking about their patient, right?"

"If they're good," I agreed.

"Well she left, and then the doctor came in, and I listened like you told me to. Then he said I could step out while he did the vision test. When I did, I literally walked into Penny. That's the nurse's name."

I'd figured. "And?"

Maricela continued, "We talked. She thought it was nice I bring my mom to her appointments. I said I don't mind 'cause everyone is so nice. I asked how she decided to be a nurse, and that made her think I want to be a nurse. I said I didn't think I would look half as good as she does in those cute scrubs."

"Nice line."

For an instant Maricela beamed at me. Then her expression clouded. I remembered Judy walking up the day that I was helping Maricela study and how I'd wondered if she'd seen Maricela poke my sunburn. I knew Maricela did not disguise her feelings well. "And then your mom saw you?"

"She forgot to give me her purse. She gives it to me to hold on my lap because she thinks that if she sets it down anywhere in the clinic, she's going to get cancer. I told her I was asking Penny if I could go back to get her purse, you know? But Penny looked so confused and then…" Maricela's eyes brimmed with tears.

"Did your mom say something?"

"No. The way she looked at us, I could see she was angry. She marched back into the room with her purse, and then Penny…she just…she left me in the hallway. When my mom was done she walked out without saying a word to me. I thought she'd wait outside for me and I could apologize to Penny. But then I couldn't find Penny, and when I came out, I couldn't find my mom. By the time I did, she was even angrier and said that she had seen you and told you to stay away from me. She told me to stay away from both you and Penny."

"I don't understand. You told me that your mom was upset because she thought I was gay."

Maricela glanced at me guiltily. "That was part of it."

I bowed my head and shut my eyes. I could not for the life of me figure the young woman out. "Why would you leave the other part out?"

"I didn't want you to know what she'd seen."

So it was shame that I had read on Maricela's face when she had pulled her mother away from the confrontation. I hated to see how Maricela was internalizing her mother's anger and fear.

"Does she know you're here today?"

Maricela shook her head guiltily. "She would be so upset. She's not supposed to get upset, you know, with her blood pressure."

"Is that why you don't want to tell her you're gay?"

"If I tell my mother, she could die."

"Still, you should tell your mother. You have a right to be yourself. Don't you want your mom to know the truth about who you are?"

"How can you say that when you know how sick she is? You want me to kill my mother? Because if I tell her, she'll have a heart attack. You saw how upset she got."

I opened my mouth to disagree but then remembered talking with Judy about how people with diabetes were already at a higher risk for any number of things including heart attacks. Could Maricela's coming out pose a health risk? I paused long enough that Maricela sat back, satisfied.

"Now you see why I can't tell her."

As much as I wanted to say Maricela could come out to her mother, the words would not leave my mouth.

* * *

My feet up on the wall and hands splayed at my side, I breathed deeply and went through my meditation.

Be well. I had that down, feeling good about the walk with Valerie and Maricela earlier.

Be content. My work was progressing nicely, and I was excited about where things with Remi were going. Monday, I'd sent a text thanking her for a good night's sleep, because we had at least doubled the number of hours we'd slept. We had texted earlier, each of us acknowledging the copious amount work that we had to do. Remi wasn't needy and didn't make me feel guilty for prioritizing my job. What more could I ask for? *To talk to her,* my subconscious suggested. I told it to shut up and concentrate.

Be calm. This is where my mind was supposed to stop returning to the worry spots of my day. I was supposed to stop thinking about Maricela and her mom, how her mother had yelled at me, and how she was likely to react if Maricela came out to her. I wanted to call Remi, return to my weekend and skip meditation. *Be calm.* I tried again. *You'd feel calmer if you talked to Remi,* my subconscious chirped. *Shut it!* I snapped at my busy brain.

Be at peace. Leave the list of things to do on the pad of paper. Don't bring them to bed. Busy brain asked whether I thought Remi was feeling peaceful, or whether she would feel more peaceful if we talked for a few minutes.

Damn. I really wanted to call Remi. I glanced at the clock. Going on nine thirty. Late for me, but not quite socially awkward. I sat up and padded to the kitchen.

You still up? I texted.

Nope came the quick reply.

On your way to bed?

After I finish this episode of Ghost Hunters.

I stared the message, disbelieving. Shaking my head, I hit dial. "You watch *Ghost Hunters?*"

"It is a great show!" Remi said.

"*Ghost Hunters.*"

"What is wrong with *Ghost Hunters?*"

"Besides the fact that there is no such thing as ghosts?" I asked.

"Before you pooh-pooh it, you have to watch at least one whole episode. I'm surprised you are not already a fan."

"Of *Ghost Hunters*. Ghosts." I didn't try to hide my doubt.

"Their methods are absolutely evidence-based. Very scientific."

"Scientific." I leaned against my bar, enjoying the sound of her voice, so serious. "You know I'm a scientist, right?"

"Yes, I also know you have trouble sleeping. Why are you not in bed?"

"I can't stop spinning on a conversation I had with the young woman whose mom has it in her head that I'm going to turn her daughter gay."

"Maricela," Remi said.

"Yes. She walked with me and Valerie today and told me about a crush she has on one of the nurses in the clinic where her mother is being treated. Her mom got angry with her, but she's still pretending she's straight. I told her she should stop lying and share who she really is with her mom. She said she can't because her mother would drop dead from a heart attack."

"That is a possibility, is it not?" Remi asked. "If she is being treated at The Miracle Center?"

"Yes. She has diabetes, so her heart is compromised. She should be avoiding stress, and here I am encouraging her to talk to her mom. I know it is not likely, but what if it did give her a heart attack?"

Remi was quiet for a moment before she said, "Yes, that would be terrible. Has she considered how she would feel if her mother died before she has a chance to tell her? It could be devastating for her to realize that her mother never fully knew her."

"So I'm not a bad mentor for saying she should share more with her mother."

"Is that what is keeping you up? Because it should not. You are a terrific mentor. Maricela is lucky to have someone like you to support her. Knowing a successful lesbian could save her life."

Her words choked me up, and I could not think of how to respond.

Remi continued, "Think of the opportunity you have already given her to talk about the subject at all. That is a starting place. When you recognize the problem, education can begin. She might ask her mother why you upset her, you who are so successful and confident."

"You're good at this, you know that? I feel so much better."

"I am a trained professional."

I dropped my voice a notch. "Sounds like I owe you."

"Yes. My fee is watching one full episode of *Ghost Hunters* free of skepticism."

"Thank you, Remi."

"Anytime, Karla."

I held the phone, reluctant to hang up, unsure of how to end the conversation. I wasn't ready for "I love you," but a simple "goodnight" didn't feel like enough. "I wish you were here."

"Do you?" I heard a smile in her voice. "For sex or for your sleep study?"

"Because I like waking up next to you," I said honestly.

"I like that, too," Remi said. "Goodnight, Karla. I hope you sleep well."

"Thanks. You too."

CHAPTER NINETEEN

I jogged up the stairs to Remi's second-story apartment two nights later with a bottle of wine and butterflies in my stomach. It was more than her fancy car that made me feel like I was punching above my weight. She had a sophistication, maybe from her years living abroad, that made me feel out of my element in an exciting way.

She answered the door in a colorful flowing skirt and loose white blouse. "I hope it is okay that I changed. I have to get out of my work clothes immediately after I get home."

I had no words. To me, she looked incredible, and I told her so.

"You are too kind." She kissed my cheek as she took the wine and beckoned me into her house.

It was like stepping into another world. Outside the doorway was a balcony like any other apartment complex. Inside the doorway, though in square feet smaller than my condo, her place felt huge. It didn't make sense because her furniture was ornate and big, starting with an end table that had legs more shapely than mine. An intricate colorful rug covered most of the standard beige carpet, and an ornate crystal chandelier made the place feel like a ballroom.

Remi sounded apologetic when she said, "It is not mine. I am renting for the time being."

"It is absolutely yours, though. Everything about it is you."

"The things, yes, but I long for a place with more light, with higher ceilings. For now, I needed something close to Neil." She held up the bottle of wine. "Shall we get started on this while I get dinner together?

"Sure," I said, following her into the kitchen. "How is Neil?"

"He is well. He has finished the Batman Lego you left with him. He is anxious to show you and see if it meets with your approval."

"He doesn't want to keep it? I got it as a gift for him."

"He is very literal. You said that you heard he could help you fix your set. He has fixed it for you and will be very happy for you to take it back." She set stemless wineglasses on the table. They looked like they had been blown from different colored glass collected at a beach. With a tool I'd never seen the likes of before, she effortlessly extracted the cork. I couldn't take my eyes off her, graceful in her every move. She caught me staring and tipped her chin. "What?"

I stepped forward and swept her thick hair back from her neck. I kissed it and checked her countenance before I kissed her lips. "You are a very beautiful woman."

"I think you forget how beautiful you are, Dr. Hernandez." She swept her hand down my bare arm, making my skin come alive. She must have seen the fire in my eyes because she tick-tocked her pointer finger and said, "but we will revisit that later. First dinner and *Ghost Hunters*. You owe me one whole episode, with an open mind."

"You never said I had to keep an open mind!"

She lifted one of her sculpted eyebrows. "I do not want to watch with you if you are going to be mean."

"I won't be mean. I promise. It's part of your unwinding, so I'm interested in checking it out."

She accepted my words and served dinner—spicy chicken and vegetables on rice—that she'd picked up on her way home. Her steady chatter abruptly came to a halt.

"What?" It was my turn to ask.

"Eat and then watch or eat while we watch?"

"Eat and watch is good with me."

We gathered food and drink, and I followed her to the living room. "What would we be watching if we were at your home?"

"That depends on whether a game my brother wants to watch is more important than the show my nieces and nephew want to watch."

"What about you? What do you watch when you are not with your family?"

"I don't watch TV." I thought of all the times Ann wanted me to join her to watch the hospital dramas and sitcoms she loved. "I don't have the attention span for it. My mind stays too busy on what I should be doing."

"Is it true what your mother said, that it is very difficult to get you to leave your work?"

"It was worse when I was a postdoc. I spent a lot of years not watching TV. If I have any time to kill, I'm more likely to poke around on YouTube and watch whatever's trending."

"Well thank you for giving this a try."

She began an episode, and I asked if she had ever watched the show with her brother. She pressed pause, and I made a mental note: no talking during a show.

"No. He watches only Lego. We have a movie night once a month and it's almost always one of the Lego movies. I have persuaded him to watch anime on occasion."

"Does anyone ever bring a date?" I asked, keeping my voice light.

"Not so far, but we have one coming up. I can see if he would permit you to join us. You were asking to join us, were you not?"

"I was. It sounds like fun."

She held my gaze, a small smile on her lips. "If you are serious, I'll let you know."

"I am. If Neil's up for it, I'm all in."

She nodded and started the show again, but I caught her glancing at me a few times while we ate our dinner like she was waiting for me to take it back. I could get used to her looking over at me while we shared a meal. Was she thinking the same thing? I really liked where I was, where we were, not just physically, though being invited to her apartment felt like another step forward for us. But emotionally too. I could tell how much it meant to Remi that I wanted to see Neil again. Learning what brought her joy felt like discovering a small treasure.

I hadn't spoken during the interview with the property owner and setup for catching ghosts, but once they got to the actual running around whispering in the dark, it got more difficult for me pay attention to the show and keep my thoughts to myself. Watching Remi's reaction was better entertainment, anyway. She was so transfixed that her food stalled halfway to her mouth. Sometimes half of the fork's contents fell back to her plate before she got there.

"Your dinner must be cold by now," I observed when her fork stalled on the plate for several minutes.

She wrinkled her nose at me. "They are so quiet that it is difficult for me to eat and listen at the same time."

"Do they think that when they whisper like that, the ghosts can't hear them?"

Remi smacked me lightly. "They are listening for signs that the ghost is with them. How would they hear a board creak if they do not whisper?"

I smiled because Remi had lowered her own voice. "You're listening for the ghost too?" I scooted closer to her on the couch. "I'll hold your hand if you're scared."

She leaned close to me. "Doesn't the hair on the back of your neck stand up when they say that they can feel a presence?"

"A house that old, it's got to be drafty."

"A draft is not going to make the EMF detector light up the way it does."

"EM-What?"

"Electromagnetic force detector."

"Is that the evidence you were talking about when you said they use scientific method?"

"Absolutely! They also use a seismograph, thermal-imaging cameras, infrared night-vision…"

For every piece of equipment she listed, I placed a kiss on her neck, moving toward her ear. "Yes, this is sounding very scientific. I'd be more impressed if they had a spectrophotometer or a thermocycler."

"This is about entertainment," she said, squirming.

"Are you entertained?" I whispered. I had my eyes closed, breathing in her spiciness.

"At the moment, I am distracted."

"Should we investigate the cause of that?"

She turned her face to me and leaned forward to capture my lips with her own. All the stresses of my life slipped away when first her lips, and then her tongue, pushed against my own. Unhurried, I savored her, happy to let the signals I was picking up with my lips ripple through my body. I kept my hands to myself, content to follow wherever she led things.

The pressure of her lips lessened, and I leaned, trying to coax them back to me. Quickly, she set her plate on the coffee table and paused the show. Then her lips were back on mine, more forcefully now and followed by her upper body. I wrapped my arms around her shoulders and pulled her to me as I reclined. She nestled between my legs, and I slid my hands down to her hips, pulling her closer. The fabric of her skirt moved with my hands, so I kept gathering it until I could get my hands on her bare skin.

She broke the kiss with a very satisfying moan, and I pushed myself against her, wanting her to feel how hot she made me. Her hands slid under my shirt, sliding along my belly and up to my breasts. I lifted off the couch enough to pull off my shirt, and she reached behind me to unclasp my bra. Both fell to the floor as she pushed me back against the couch. Her mouth latched onto one nipple as her hands explored my exposed skin.

I didn't want her to stop, but I wanted so much more. "I want your hands everywhere. I need you inside."

She answered with such a hard pull on my nipple that a shock of electricity shot straight to my clit. "Don't you want to finish the show?" Her face hovered over the other breast, and her fingers kept the electricity pulsing between the nipple she had wet and where I so desperately wanted her hand.

"Remi," I pleaded. "Take me to bed."

A string of melodious words left her mouth sending shivers up my spine.

"I hope you said, 'I thought you'd never ask.'"

More words I didn't understand but more familiar. "Was that the same language? Or did you say the same thing but switch to French? That sounded like French."

"I said, but you hardly know me. You do not even know all the languages I speak."

"I thought I knew you pretty well." I ran my hand up her bare leg again, dipping my hand under her panties. She moaned with me when I discovered how wet she was.

"You know some," she whispered, shuddering as I continued to tease her. "But you have not guessed the last language I speak."

"I think it is a love language, and if I try hard enough, you will divulge it in bed."

"Ah, an interesting experiment."

"Remi," I pleaded. "I need to feel your skin on mine." I tried to get my hands under her shirt. "But my access is severely limited here."

She turned her attention to the television again. "We have not learned if the ghost is upset about the owners selling the house."

Was she serious? I opened my mouth, snapped it back shut and scrambled for something to say. "We could come back to it?"

Her thick hair tickled my face as she lowered herself to kiss me. She hovered there and said, "Later?"

Had I miscalculated how turned on she was, or was she going to torture me by making me wait until the show was over? "That depends," I said.

"On?" she asked.

"Whether you can get out of bed after I do all the things I want to do to you."

Her eyes sparkled as she studied me.

"This is your theory? That your lovemaking will make me unable to leave the bed?"

"Hypothesis," I corrected. "A hypothesis requires proof to validate the claim."

"Let us test this hypothesis of yours."

She switched off the TV and led me to her bedroom, stripping her clothes as she went. By the time we hit her sumptuous sheets, both of us stripped naked, I was confident that we would not be leaving for the rest of the night.

CHAPTER TWENTY

As predicted, we did not make it back to finish the episode of *Ghost Hunters*. I'd slept soundly next to Remi in her luxurious bed—more data for my sleep study. I did not argue when she insisted that I still owed her a whole episode of *Ghost Hunters* without judgment, even when she had rested a single finger on my chest and said there would be no kissing until the show ended.

The following nights alone in my bed, I returned to tossing and turning. I missed the blissful sleep I logged when I was with Remi. In grad school, papers I was reading or experiments that weren't going as planned kept me up. Until I met Remi, troubleshooting my work filled restless dreams, often pushing me out of bed to jot down ideas. I was used to my work keeping me up. I was not used to a woman keeping me up even when she was not present in my bed.

Though I meditated and wrote down the things I was supposed to stop spinning on, Remi continued to fill my thoughts. First, whether Neil would say yes to my joining them for the movie gnawed at me. Once he agreed to our plan, I stayed awake ruminating about how to make the second meeting go as well as the first one. I talked to Remi nightly, and she told me not to worry about the movie. She argued that the distraction of the film was likely to make it easier than our first introduction as long as I didn't talk during the show. That, of course, got me to thinking about Remi's scolding expression during *Ghost Hunters* and how I would have to keep my hands and lips to myself the next time we watched the show together.

By Thursday, lack of sleep had me dragging so badly that only the thought of how pissed Judy would be about my tardiness got me out of bed. I usually tried to be in the lab before eight. Unless Judy was at a conference, she was always in her office well before that, and I imagined her standing by my empty chair glaring at her watch if I wasn't in early as well. It was ten after eight by the time I pushed through the heavy glass doors to my building and bounded up the stairs, grateful for all the days exercising with Valerie. I swiped my badge and had just gotten the green light to enter when I heard my name.

"Dr. Hernandez?"

It felt like a bucket of ice dumped over my head. I turned but didn't recognize the woman standing in the doorway to my left.

"Judy asked me to keep an eye out for you?" Hair so black it had to be dyed fell in her face as she consulted a piece of paper. She was so pale she looked unwell. I crossed the foyer and peeked at what she held which turned out to be pictures of the dozen scientists who worked for Judy.

"I'm the new administrative assistant? Ashleigh?" She held out her hand, letting the automatic-locking door close behind her.

I gave her hand a perfunctory squeeze. When I'd learned how quickly Judy went through office administrators, I gave up getting to know them. This one was not going to last long if she didn't change the uptick that made all her statements sound like questions.

Ashleigh turned back to the door and stopped. I watched as the realization that she'd locked herself out sank in. Instead of offering my own badge, I watched Ashleigh pat her pockets, front and back, in hopes of finding the key card that probably sat on her desk. Ashleigh's gaze drifted to Judy's office door, and though I would not have thought it possible, she paled even more. At least Ashleigh had the sense to look panicked. Seeing that, I extended my badge from my hip on its zip string.

"You've got to wear it somehow." I let Ashleigh through first. "A lanyard works too."

"Thanks for the advice. Dr. Vogelsang said…"

"Karla!" Judy interrupted, gesturing me into her office. She held up a finger before focusing her attention back to her phone call. She sat at a desk set up like a fort with three working surfaces surrounding her. Multiple monitors sat on one desk, and stacks of folders covered the others. The longer I stood there studiously not listening to Judy's side of the conversation, the more I thought about her life. Here she had this gorgeous view of the Pacific Ocean, but did she ever take the time to admire it? If I were talking on the phone, I would have been staring at the horizon. I wondered how often Judy allowed herself time to appreciate it or took the time to talk to her spouse in the middle of the day. The familiar urge to call Remi hit me again.

"I'm scheduled to give the luncheon address at the International Diabetes Association Conference in Seattle," she said without preamble.

I tried to hide that she'd startled me. I hadn't heard her end the phone call. "Is there something you need me to do in the lab over the weekend?"

"I need you this weekend, but in Seattle, not in the lab."

"You want me to go to the conference?" I tried to keep my voice from squeaking in surprise.

"You are equally qualified to present our material, yes?"

I gulped. I had thought she was inviting me to attend, not to present! The yearly event gave scientists a chance to discuss research and graduates a chance to network and feel out possible postdoc positions. "Me?"

"The FDA have contacted us about securing fast-track status, and I must be here to meet with them. Can you do the presentation on behalf of the lab?"

A zing of adrenaline shot through me. "Absolutely."

"Good." Judy rose and easily squeezed through the small gap she left between two of her desks. She sat next to me. "It's time for you to start taking on more responsibility. When we move into phase one of the clinical trial, it will demand more of my time, and I will need to count on you to keep things running smoothly here. I want you to resume the initial studies of our drug on kidney disease and head up that program."

"That would be…" I had no words. Taking the lead on the kidney research would be a huge step up for me, and the way she was watching me said that unless I fucked up, it was mine. I thought about my insomnia and could easily imagine the effect the new research would have.

The thought must have registered on my face because Judy said, "Is something the matter?"

I chased the worry about sleep from my mind and arranged my professional expression. "I'm sorry. I was distracted. A friend of mine just found out that she's pregnant."

"Oh! That's a distraction, indeed! A child will certainly complicate her career. She's here at The Miracle Center?"

"She's in cancer research," I said, not wanting to expose Valerie.

"Well I am fortunate that it is not you. You've invested thousands of hours on this project and deserve the chance to see it to fruition. A pregnancy would certainly sideline your career." A stillness fell over the room, and I wasn't sure if I was supposed to agree with her. She nodded as if my silence had satisfied her that she'd made her point.

"I'll email you my slides. We can run through them after you've had a chance to take notes. I'll have Ashleigh work on your itinerary."

"Absolutely. I'm so honored."

"Of course you are!" She smiled as she walked back behind her fortress, her back to the picture window.

I sprinted to my office, calling up Valerie's number. "You won't believe this!"

"You're pregnant!"

I couldn't help but guffaw. The noise caused Ashleigh to look up from her work. I waved an apology and slipped into my office. "Idiot, that's you! Guess who is going to IDAC this weekend! Me! Judy asked me to do the talk for our lab!"

"Ace! How'd you score that?"

"Judy has to meet with the FDA."

"Great exposure for you."

"Right? You're a good friend, you know. Better than me. I would hate you if you called to tell me you got a talk."

Valerie laughed. "Yeah, well we already know your career is roses and mine is crap. Now that you've found your mystery woman, I'm fucked."

"Shit." I fell back in my chair.

"What?"

"Remi. We had plans this weekend."

"Nothing that can't be rescheduled, right?"

"Right," I said, though my mind was still spinning.

"Call me when you're back. I want to hear how brilliant you were!"

I agreed and hung up. I had to text Remi. She had been on my mind all night, and I had just been thinking about talking to her, yet now I dreaded texting. I had to go through the slides and get back into Judy's office. But first I had to face the fire.

Have to cancel Saturday

I hated to hit send, but I pulled up my big-girl chonies and did it.

Will explain later

Going to a conference was not me blowing off our plans. She would understand what a huge opportunity it was, right? The longer my two texts sat unanswered the more convinced I was that the cancellation was going to create a big problem. She'd been so excited when Neil agreed to my joining them for their monthly Saturday movie night. I worried that changing the plan again wouldn't go well. I tapped my phone against my thigh. I had to get back to work.

Really really sorry! I typed out before shoving the phone in my pocket.

CHAPTER TWENTY-ONE

"No Maricela?" Valerie asked on Tuesday when we met up for our workout.

"Her mom has an appointment."

"She went back to see her nurse friend? Ballsie! I like that one."

"Maybe she's trying to convince her mom that she wasn't flirting. I don't know."

"Someone's a misery bag today," Valerie chastised.

"Sorry. Too many nights of bad sleep."

"Don't say that to a pregnant lady."

"You're barely pregnant. Not even showing pregnant. Why are you complaining about sleep?"

"Heartburn, mate. Getting up three times during the night to pee. And every time I get up, I have to shut down all the mental questions about pregnancy and parenting that fire up the second I open my eyes."

"Think about how it's preparing you for how often you'll be getting up with an infant."

"You're not helping."

"At least you have a reason and a prize that makes it worthwhile."

"C'mon. I'd call your insomnia experiment a hellofa good way to get Remi into bed. If I were you, I'd be talking to her about needing to gather enough evidence to achieve statistical significance!"

I hmphed and sped up.

"What's that about?" Valerie easily kept in step with me.

"I would love to talk to her about gathering some more evidence to back up Rosa's findings that I sleep better when I'm not alone, but we haven't really talked since I got back from the conference."

"What happened? Did she have to cancel something significant or something?"

"Plans with her brother."

Valerie rubbed her finger in her ear and scrunched up her face. "Sorry. She had tickets to what?"

"We had plans with her brother."

"Sorry, mate. I'm not following on why that would cause a row."

"He's big on consistency. She'd already talked to him about doing something different than they usually do, and then she had to change it all again."

"Is she punishing you, then? For having to present your work at a major conference?"

"I don't think so. She said she understood that I had to go, but remember that thing you said way back about checking out the competition?"

"At Sloan's?"

"Yeah. She told me that for some people, her brother could be seen as the competition. Since I got back, she hasn't had time for us to get together, and it makes me see how someone could feel like Neil comes first."

"Did she say that she's having to deal with fallout from her brother?"

"No, she's been super busy at work, which I get. I was busy with work over the weekend, so it's just bad timing, right?

You and Emma said that having someone who was as equally invested in her work as I am in mine is what I needed."

"Maybe," Valerie said.

We walked in silence for a few beats. "What's that supposed to mean?"

"I don't know. It sounds more…complicated than that." She sounded apologetic.

For Valerie, calling something complicated was a step away from saying the downsides outweighed the benefits. I wasn't one to hold a set of scales in my head like that. "Not complicated," I said. "I get that things are different with her brother. He's autistic and routines are super important. I asked to interrupt his routine and then didn't follow through, so it probably made things difficult for her." I put myself in her shoes, trying to smooth things over with Neil. Was what was happening with us worth the trouble I'd caused? "Shit."

"What?"

"What if she thinks like you and is weighing whether I'm not dependable enough to invest any more of her time?"

"You two can't have been dating long enough for her to feel like your flakiness outweighs the sex."

"Punctuality is important to her, and I was running late the day that we went horseback riding."

"You work in a lab. It's not always easy to predict when you're going to wrap up and walking away without finishing can cost you weeks of work. That was sort of hard for Emma to understand. Her class ends, and she comes home. It doesn't unexpectedly go twenty minutes over."

"Maybe she should meet Emma, so she can explain how it comes with the territory."

"Great idea. Invite her to dinner. Emma would love to meet her."

"Thanks. That might be exactly what I need to break through this awkwardness."

* * *

The dinner was perfect. I could not have asked for anything more. Valerie was cranky pregnant but engaging. Emma was warm and welcoming, and Remi and Emma fell into an easy discussion about how dance could be used with children with autism. She fit in as if we had all been friends for years. Catching Valerie's eye across the table, I could tell she was thinking the same thing. We had learned to keep our shoptalk to a minimum, but typically had to remind ourselves. Tonight, the only time Valerie brought up work specifically was when she called me a lab rat.

"I am not a lab rat. I get outside plenty," I argued.

"Now that we're mates, but before that was a different story. I have proof of how far gone you were when I met you."

"What are you talking about?"

Valerie ignored me, thumbing through her phone. The width of her smile when she found what she was looking for finally engaged my memory. "Don't," I said, cringing without even needing to see the picture again.

"Remi, you're going to want a copy of this one," Valerie chortled. "What's your number?"

I could see Remi's eyes on me through my hands covering my face. She squealed after her phone pinged and she opened the image. "Is that you, Karla?"

I moved my fingers a smidge. "That was a long time ago."

Valerie showed Emma, and they all laughed together at my extreme science getup: gown, goggles, and face mask, gloved hands holding a Geiger counter. "You don't wear all that, do you?" Emma asked Valerie.

"I don't even wear all that normally," I interjected. "Back then I was trying to make a transgenic mouse and was attempting a Southern blot. Once! And I made the mistake of sharing that picture with Valerie. You promised you wouldn't show anyone."

"Did I?" she asked innocently, tucking the phone away.

Remi reached out and casually placed her hand on my thigh. "I think you're adorable. You know my thoughts about a woman in a lab coat."

Both the words and contact brought a blush to my face. Emma and Valerie shared a look. They'd seen the gesture and my reaction, and I could tell they approved.

"At the risk of sounding like an arse, I have to say how much fun you are," Valerie said to Remi.

"How exactly does that make you sound like an arse?" I asked.

"I have to admit I completely hated the toad you dated before."

Laughter filled the room. "Like that was ever a secret," I said.

"As happy as I am that Karla has found you, I have to agree," Emma said. "If you'd been in the picture when we met Karla, I would have had to hate her."

Remi turned a confused expression my way. "Whatever would make you hate her?"

Emma's lips were pinched in a tight line before she said, "Envy. I don't know if Little Miss Lucky has filled you in on how many roadblocks we've hurdled in the last few years."

"I understand getting pregnant was difficult," Remi said, her voice gentle.

Emma reached over and placed her hand on Valerie's growing belly. "It was, but we stuck with it and finally had our luck turn there."

"And you got that *Cell* paper," Valerie said. "You joked about it that night you found Remi, and I laughed it off, but it's kind of hard not to get jealous when your bestie gets every single thing she wants."

I didn't have a snappy comeback for that because Judy's sending me to the conference was yet another step in the direction of achieving what I wanted.

Emma continued. "I don't know how you feel about being a work widow, if Karla's as bad as Valerie was. Before she got pregnant, Val was putting in all these hours, gone before I got up, back way after dark…" She and Valerie shared a look. "It's one thing when those kind of hours end up with a paper in *Cell*.

It all feels worth it, but Val's lab...It was like she was putting in all the same effort and getting nothing."

"Till I got pregnant."

"You told Seonwoo? You didn't tell me that!" I exclaimed. I clarified for Remi. "Seonwoo is her PI. I thought he was going to flip when he found out that Valerie was pregnant."

"Just the opposite. I had the most amazing talk with him. He was so excited! We planned out the rest of the experiments I need to complete for my paper, and he said he doesn't see a problem with me finishing it this summer. This summer! I thought it would be December at the earliest, but he pulled it all together."

"That's not even the best part," Emma interrupted, "He was happy to map out what needs to be done before maternity leave and will save Val's project for when she goes back. He actually asked Val if she preferred partner or wife when they were talking about me! Now when she's at the lab late, he reminds her that she needs to be kind to her body, so she's making it home for dinner a few nights a week."

"I feel bad for all the times I've criticized him. What I thought was laziness is looking more like better balance between life and work."

"That's such good news," I said. I hoped I sounded more enthusiastic than I felt. For so long, I'd been the one with the coveted boss in the cutting-edge lab pushing for the big papers. Holding the two bosses side by side now, I envied Valerie's less flashy PI who valued more than the lab work. I recalled Judy's reaction when I told her about Valerie's pregnancy. She didn't see pregnancy as something to accommodate. She defined it as a problem that sidelined a career. What if success was not excelling to the exclusion of all else but having a life worth living as well? I didn't realize how long we had sat in silence until Remi ran her hand along my thigh.

"You okay?" she asked.

"Sorry, I spaced out there for a minute," I said.

"What's up, mate?" Valerie leaned forward from the awkward posture she'd been holding in an attempt to get comfortable.

I grasped for words. "I'm surprised Dr. Seonwoo's being so supportive. I'm trying to wrap my head around it."

Valerie laughed. "Exactly! Blew me away talking to him."

"There's no way I could go to Judy with something like that. When I told her a friend of mine was pregnant, she said 'thank goodness it's not you.'"

Emma and Valerie wore twin expressions of surprise.

"The Goddess?" Emma asked.

"Goddess?" Remi asked.

"You haven't met her?" Emma feigned a swoon in her chair. "She is so sexy. And the fact that she's driven on top of that? Val and I both don't get how Karla can see her every day and not jump her bones."

"You never said she's attractive," Remi said.

"I have never shared their obsession," I said.

"That's the truth," Valerie said. She looked concerned about the turn the conversation had taken. "Karla's always said I'm a disgusting pig for talking about her boss like that."

Despite Valerie's attempt to swing the conversation to lighter topics, I could not dispel the dark mood I had been struggling to suppress. I was happy to let Valerie continue until she began to yawn, signaling that we should go and let her get to bed. It should have made me happy to hear Remi and Emma talking about getting together again soon.

Valerie leaned in for a hug and dropped her voice. "Sorry to be crass about your boss. I don't know what I was thinking. Is Remi going to chuck a hissy fit about it?"

"Not at all. You saved it saying I've never crushed on her."

"You sure it's okay? You don't seem right. I can talk seriously if you need to."

"I know." I hugged Valerie goodbye. "I appreciate it. Tonight was great."

"First rate!" she agreed. She was smiling happily with her arm around Emma as we parted.

Remi crept through the beach traffic, occasionally glancing in my direction. "I enjoyed meeting your friends," she said, breaking the silence.

"They loved you." I peeked at her to see if she had reacted to the word "love." Why had I said that when I hadn't even used the word myself? She kept her eyes on the road ahead. If we were talking love, we were going to talk about priorities and whether Remi had a problem with the increased hours I might have to keep. I had noticed that she looked at me when Emma said that she was excited to have Valerie at home for dinner a few times a week. Was Remi someone who expected her girlfriend at home for dinner every night?

"What made your ex a toad?"

I thought carefully about my answer. "You know Valerie is a researcher too." Remi nodded. "She felt like my girlfriend didn't support my research enough."

"How so?"

"Mostly in the hours I keep. For both of us, science comes first."

"Still? It seems like she has had to become more flexible."

I couldn't deny that. But I remembered when Valerie first talked about getting pregnant. "She was definitely flexible about switching ovens," I said. "But it scared her. When I asked what she would do about work, she said she'd jump off that bridge when she got to it. I'm glad she got so lucky with her jump. I'm glad her PI has made a plan with her, but not everyone would be as accommodating."

"Not yours?"

"No." Her comment frustrated me. Inviting her to dinner was supposed to have given her a look at how Emma and Valerie balanced their relationship with Valerie's demanding career. The safety net Valerie had fallen into had skewed that message. "Judy said a pregnancy at this stage of our research would sideline my career."

She drove in silence for a block. "You think she would say the same about a relationship."

I bit at a rough spot on my lip. "If it impacted my work, yes."

"For example, if you weren't able to go to a conference at a moment's notice."

There was no use in arguing. "Right."

Remi was quiet for a long time, and what she was likely thinking stirred up a mushroom cloud of panic. I was sure some of it was sorting through Neil's reaction. To me, it sounded like he'd accepted the change in plans fairly well, but I didn't know him like his sister did, and I also didn't know whether Remi had given me all the details.

I leaned my head against the soft leather of the Ferrari's seat and soaked in Remi's beauty. Her thick hair was tucked behind her ear, exposing the clean line of her chin and a particularly intricate dangly earring. Her delicate features contrasted her fiery strength, and picturing her eye to eye with hard-ass school administrators to advocate for special-needs children made me smile. She broke the silence.

"What a risk," she said.

I'd been swimming in my own thoughts for so long that I didn't follow. "Risk?"

"Valerie took such a risk getting pregnant. To say she would jump off a bridge when she got to it…That is a leap of faith, one she made for her wife because she loves her. That is a beautiful thing."

I wasn't sure how to respond. It was a beautiful thing. I had often admired the strength of my friend's relationship. Was Remi asking whether I was capable of making a leap like that? I honestly didn't know myself. Nothing I had ever done in my life had required that kind of blind leap. Since I didn't know what to say, I said what I did know. "I'm am so incredibly sorry that the timing of my conference sucked so bad."

"I know you are," Remi said.

She didn't sound mad. I hoped she understood how important it was that I was able to stand in for Judy when she'd needed me. I hadn't told her how she was angling to begin a new project and I would have even more responsibility, even more demands on my time. I shifted my gaze out the window. Driving solo, you only had to think about where you were going. Adding a passenger added the question of whether both people wanted to go to in that same direction. I could only hope that she would understand the importance of the road I was traveling.

I couldn't wrap my head around something that big yet. Tonight, all I wanted was for Remi to drive us both to my house and for her to stay. I reached across the console and rested my hand on her thigh. She slipped her hand under mine, met my eye and smiled.

"You're sure?" I asked.

"*Bien sûr.*"

Remi's switch to French lightened my mood. "You know how to cheer a girl up."

"*J'en sais plus que ça,*" she said with a hint of promise in her voice.

"I hope the translation of that involves some kissing," I said.

"Of much more than that. You can be certain."

CHAPTER TWENTY-TWO

"What do you want to watch?" I handed Remi a plate of enchilada and rice. Before she answered, I added, "No more *Ghost Hunters*." I'd fulfilled my requirement to sit through a full episode with no disparaging remarks and no wandering hands or lips. Now we could see something different.

"Fair enough. *Finding Bigfoot*?"

"You're joking, right?" I settled on my couch next to her.

"You discredit fellow scientists so easily?"

"Fellow scientists," I snickered. "How about *Biggest Loser*?"

"Since when do you watch *Biggest Loser*?"

"It has a good message. Work hard. Eat healthy."

"Sounds thrilling."

"It's accurate. Measurable results. Way more scientific."

"Don't you get enough of that at work?"

"Is that why you like shows about ghosts and Bigfoot?"

"Yes. I need a break from real-life problems." She took a bite of enchilada. "Delicious."

"Don't get too excited. It's pretty much the only thing I know how to make."

"Ah, perfect solution. A cooking show."

I was about to ask how she thought I could learn from accomplished chefs on television when she suggested *Nailed It.* I didn't even have to pull it up to know that it was not serious. Still, it wasn't *Ghost Hunters*, so I handed over the remote to Remi.

As she pulled up an episode, a line formed between her sculpted eyebrows. I couldn't imagine what would make it so hard to choose an episode, and even after she cued one up, she didn't hit play. She rubbed her thumb across the play button and glanced at me.

"What's up?"

"The second Lego Batman movie is out in theaters now."

I hated how tentative she sounded. I knew the hesitation came from setting up something that hadn't turned out. I was glad she was still asking me. "Neil must be psyched. When are you taking him?"

"Tomorrow."

"Oh!" I kicked myself for the knee-jerk exclamation.

"Would you want to go to the first matinee with us?"

"Absolutely," I said. I wondered if it had been their plan for a long time, and she'd been waiting to see if I was going to disappear for the weekend again. "Does he know you're inviting me?"

"He kind of has an armor he puts on when he goes out in public. He should be fine."

I nodded. Realizing that ditching him had affected him to that extent felt shitty. And it stung that she had extended an invitation where he was prepared to protect himself, but I deserved that.

"Thanks for inviting me. I have some cells to check in the morning, but it won't take me long at all."

* * *

Stupid. Stupid. Stupid. Stupid. The word spun in my head. What had I been thinking jinxing myself by saying that I shouldn't be long at the lab? Had I not said anything, I could have rolled in, treated my cells and made it to the movie theater with time to spare.

As it was, even skipping lunch had not helped me deal with the unexpected contamination in the incubator. I was relieved to get all my samples relocated, but since Judy wanted me to start taking more of a leadership position, I had to stay and help resolve the issue.

I'd texted Remi that I'd meet her at the theater when it was clear how long that was going to take.

Everything okay?

Not really. Working fast.

My phone buzzed. I felt like I had just texted Remi, but almost an hour had already passed. *Neil doesn't like to miss the previews. Almost here?*

I hated that I was causing her stress. *Not quite. Meet you inside. Where do you sit?*

I paused, wanting to finish the exchange before I put my gloves back on to clean up the hood I had been using. The longer I waited, the more uncertain I became. I put my gloves back on and got back to putting my pipettes and cell-culture media away. Writing out a note for the lab manager, I wondered if it would be better to show up late for the movie or not at all? I should have asked instead of presuming. Should I ask now? I did not in any way want her to think that I was angling for an out. *Shit. Shit. Shit.* How had this happened again? I heard Valerie shrugging it off, saying, "It's science, mate," but that didn't calm my nerves. My phone buzzed again and I threw my gloves in the trash before pulling my phone out of my lab coat.

Three rows from the front.

Got it.

I shoved my phone in my pocket, heading to my office to wrap up. My phone buzzed again.

Not a good idea to come in if movie has started.

Shit!

You have about fifteen minutes.

Which meant I was out of time. I'd have to finish my email to Judy later and pray that she didn't hear about the contamination from the lab manager before she got it. Throwing my lab coat at my desk, I raced to the parking lot and drove like Lego Batman out of hell to get there.

I literally ran directly up to the window, relieved that I didn't have to wait to get my ticket. "Has it started?"

He turned to the clock, costing me precious time to grab a snack so my stomach didn't growl during the movie. "Starts in five."

I thanked him and ran through the door after the ticket man ripped the ticket and pointed out my theater. Anxiety knocking against my pounding heart, I fidgeted in line, checking my watch every ten seconds. With about thirty seconds to spare, I ran to the theater and slipped in for the last ad before the movie, asking people to silence their cell phones and enjoy the show.

I easily spotted two single silhouettes near the front and slipped in beside Remi. "Made it!" I whispered.

Neil shushed me loudly.

I mouthed *sorry* to Remi and leaned back to catch my breath. I tipped my head to the side to smile at Remi and saw her eyes glued to my popcorn. I extended it toward her. She shook her head vehemently, glanced worriedly at her brother and then focused on the big screen.

"I skipped lunch," I whispered as quietly as possible. Still, I pictured my words going straight through Remi's head and out the other ear to accost Neil.

Remi tipped her hand up at the wrist.

What did that mean? That she got it? That I'd blown it? Should I eat it?

My stomach rumbled loudly, and I caught Remi looking at me out of the corner of her eye.

I should have stayed at the lab.

Having already been shushed by Neil for whispering, I worried over how to eat popcorn quietly. As delicately as possible, I pinched a few kernels of popcorn and placed them in my mouth. I willed my cheeks to absorb all the sound. Still, Neil folded his arms across his chest. What happened to his having armor he put on in public?

I took one piece of popcorn from the top and chewed as slowly as possible.

Neil started tapping his elbow.

How could he possibly be hearing my chewing? It didn't seem possible, but Remi touched his elbow briefly, so I knew I wasn't making up Neil's discomfort. I began to lower the popcorn to the floor, but Remi stayed my hand with hers. "Neil's very sensitive to eating sounds, but he knows they cannot be avoided entirely. Eat your popcorn. Please."

Neil shushed his sister. I wondered if they sat so close to the screen to avoid being near anyone who might make a noise.

"I should move," I whispered.

"Stop worrying. You're hungry." Her smile was tight.

I wanted to argue, but I knew better than to continue to talk with the previews going. I would hold the popcorn and not eat it. Remi couldn't force me to eat it. My stomach grumbled again. Shit! Was Neil going to shush that too? I put a piece of popcorn on my tongue, waited until my saliva made it soggy, and then mushed it against the roof of my mouth with my tongue.

Remi smacked me lightly on the arm. "Don't be weird."

I raised my shoulders in question.

"There is no quiet way to eat popcorn. Neil and I can move if it bothers him."

"I'll move."

"You're too loud," Neil said loudly. Remi tensed and whispered something to Neil. He nodded, his eyes boring into me. Still looking at me and not the screen, he moved over a seat.

I wished I had thought to ask whether they had a protocol they followed before the movie. But then, I wished I had eaten a real lunch, met Remi at her place, and picked up Neil together.

My stomach had soured to the point where I could not enjoy the popcorn. Remi quickly noticed that I had stopped eating. "Eat," she whispered. "He has to learn that he can't always control what's around him."

I dutifully placed another few pieces of popcorn on my tongue, too aware of the tension buzzing between Remi and Neil to take in any of the movie at all. Neil lasted in his new seat for five pieces of popcorn. Then he moved farther down the row. Three more handfuls, he left our row and moved to the row in front of us. Remi turned in my direction before she got up to join Neil, but it was too dark for me to read her expression.

I ate until my stomach stopped growling. Keeping Neil in his seat became my main concern, and by the time the movie ended, I had two-thirds of a bucket of congealed popcorn to toss. Not wanting Remi to see how much I was throwing away, I left the theater when the credits began. I wasn't surprised when Remi and Neil followed on my heels. Remi paused by me, but Neil kept walking without acknowledging me.

"Neil, we need to say goodbye to Karla."

"You should eat at home, not in the movie theater," he said.

Despite knowing about his autism, his words stung. "I'm sorry, Neil. Pretty much nothing happened the way I thought it would today."

"You should plan better. I have a planner."

"She apologized, Neil. Can you accept her apology?"

"And then we can go?" He was only looking at her.

"Then we can go." Remi sounded tired.

"I am really sorry," I repeated.

"I accept your apology but…"

"That's all," Remi interrupted. "You accepted. Thank you."

He turned and began to walk toward the exit. "You said we could go now."

I could tell that Remi was frustrated when she started to walk backward. I took a step but she held up her hand to stop me. She placed the tiniest of kisses on her fingertips which she tipped in my direction. "I'll call you."

I wanted her frustration to be because of Neil dragging her off the second the movie ended, but I worried that everything had gone south because of me. If I'd been there on time having eaten lunch beforehand, would we be walking together talking about details about the movie? I probably wouldn't get another invitation to find out.

CHAPTER TWENTY-THREE

I had mass with my parents in the morning. My mother was not sending Rosa over to make sure I was eating since I had told her I might be eating with Remi. We usually did something between mass and Sunday dinner, but after the disaster at the movie theater, and her "I'll call you," I thought it would be best to wait.

I had things to do, anyway. I ran a load of laundry and scared Petri with the vacuum. I went shopping for the week and cleaned out my pantry. To encourage her to call, I started a paper that I'd been meaning to read.

I'd gotten discouragingly far before I admitted defeat and walked over to my parents' house for dinner.

"What is bothering you," my mom asked as she served the enchilada casserole.

"Nothing," I said.

"Are your mice infected again?"

"Ma, I don't even work with mice right now. There was a problem with cell contamination in the lab yesterday, but I got it under control."

"But you still sound worried. Will your boss be angry?" my mom asked.

"She doesn't spend very much time in the lab. Running the lab is a whole different ball game." I remembered explaining the difference between being a postdoc and a research scientist to Rosa. The difference between what I did and what Judy did was vast. And the more time she spent working with the sponsor and the FDA, the more those responsibilities would fall to me. I would be spending more time writing grants, traveling to conferences, and troubleshooting problems that would undoubtedly come up in the lab.

I had anticipated that kind of responsibility my whole career, yet now that I was on the cusp of securing that role, I worried about what Remi would think. That paused my thoughts, and I noticed the quiet at the table. What were we talking about? Running the lab being a whole new ball game. I saw an opportunity to switch the subject and took it. "Maybe I should take Remi to a ball game. I've been trying to think of another good date idea. You score any tickets?" I asked Luis.

"Not lately," he said. "My timing is off. I was pretty sure you stole it when you picked up your lady friend. Thought you'd be getting plenty lucky."

"Luis," Antonia, my mother and I all said at once.

He threw his arms in the air. "Just sayin'. Where is your girl, anyway?"

I flushed hot at his question, my silent phone heavy in my pocket. It wasn't bad that she hadn't called or texted all day, was it? I certainly wasn't going to offer that question to my family. I'd been busy today. She could be busy too. Luckily, Antonia saved me, jumping into the conversation.

"I hope you're going to the movies and eating at restaurants that don't take kids. You could go on a road trip, head out to Santa Barbara or Las Vegas. So many things you can do. I love my kids, but I miss the stuff Gustavo and I used to be able to do together when it was just the two of us."

Giselle ribbed Luis and said he should be taking notes from his sister because she was tired of going to ball games, and Rosa asked her grandparents to talk about when they were dating.

I sat back and soaked in how lucky I was. How many families would so easily move into talking about their own dating after the lesbian said something about hers? My family had never once called me a dyke, had never made me fear rejection. I wished I could bring Maricela home to show her how accepting families could be. Or maybe I should bring Maricela's mother to give her a lesson on how family should treat each other.

I stayed late enjoying the rapid-fire conversation between my brother and sister, which kept my mother from asking what was swirling in my thoughts. Her eyes were on me, so I knew there was a follow-up question about what was bothering me in store. Not tonight, though. After my brother and his family left, I walked home with even more to think about. My mother's question about my boss made it impossible not to think of the impact more responsibility at work would have on the time left to spend with my family.

There was just enough ambient light from the lengthening days to navigate to my room and change into my pajamas for my nighttime routine. I wondered what Remi was doing and then decided it was stupid to spend any more time on it. I didn't want to play games. I wanted to know how she was.

My family asked about you at dinner.

A happy face popped up. Then, *Duplo has arrived to destroy me.*

I furrowed my brow. Duplo? As I put toothpaste on my brush, I figured out that Remi was referencing a scene from *The Lego Movie*. I sighed. She was with Neil. Had yesterday's movie experience required an all-day intervention? I remembered when Remi shared that her brother could be viewed as the competition by some. To have any chance at a relationship, I could not view Neil as the competition.

Not Batman Lego tonight?

Go figure. Neil insisted. Almost over. Okay to call you on my way home?

Sure.

I finished brushing my teeth and arranged myself with my feet up on the wall to run through my meditation. On *Be Content*, my phone rang.

"It's late. I'm sorry," Remi said.

"I'm glad you called. I was so wishing that you were at dinner with me tonight."

"Why is that?"

"If you were there, they wouldn't be able to tease me."

"If I remember correctly, they still teased you when I was there for dinner."

"But then you were there to smile and take away the sting."

"What did they say tonight?"

"My brother says once I met you, I stole his luck."

"That sounds sweet, not like teasing."

"I edited it to take out the crassness."

Remi laughed. "I wished you were with me, too."

"With Neil?"

"With Neil."

The line was silent for several beats. I scooted my legs off the wall and sat cross-legged on the carpet, picking at cat hairs. "Lay it on me. How bad was the popcorn?" I hadn't expected Remi to laugh and was startled by the burst that erupted from her. Despite my trepidation, I smiled.

"That will be your name for a while, I'm afraid."

"What does that mean, my name? He calls me popcorn?"

"Why was Popcorn late?" she said in a deeper voice, mimicking her brother.

I winced. "There was unexpected contamination at my lab yesterday. I couldn't leave until I had it contained."

"I understand that your work is unpredictable…"

"Neil doesn't," I said.

"He has trouble understanding that not all jobs start and end at an exact time."

"That's a problem."

"It is a new challenge that we will figure out. I think he is working on it in his own way."

"With Lego?" I asked.

"Yes. It has been a while since he has chosen *The Lego Movie* to watch, the first one," she clarified for me. "More often he wants to watch *The Lego Batman Movie*. That one explores family dynamics, but *The Lego Movie* is about dating."

"I love how you talk about movies. It's not a fluffy kids movie to you."

"No, it is significantly more than that. And the first one has more romance than I remembered. It made me think that maybe he comprehends more than I give him credit for."

"You think he is trying to figure out why you want to spend time with me?"

"I do. He was very intent when the music slowed down and Wyldstyle swung her hair around."

"Everything pauses and Emmet is mesmerized. That is so me when I see you. I'm the dorky nerd wondering why it didn't work out between you and Batman."

"Batman has issues. That is most likely why Neil fixates on *The Lego Batman Movie*. He's got issues."

My blood froze. Was she calling to tell me that trying to date was too much? "You told me before," I said. It felt like she was quiet for minutes.

"Tonight, we didn't watch the Batman one. We watched the romantic one, and I do not think it was a coincidence. I bet he will choose it again next week. Would you want to join us?"

Her invitation was so unexpected tears sprang to my eyes. It felt huge after I'd so badly mangled the movie theater. "Yesterday didn't go so well."

"I don't know. Getting a nickname could be good, Popcorn."

"I'm in. Thank you for inviting me. I was so worried that you were calling to say I blew it."

"My brother is complicated. Life is complicated. Where would we be if people didn't try again when something went poorly? Isn't that how science goes, Popcorn?"

"You said Neil called me Popcorn. I don't know if I want you to call me Popcorn, too."

"Fair enough."

"You sure it'll be okay?" I asked.

"I am sure about one thing only."

"What's that?" I asked. I swung my feet up on the wall.

"That I want to sit next to you and hold your hand."

"Then it's a date. All that time my family spent plotting out what we could do next, and you had it figured out already."

"What's this?"

I closed my eyes and recounted all their memorable dates my family recalled at dinner.

"That is the sweetest thing I have ever heard. I am sorry I was not there to hear it in person."

I agreed and lay there on my back, nothing more to say. More and more I found myself wishing Remi was with me. Remi was equally quiet, and I searched for words, something that wasn't "Come over. Please come over right now and stay with me."

"What was that?" Remi asked.

I held my breath. Had I said that out loud? What did I say now? "I know it's late and you have a long work week ahead." I took a deep breath. "But I really wish you were here."

"If you had a genie, would you use that as one of your wishes?"

"Yes, absolutely, and I wouldn't even need the other two wishes."

"You are sure?"

"What more would I wish for?" I laughed.

"No, I meant about wishing I was there. Were you serious about wanting me to come over?"

It was late. I was headed to bed, and Remi knew that. If I said yes, I was actually inviting Remi to bed and so far we had not tried collecting any data on how I slept next to her without having sex first. My body thrummed just thinking about Remi in my bed. "Yes. I was serious about wanting you here."

"Oh good."

There was a knock at my door.

"Shit!" I said, leaping to my feet, my heart pounding. "Shit, shit, shit. Someone's at my door."

"You sound very surprised for someone issuing invitations."

"What?" I froze, trying to understand what Remi was saying.

"You said you wished I was here."

My feet caught on faster than my brain and carried me to the front door. I peeked out the window. Remi waved. "You're here," I said into the phone.

"Not quite." Remi pointed to the door.

"Sorry!" I unlocked the door to let Remi in. "I guess I can hang up now."

Remi tucked her phone in her purse and set it on the couch. Her eyes scanned my body. "Nice pajamas," she said. Her stretch pants and tee were not such a leap from the tank and boxers I slept in.

"I didn't know you would be here. If I had…" I swallowed hard thinking about how much fun Remi and I could have with lingerie. Strangely, I felt utterly exposed in my close-fitting tank. I was certain my nipples were pushing at the fabric and fought the temptation to fold my arms across my chest. "How are you here?"

"I couldn't stop thinking about you." She ran her fingers up my arm. "When I left my brother's, somehow the car pointed toward your place. I was trying to figure out how I could invite myself when you said you wished I was here. So…here I am."

"Just like that?"

"Just like that."

I wrapped my arms around her. She felt so good nestled there, and I felt how deeply it would have hurt if she decided that dating me was too stressful. I held on tighter.

"Hey." She squeezed me back. "Are you okay?"

"I'm so relieved you weren't calling to tell me this isn't worth the trouble I'm causing."

She took my hand. "Let me show you how worth the trouble this is."

I followed her to the bedroom and let her show me to her heart's content.

CHAPTER TWENTY-FOUR

"This is awesome! Are you sure you can't use them?"

"It's a family four-pack. I thought you and your lady could come with me and Giselle."

I leaned back in my chair, easily picturing me and Remi at the San Diego Padres game Thursday night. Me and my brother and our ladies in front and center top deck seats sipping beers and eating dogs. It would be a perfect date and taking Remi to hang out with Luis and Giselle sounded fantastic.

But Remi had dinner with Neil on Thursdays. "I have to pass, bro."

"What? Ma said you're not working as late. Come hang with me and Giselle."

"I'd like to, but I'm pretty sure it'll be a no-go. Remi has plans with her brother every Thursday. She doesn't mess with his schedule."

"Aw man, if you don't come, that means Giselle will bring her sister and you know that she and her guy will be talking shit about the Padres all night."

"The Dodgers are having a great run," I agreed.

"It's going to be a killer game, sis. You don't think you could convince Remi?"

"I've asked Remi to mess with Neil's schedule before. It's important that I do stuff with them. I'm sorry."

There was a long pause before Luis said, "You can have all four. Then her brother can go, too. You said before it would be a good date."

For a second, I thought about calling Remi to invite her and Neil, but only a second. After that one brief moment of wishing we could, I knew how awful that experience would be for Neil. If the sound of popcorn bothered him, there was no way he was going to get through the experience of pushing through the crowds and sitting in a baseball stadium filled with fans yelling their heads off. "It would be such a good date, but I'll get tickets another time when Remi and I can go. You're stuck with Giselle and her Dodger-loving sister."

He grumbled but accepted my answer and signed off.

I was right about Neil, wasn't I? Or had I spoken too swiftly? I sent a quick text to Remi.

My brother scored tx to the Padres game Thurs. 4 tx. He said I could have them.

I hit send and immediately added *Bad idea, right? Was I right to say I'd pass?*

As I hit send again, her reply to my first message came in. *You want to go?*

Tempting, I typed. *But I can't see Neil at Petco Park.*

No. He'd be miserable.

That's what I thought. But I wanted to check.

Tnx. She fired back. *You could go without us.*

Would rather catch The Lego Movie if I'm still invited.

A thumbs-up and then *Give you a lift?*

Will have to leave from work. Text me Neil's address. Meet you there. Six?

Her reply took more time, and I could easily hear her worrying about whether I would be late. When the address and *Yes, six* came through, I sighed in relief that I had said the right thing about the tickets and had a chance to prove that I could make it to Neil's on time.

* * *

I took precautions to make sure I left work at five on Thursday, my plan to beat Remi to Neil's place. I arrived a good fifteen minutes early and still ended up parking next to Remi's beautiful Ferrari.

"Are you here early to check up on me?" I asked, leaning on the doorframe of her open passenger-side window.

"What do you mean?"

"You were worried about me being here on time."

"I was hoping you would be here early, so we could have a few minutes before we went in." She leaned over to open the door. I slid into the luxurious leather seat and leaned across the console for a hug.

"It had nothing to do with wanting to know whether I gave myself time to spare?"

A smile played at her lips. "I am glad you are here, but I do not understand why you are so interested in talking when we could be kissing."

In total agreement, I brought my lips to hers. Melting into the silken softness of her lips, I was so glad that I had turned down the tickets and so glad that I had left time for a sensual hello. It felt so much better than the movie-theater episode.

When Remi pulled away, she ran her fingers through my hair. "It means a lot to me that you chose to be here with me and Neil."

"There will be other games," I said.

She squeezed my hand, and we headed in for the show.

"Hey, Neil!" she said after knocking on his door. "Anything exciting happen today?"

Neil looked up, but before he answered, his gaze jumped to me. He shrugged and went back to flipping through a massive book. "You brought Popcorn."

"I told you Karla wanted to watch *The Lego Movie* with us this week."

Neil set down the book, and I caught from the title that it contained thousands of things you could build out of Lego. It made me think of all the insane things I'd seen on the *Lego Masters* show. "Have you guys ever watched *Lego Masters?*" I asked.

Neil looked to Remi. "We haven't tried it," she answered.

"She doesn't want to watch *The Lego Movie*," Neil said.

"I do," I quickly countered. "Your book reminded me of a show I've seen with my nephew is all."

Remi caught my eye and lifted her eyebrows a smidge. Somehow, I knew that meant it was better if I followed along. I could do that.

A loud bottle cap sound came from my pocket. I quickly extracted my phone to silence it. "Sorry," I said to both Remi and Neil.

"I told you Popcorn is too loud. She's going to ruin this movie, too."

"It's on silent now," Remi assured him.

I nodded, but neither sibling was looking at me. Remi moved to the TV to cue up the movie, and I stayed by the door. Since I'd swiped into my phone to silence it, I checked the text.

Grand Slam first inning Baby! Padres are going to kill tonight! I shoved my phone in my back pocket and put the game out of my head. It was important to be with Remi and Neil, and I was not going to mess up again.

Later, when I had followed Remi back to her place, I remembered my phone and pulled it out to see no fewer than twenty texts from Luis that captured every exciting play of the high-scoring game. I was distracted thumbing through his increasingly excited texts when Remi slipped her arms around my waist and raised herself on her toes to see over my shoulder. I held up my phone. "They were on the Kiss Cam."

"It sounded like an exciting game," Remi whispered, sending all sorts of wonderful shivers down my spine.

I set my phone on her table and turned in her arms. "How do you know?"

"I listened to some recap on the drive over. The Padres won in extra innings. Are you upset that you did not go?"

I pressed my lips to hers and then added my hips and breasts. Her lips were supple under mine, and she readily parted them and pulled me deeper into a kiss that did not stop until we both needed to come up for air. Between breaths, I said, "I was exactly where I wanted to be."

"What was that? I think I got it. But just in case…tell me the whole thing again, I wasn't listening."

I recognized the line from the movie. I hadn't fully appreciated how clever the dialogue was when I'd seen it with my young nieces and nephews. Watching it with Neil and Remi, I recognized many of the lines as things Neil used in his communication. Interspersing my words with kisses, I said again, "I was exactly where I wanted to be."

She took my hand, and it was easy to see how right my decision to turn down my brother and spend time with hers had been. "Come with me," she said, leading me toward her bedroom.

I could not resist adding, "…if you want to not die."

Her laughter sweetened our next kiss, but when she pulled away, her eyes were so serious. She reached out and traced my jaw with her fingertips. "It means the world to me that you were with us tonight. It helps him understand what you mean to me."

"You mean so much to me. You are everything I have ever wanted in a partner. You're so smart and so sexy." I had more to say but putting it into words was taking too long. I added my hands to the conversation, tucking them underneath her shirt to run up her back. Her shirt rode with them, and she pulled it the rest of the way over her shoulders. Her breasts lifted with her quickening breaths. Pulling her close, I lavished kisses above the fabric of her bra.

Then she was unbuttoning my shirt and rolling it off my shoulders. I stepped to her, feeling heat radiate between our bodies. She took a step back, and I moved with her. She placed her hand on my chest. "I want you in my bed." She turned, carrying both our shirts to her room where she draped them over a chair in the corner. Her eyes never leaving mine, she added her bra to the pile before slipping out of her skirt and underwear. She was unhurried but her desire was plainly visible.

I added my clothes to the pile while she turned back the covers. Each action felt significant despite its mundanity. The way Remi's eyes roamed my body silenced the whisper in the back of my mind about why Remi would choose to spend her time with me. "When you look at me like that…" I was having trouble putting my feelings into words and crossed the room to sit on the edge of the bed.

Remi raised herself on her elbow and reached out to trace my thigh with her fingertips. "When I look at you…?"

"I don't know. It's like you bump me up a notch when you look at me like that. I feel like a better me, definitely a sexier me. You make me feel like this is where I belong."

She leaned to me and kissed me deeply, somehow pulling me with her as she lay back down, wrapping her legs around me to bring our bodies into full contact. "This is where you belong." I wound one arm around her shoulders and another around her waist, fusing our bodies as our kisses grew hotter. Remi's mouth was mine, or mine was hers, parrying our tongues though not to win anything, simply to appreciate the other's great skill. I could not get close enough.

I tore myself away from her kisses, gently nipping my way down her body.

"I liked you there," Remi said, trying to hold me.

"I have to taste you. I have to feel all of you." I could not linger on her beautiful breasts or tease her with hints of a touch or a hot breath nearing her center. I found her clit with the first swipe of my tongue and reveled in the gasp that followed. I plunged again and felt her push against me, inviting me deeper just as she had when we kissed. Tonight, the tilt of her hips invited me further than she ever had before. My lips sealed to hers, and I lost myself in her heat, in her ragged breathing, in the way she rocked beneath me.

I had to have more and slipped inside her. I'd never felt her so ready and pushed deep inside, my lips sealed around her clit, tongue flitting across it. I teased her opening with a second finger, and she opened wide to me, pulling me deeper and deeper. I ran out of breath and replaced my mouth with my thumb, pulling myself up to capture one of her perfect nipples in my mouth.

"More," Remi breathed.

"Here?" I asked, pulling on her nipple more forcefully.

Remi shuddered beneath me. "Deeper."

I obliged, wrapping my free arm around her shoulders, fusing our bodies again. When I ground my own center on her thigh, Remi groaned. I slowed my fingers and matched the rhythm of my hand to my own hips.

"Don't stop! Oh, don't stop," she said.

I wasn't stopping, but I was going to pull as much pleasure out of her as I possibly could. I circled her clit with my thumb again and again, forcing myself to go slowly, to read every one of Remi's breaths and undulations.

I watched emotions play on her face, concentration mixed with pleasure. Eyes still closed, she looked as if she could see her orgasm approaching. Closer and closer until it was upon her and she was quaking beneath me. Her eyes fluttered open, locking on mine.

"You…turn me inside out," she whispered.

Her words tipped me over into my own release. I hadn't realized how close I was, and the orgasm caught me quick and strong. I cried out and buried my head between her breasts enjoying my own pleasure with hers.

Out of breath, every muscle jelly, my sweaty skin stuck to hers, I attempted to pull away, but Remi grabbed my ass. "Not yet."

My eyes met hers again. I felt utterly satisfied. "Well, I'd call that a grand slam," I said.

"So you were thinking about baseball all night!"

I eased out of her and nestled myself in her arms. "Only you, Remi. Only you."

"You make me feel like we could have it all, Karla Hernandez."

I squeezed her tight. In that moment, I believed we could.

CHAPTER TWENTY-FIVE

Weeks passed, and though Remi sometimes called me "Popcorn," she said it in a way that made me feel included in her life instead of reminded about the movie theater mistake. Remi and I fell into a routine where she slept over several nights a week, adding data to verify Rosa's hypothesis. As long as she was with me, I dropped off to sleep without issue. I watched *The Lego Movie* and spent most days humming "Everything is Awesome" as I pictured curbing vision loss in diabetics like preventing the Lego city from being stuck permanently with Kragle.

The buzz of my phone paused my soundtrack, especially when I read Remi's text.

Had THE WORST IEP meeting ever. So looking forward to dinner.

Me too. Sorry about the meeting.

She sent a kissing emoji and I tucked my phone back into my pocket, grateful, as always, that Remi and I worked with the same level of dedication and focus.

I resumed my work and my song and was happily typing when Ashleigh found me at my desk. "Judy wants to see you?"

"I don't know," I answered even though I knew that for Ashleigh the question was a statement.

"She wants to see you? She said for me to wait for you?"

That wasn't like Judy. Usually she understood that I would come when I found a natural pause in what I was doing. Luckily, it was easy to save my work and follow Ashleigh immediately.

Judy was standing when I got to her office, and she was angry. I had never seen Judy angry, and instantly I flashed hot.

"Explain this to me." She extended a letter but before I could take it, she snatched it back. "It's from the Miracle Center's institutional review board with a complaint about our project. Apparently, one of the volunteers has withdrawn because..." She skimmed through the letter. "The research conflicts with her moral beliefs."

I felt so sick to my stomach, I had to sit down. Judy towered over me.

"Do you know what she could be talking about? She says that being around gay people in both the clinic and the lab has ruined her daughter."

Maricela must have told her mother. I shut my eyes.

Judy paced along her window, never once looking out at the view. "Such ignorance! To believe that being exposed to gay people will somehow infect her child? Who is this child and who is this gay person she has worked with in my lab?"

Heart hammering in my chest, I managed to say, "Me. I'm gay."

She whipped around and stared down at me. Life slowed like it did in *The Lego Movie*, but not like it did when the romantic interest entered the picture. This was the scene that could wipe out the protagonist, and I had no clue what to do. She threw her arms in the air, and I prepared myself. Could she fire me for mentoring Maricela when I knew her mother was one of our volunteers? "Why would that even matter? I don't care if you're gay. I care that you can design good experiments and interpret data. Who the hell cares if you have sex with women? You could screw a god-damned goat in the middle of campus at high noon and I wouldn't care so long as you were doing your work."

My phone buzzed in my pocket, and I thanked my lucky stars that it was on silent. I didn't take my eyes off Judy.

"How the hell does she even know you're gay?"

I heard the waver in my voice when explained how I had tutored her daughter while she was working in the neighboring lab.

"She did no work in our lab?"

"None," I said. "But she is Latina, and she was floundering in Bautista's lab trying to understand the Chinese postdoc who was supposed to be helping her. At first, I was protecting the equipment from her inexperience, but when I found out she was struggling in her college class, I offered to help."

My phone buzzed again. Remi never texted this often. Neither did anyone in my family, but I didn't dare pull it out to look. Not when I was caught in Judy's crosshairs.

"This is a critical time. If she broadcasts this message to the community, it could seriously impede recruitment."

"She's the only volunteer I encountered. I haven't pissed off anyone else, I think."

"Do you know how many of the volunteers are Hispanic?"

"Eighty-three percent," I said. I ran the data, and besides that I had personal knowledge of the increased probability of diabetes in that population.

"I do not like hypothesizing about how many of those Hispanics happen to be Catholic and hold the same moral views as the mother you pissed off. What is to stop this woman from spreading her ignorance to other Miracle Center patients?"

"It's personal. It's about her daughter. She wants to punish me and her daughter, not ruin the trial."

"Of all the things…" Judy kept pacing, the letter clutched in the fisted hand on her hip. I sat mute and trapped when my phone buzzed with an incoming call. "We will have to respond to the IRB. This is a good time for you to take more responsibility. Give me a draft within the hour."

I glanced at my watch. I was going to be late to dinner. "Understood," I said to Judy. I strode from the office, behaving how Judy would expect a research scientist to take the helm. I checked my phone on my way back to my desk.

Call me when you can talk?

I hit the phone icon at the top of the screen and waited impatiently for the call to connect.

"Looks like it's a crap day for both of us," I said when she answered. "Maricela's mom sent a letter of complaint, so now I'm in the hot seat explaining my relationship with them as well as my sex life to my boss. I have an hour to respond to the letter Judy received from the IRB, so there's no way I'm going to make it to dinner."

I sat down at my desk and opened my email, phone squished between my shoulder and face. "Call you later?" I asked.

"If you have time."

"Great. Thanks! This is...ugh. I have so much to do."

"I'll let you go."

I thanked her again and pocketed my phone. Before leaving it there, I reflected briefly on Remi's tone. Her voice sounded tight, but I was certain she had not been crying. If whatever she wanted to tell me about couldn't wait, she would have said so, right? Blank document in front of me, I got to work.

* * *

By the time Judy nodded her approval and let me go, my eyes burned, my back ached and I was starving. My growling belly reminded me of the dinner I'd missed with Remi, and I dialed her number on my way out of the building.

"Hey." Remi did not sound like herself at all.

"You sound how I feel," I said.

When she didn't respond, I peeked at the phone to make sure we were still connected. We were. "Want to tell me about the terrible IEP meeting?"

"Not really."

"I don't understand. You said earlier that your day sucked because of a meeting."

"Is that all you read? You did not read any of the other texts or listen to your voice mail?"

She'd left me a message? I stopped walking. "Should I read the texts?"

"Whatever you want, Karla."

Remi's words made my body go cold. Something was wrong. I clicked Remi onto speakerphone and opened the texts. I thumbed back to the IEP message and quickly skimmed the following texts.

Prob w Neil. Can you talk?

Neil had an accident in the kitchen. Staff says he is still quite agitated. On my way there.

Worse than I thought. Where are you?

On our way to the hospital. Can you call?

Are you still working?

Karla?

I gasped. "Remi, I'm so sorry I didn't see these this afternoon. I didn't mean to go radio silent on you today. I just…" I pressed the palm of my hand to my forehead. "There was literally no time for me to stop today." Too much time passed in silence, but I didn't know what to say. "Remi?"

"I think it is best if I say goodnight."

"Remi, no please don't. I'd like to hear what happened with Neil. I can be at your place in twenty minutes."

"That is what I needed hours ago. It is late, Karla. I cannot talk now."

"I know how bad this looks, that I was stuck at work again. I wish…"

"Stop. Please."

I wanted to talk a mile a minute thinking that I could somehow find words that would soften Remi to me. I wanted her to change her mind and ask me to drive over. But she had said stop, so I did. I stopped my feet and my mouth and waited, my heart in my throat, my pulse pounding in my ears. Stupid. Stupid. Stupid.

"I have faced this dilemma before, and my feelings about my brother haven't changed."

"I understand that…"

"Please let me talk. What is happening between us…" Remi paused, and I dreaded hearing what she was trying to put into words. "It is stretching me in two directions, and it is affecting

Neil. I thought that I could explain to him who you were to me, but it is taking a toll on him. His difficulty coping today…This, dating you…I am afraid that it might not be possible for me to have a relationship and maintain my brother's care."

Her words squeezed my heart until it hurt so badly I pushed the palm of my free hand to my chest.

"Can you at least tell me what happened to Neil and whether he is okay? I care about him, and your being at the hospital worries me."

"He was learning how to make a BLT. He caught the handle of the pan somehow and the grease splashed onto his legs."

"Did it come in direct contact with his skin? Is it blistering?"

"I must go now. I have to concentrate on Neil."

There was no arguing with her. "Can I call you tomorrow?"

"Give me some time, Karla. I don't know when he will be released from the hospital."

I waited for her to say more, hoping that once she started talking, she would see that I was available now and ready to support her.

"Goodnight, Karla. I will call when I can."

She hung up, and my screen went dark. I stood alone on the sidewalk as the night air chilled. I told myself that it could be worse. I still had my job. It would be awkward tomorrow, but Judy prioritized science, and I was still a good scientist. And Remi had not said goodbye. She'd said goodnight. She had to care for Neil and didn't feel like she could count on me. I would give her time to see that she could. I would find a way to prove it.

CHAPTER TWENTY-SIX

I was in my bedroom changing into pajamas, emotionally wrung out from two days of waiting to hear from Remi. I should have been on my way to my parents' house, but it was late, late enough that I wasn't going to bother going over. Still in my closet, I heard the front door slam.

"You are so dead!" Antonia hollered from the kitchen.

"Luis doesn't care if I'm at his birthday party or not. More cake for him."

"Mom does."

My guilt deepened as I listened to my sister putting the leftovers my mother had sent into the fridge. I'd purposely avoided driving by the house hoping I'd be able to tell my mother I'd gotten in too late to go over. "They're not waiting on me for cake, are they?"

Antonia's silence worried me. Cheerful barbs, I could handle, but the silence meant there were real hurt feelings to fix. When I joined my sister, I was surprised to see her sitting on the couch with two beers, one extended toward me. Cautiously, I crossed the room and perched next to my sister on the couch. "Why are you being nice to me? Is this my last beer or something? How'd you know I was here, anyway?"

"Mom had a sense."

"How mad is she?"

"She didn't talk at dinner."

I took the beer and sank back into the couch. Petri jumped up next to me, and I stroked her fur. I tried not to think of my mother's silence. The more my mom had to say, the quieter she became, and no amount of badgering could get her to come out with what she was thinking. When she had figured out how to put her disappointment into words, without fail, those few words would cut clean and deep. "She didn't give you orders to drag me home?"

"Dad said to hear you out. He gave me a hand signal to use if your excuse is legit."

"And if it's not?"

"Then it's been nice being your sister."

A small smile pulled at the corner of my mouth.

"You look terrible. Are you sleeping at all?"

"Not so much."

"Something wrong at work?"

I stared hard at Antonia. She always claimed she knew nothing about my work. "You really want to know?"

"Are you kidding? No! Rosa said to ask you. She's worried about you."

"The research is fine. I'll tell her."

"You're coming back with me?"

"After I finish this beer." I rested my head against the back of the couch and closed my eyes, already feeling the alcohol relax my limbs. It felt so good, I added, "and yours." I downed the rest of mine and held out my hand.

"So why aren't you sleeping if work is fine."

"I didn't say work was fine. The research is fine. My work sucks since my mentee's mom filed a letter of complaint and outed me to my boss. She saw that as a great opportunity to give me more responsibility which means putting in longer hours."

"That does suck. Especially if it cuts into time you can spend with Remi."

I drank Antonia's beer in silence thinking about the messages I had left Remi asking when I could see her again. "It's worse than that, I'm pretty sure I fucked that up."

Antonia smacked me. "No! We like her! What did you do?"

I explained how I'd had to ignore her texts and call while my boss filled me in on Maricela's mom refusing to continue as a volunteer and berate me about the potential effect her idiocy could have on recruitment for the trial. I didn't have to look at Antonia to feel her disappointment and know that she didn't fully understand why I couldn't have held up a finger to check my messages. She didn't have to voice her question for me to offer my excuse that sometimes I can't interrupt my work.

"If you were a brain surgeon, I'd give you that." She frowned in thought and then took it back. "Nah. You know what, even that would be bullshit. I'm sure brain surgeons have someone who could read them a message, and if it's an emergency, you face it right then."

"You have me in the wrong spot. My boss could have checked her phone, but not me! You think the person doing suction can say, hold up a minute, my phone keeps going off?"

"How many times did she text you?"

I hung my head. "Maybe six. And she called."

"Shoulda picked up."

I hadn't even told my sister how I'd talked to her after my meeting and didn't even bother asking whether something was wrong. I'd been so focused on myself that I didn't let her get a word in edgewise. Lead settled in my belly. I had messed up so badly, and I had no idea how to fix it. "I let her down."

"Come on." Antonia took back her beer, stood and took my hand to pull me to my feet.

"What? I'm not ready."

"I can't fix this alone. You're going to have to talk to mom."

I groaned but followed orders, knowing I would eventually have to tell my mother everything. Antonia waited as I pulled sweats over my pajama bottoms, put on shoes and grabbed a light jacket. We walked to our parents' house in silence, and my mom managed to ratchet up my guilt with the once-over she gave my outfit.

"I'd just gotten home," I tried to explain.

"You didn't stop here to wish your brother a happy birthday."

"Happy Birthday, Luis!" I shouted toward the living room.

"Thanks for your slice of cake!" he said, shoving a big bite in his mouth.

I knew he wouldn't care. My mother, on the other hand…I could still feel the heat of her glare.

"It's not just work," Antonia said. "It's girl trouble. That's why I dragged her over." Having done her duty as older sister, she gave me a side hug and bowed out with the excuse of Olivia's bath time.

"What kind of trouble?" my mother asked when I turned back to her. Her eyebrows were pinched together and her arms crossed tightly across her chest. I opened my mouth to respond, but then she held up her hand. "Did you eat?"

I shook my head.

"Food first." She hustled into the kitchen.

I looked at my dad who shrugged. "Eat a big dinner. That'll make her happy."

"I'll be happy when she stops working too hard," my mom responded from the kitchen.

"That means she'll never be happy," I quipped.

My dad wrapped his arm around me. "There is no shame in that," he whispered. "You work as hard as you need to. This project of yours, it's good?"

"Yeah, it's fine. My PI is busy helping set up the clinical trial, so she's been handing off a lot of the administrative side of this one to me. It's great experience, but it means more travel, more late nights."

"The kind Ann used to complain about? Is that why you look so guilty?" my mother asked.

"It's not the same," I said.

My mother pursed her lips and sent some sort of signal to my dad. He patted me on the shoulder and retreated to the living room. "Why not?" she asked once we were alone.

I watched my mother put together a plate for me and tried to sort out the difference. I remembered Emma telling me that I needed to be with someone who had her own drive, not someone who expected me to hold her on the couch every night. "Ann wanted all my time. When I got home, it felt like she had everything on hold waiting for me. Remi's not like that. She has her own work, so she understands that my work can be demanding."

"Then why do you look guilty?"

"I pushed her understanding too far. She gets it, but her brother does not, and they are very close. He functions on a very strict schedule, and a few weeks ago, I had to cancel on them which caused some tension." I spooned *carne asada* and *pico de gallo* onto a steaming tortilla, folded it and took a big bite which muffled the part about how I'd blown it enough that I was worried she was thinking I wasn't worth the grief I was causing Neil.

"Say that again without the food in your mouth," my mother ordered.

"I messed up and she said that she needs some time. She's not sure she can date with how much her brother needs her."

"How did you mess up?" My mother stared at me, and I swear *she* was weighing whether I was worth it, and what I had done would be the determining factor. I wondered if my being her child tipped the scale in my favor. Her expression suggested not.

"I missed a string of texts," I said guiltily. I slid my phone across the table queued up to the messages that haunted me. I explained that I had been in a meeting when the texts came in.

My mom read them and pushed the phone back to me. "After your meeting, did you call? Did you even *read* all her texts?"

I looked down, too guilty to meet my mother's gaze. "I did call, but only to tell her why I would not make dinner. I assumed she was just blowing off steam texting. It didn't occur to me that someone as confident and capable as Remi would need me."

"Even the strongest people have moments that test their strength."

"I realize that now. I'm worried it's too late."

"Why was her brother in the hospital?"

"He had a grease burn."

"And why didn't you drive to the emergency room to see how bad it was?"

I stopped chewing. Why hadn't I? "She said I was too late."

"When *did* you read her texts?"

"After I was finished at work. It was going on nine."

"Maybe she did not want to ask again. Maybe she wanted you to demonstrate to her that you were sorry. Instead you did what? Sat on your couch and pouted and waited for her to miss you? Is that what you have been doing?"

"She told me she needed time."

She clicked her tongue and pointed at the phone. "Was it only this?"

I took another bite, gathering the energy to tell her about the movie theater.

When I finished, she said, "Was there no one else at your work to handle the contamination?"

So many times in the past, my mother had asked me about my cells being infected. That she did not take the opportunity to tease me about my work added another level of gravity to the situation. "Not when I am showing my boss that she can count on me to take on more responsibility."

My mother gave me a tired sigh. "What about delegating some of your responsibilities? Isn't that part of being a leader? If looking good for your boss is what is most important, then maybe your Remi is right. I thought she was the one who would help you see that there is more to success than work."

"That's not fair. I have a lot on my plate right now."

She looked pointedly at the food she had heaped on the plate in front of me. I would never be able to finish it, especially after all the beer I'd downed. "Why are you not eating?"

"You're the one who piled up my plate!"

"What will you do? Eat it all, even if it makes you sick?"

She and I both knew I would take home more leftovers. I would choose when to stop eating even though making my mother happy was a high priority in my life. "It's one thing with the food that's literally on my plate. But the metaphorically loaded plate isn't that easy."

"Life is about balance. If you want to fit something else on your plate, something must give. The question is what it will be."

"What about her plate? Her brother takes up a lot of room on her plate."

"I never said it is only your plate that needs to change. I said life is about balance. But if you load work on your plate as a priority, why would it surprise you if your Remi does the same with her brother?"

I chewed on all that my mother had said, and she left me to think as she puttered around the kitchen. "I want my plate to look different," I said when I took my plate to the sink. "I want to make room for Remi. She's…" I couldn't find the words to express what I was feeling for Remi.

"I know." She patted my shoulder and finally smiled at me. "Now you need to find a way to show her."

CHAPTER TWENTY-SEVEN

Though I'd been tempted to call Remi as I walked home from dinner, I had some thinking to do. I used my evening meditation to write down everything I had on my metaphorical plate and think about what was most important to me. I'd lectured Maricela about making better choices about what food to put on her plate to keep her healthy, yet night after night, I found myself chasing sleep. What if the key to healthier sleep was tied to the amount of work I elected to put on my plate and not who was in my bed?

The path that led me to my doctoral program logically pointed to a future either in research or industry. My priority was not the paycheck that came with industry jobs. I had been drawn to research because I thought I could help people. My research looked promising for diabetics, but at what cost to my own health? The demands of my job were beginning to make me unhappy. Remi made me happy. Her help with my sleep study had made me happier than I ever remembered, and that happiness went deeper than the physical connection and rest I experienced when I was with her.

Remi and I engaged on so much more than a physical level. She'd awakened a lightheartedness with her silly "scientific" television shows, and our date challenges had given me some of my best memories. I wanted to share my days with Remi. I valued her insight when we talked about work. I loved the trust she had in me to talk honestly about the challenges Neil brought to her life, and I knew that developing a connection with him was important to Remi.

And then I went and screwed that up trying to do everything at once. I pictured losing part of a meal by piling too much on my plate. As good as it looked, I wouldn't eat it off the floor, no matter how many times my family yelled "Five second rule!" As if bacteria gives you five seconds before they contaminate the food. Had I contaminated things with Remi, or could I call five-second rule and make some adjustments to my plate?

I was relieved when she began returning my texts again and stayed focused on making sure Neil was okay before I approached the topic I wanted to discuss. I thought it would be best posed at dinner and plotted my invitation carefully. I sensed that Remi was waiting for me to stop texting because of the snag we had hit, but I was in no way ready to give up. I said that I wanted to apologize to Neil and wanted him to join us for dinner.

She pointed out that changing his routine had resulted in a trip to the hospital.

I felt like she was blaming me for what had happened to Neil but wanted to keep talking about the future, not the past, so I countered that scientists didn't give up when they didn't get the results they wanted. Scientists persist. We plan a new experiment, tweak the method and hope for different results. I planned dinner at my house. I would be on time. I would have Lego.

Finally, she accepted. Even though we did all of this through texts, I could tell that she'd begun to steel herself for the end of our relationship. I really hoped I could prove her wrong.

When she arrived with her brother, Remi looked as fabulous as ever, not a hair out of place, and I wanted so badly to wrap my

arms around her and lose myself in her scent. Instead, I gave her a loose hug and asked Neil how his burn was healing.

"It was hard to sleep at night when I had to keep ice on it, but it doesn't keep me from doing Lego." With that, he walked into my house to begin a silent appraisal of its contents.

I ushered Remi in, ready to convince her that I had learned from my mistakes in the last weeks. Thinking about his sensitivity to the sound of popcorn at the movies, I'd chosen soft flour tortillas instead of hard corn tortillas, no tortilla chips, and was feeling pretty confident that the night would go well. I could already check off being ready on time.

I arranged the colorful bowls of sliced chicken, grated cheese, shredded lettuce, diced tomato and olives, sour cream and fresh guacamole. I pointed to the warm tortillas and told them to make as many as they would like. Remi took a plate and two tortillas, adding ingredients in a line down the center of the tortilla, leaving plenty of room to fold it. Neil asked for two tortillas as well and loaded them with cheddar cheese.

He turned toward the table, and Remi saw his plate. A look passed between brother and sister. Neil frowned and sprinkled a tiny bit of lettuce off to the side.

Remi turned a pained expression toward me. I shrugged. How he ate his taco didn't matter to me.

"A little chicken as well," Remi instructed.

"I like cheese," he said.

Remi took a bite of her taco. "It's delicious. The chicken is not at all spicy."

"Cheese."

I didn't see the harm in his eating cheese, but I wasn't going to contradict Remi. I loaded my tacos, aiming for something that would be as neat as Remi's but overloading them to the point that I was going to lose stuff every time I took a bite.

"At least put one scoop with your lettuce."

Neil frowned at his plate. Remi frowned at me as if to say *See? This is too difficult.* I wasn't buying it. He was in my house, and he did as instructed and sat at a table with the two of us. Thinking about how upset Neil had been at the movies, I made sure to take small bites and chew as quietly as possible.

Neil plucked cheese from the tortilla with his fingers and filled his mouth.

"Use your tortilla, please. It is not civilized to eat with your fingers," Remi said.

"She is," Neil said, pointing at me.

As I'd predicted, I started losing tomato and olive the minute I bit into my taco and had pinched a few escapees into my mouth. "Should I get us forks?" I said around my food.

Remi shut her eyes. Shit! Why hadn't I fetched the forks without talking with my mouth full? I pushed back from the table and returned with three forks. Neil used his finger to push cheese onto the fork. I used the edge of my taco to pick up the overflow. Remi's fork sat untouched as she ate her taco without a single thing falling out.

Having emptied the tortillas of cheese, Neil stood.

"Not before your chicken and lettuce. It would be nice if you tried it in the tortilla."

Neil frowned, scooped the chicken and lettuce up in his fist and shoved it all in his mouth. He looked from his sister to me, working hard to keep his mouth closed as he chewed the mass. I did my best not to crack a smile. Remi's expression told me it was important that I did not encourage barbaric table manners.

"Thanks again for fixing my Batman Dragster," I said.

"The cat didn't break it?" he asked, his eyes directed toward the counter with all the food.

"I put it in my office and shut the door, so Petri can't get to it. My niece brought over some of her Lego that she doesn't want her little sister to break. You can check it out after dinner if you want."

"Can I see it now?"

"Are you finished with your dinner?" Remi asked.

Neil nodded and started to stand.

"Water, too," Remi said.

Neil gulped it down and looked to his sister once more. "If it's okay with Karla."

"Sure," I answered.

"Clear your dishes."

Neil piled cup on plate and deposited them in the kitchen. I walked him to the office and left him inspecting the Lego-Friends collection Rosa had agreed to lend me for the night.

"We are working on table manners," Remi said when I returned.

I was hoping the room would feel less tense once Neil turned his attention to the Lego. Unfortunately, Remi had not warmed at all. I tried to lighten the mood. "My mom's still working on Luis."

Remi's eyes did not dance in reply. Her read on the night was vastly different to mine, and I wished that it was as easy as offering some Lego to play with to get her to see things as I did. I reached for her hand but then realized I needed both to eat my tacos. She had nearly finished hers. We ate in silence for a few minutes before I found something to say. "Neil seemed to do okay with dinner."

"He didn't like the tacos."

"But he ate the meat and cheese. My sister would call that a win."

Remi inclined her head, acquiescing.

"How was your week?" I missed hearing the details of her workdays.

"Long. I should be doing testing for a fourth grader who is struggling badly, but the campus is dragging its feet. She's passing all her subjects, so they don't see an issue. They don't care that she's working three times as hard as her classmates to barely get by. Working with a resource specialist would help her significantly..."

Her thoughts drifted from the subject and she didn't continue when she brought her focus back to me. It felt like when we'd spoken on the phone and she realized she was starting a conversation that would let me back in.

"But that costs money."

"It's always about money," she said.

Was that directed at me? Did she think my choice to stay at work and respond to Maricela's mother's accusation had to do with money? I didn't know what to say and didn't want to get us back on the subject of how I'd let her down.

"It was nice of you to invite us," Remi said when she finished her dinner.

Her beer was nearly empty. The night was slipping away from me, and I hadn't eased the tension between us. I set down my unfinished taco and took her hand. "Thank you for accepting. I really miss seeing you."

She brought the bottle to her lips and swallowed. Though her eyes were on the remainder, I could see gears in her head turning and wished that I had access to her thoughts.

"I get that..." she began.

Neil stuck his head out of the office. "Can I move the Lego?"

"All you want," I said.

Remi got up and cleared our plates. She didn't sit when she came back.

"Can we talk?" I asked. "I've been thinking about the time I invest in my work."

"With Neil here..." Remi tried again.

"Look! Karla has science Lego!" Neil returned to the table, setting down the chemistry lab set that I'd given Rosa for her birthday. "See the beakers? And the periodic table? It has rats and..."

Remi's eyes never left mine as he rattled off more features he liked about the pieces. Could she tell from my expression that I wanted all of it? That I wanted her with every one of her life's complications? Neil happily continued despite the fact that neither of us responded to him. Remi sighed deeply, another cue he didn't catch. I wanted to say it didn't matter, but I knew it did.

"That is very interesting," Remi said. "Time to put it away, though."

"Five more minutes?"

"Two," Remi answered

"Compromise, three."

"Three, okay." Remi watched as he ducked into the office again and took out her phone to set a timer for three minutes.

What could I say in three minutes that would bring back her smile? In three minutes, I would never be able to say enough, so I stepped closer to Remi and kissed her. Her lips were warm, but her kiss guarded. I added the tiniest bit of tongue, a little tease along her bottom lip. She sighed and stepped closer to me, resting her hands on my shoulders. She leaned forward and pressed her lips to mine, so intimately supple, I felt the contact down to the backs of my knees.

"Your cat *is* a problem. It eats Lego. Why would it eat Lego?" Neil's voice snapped me back to attention. He stood before us, holding Petri against his chest. My traitorous cat curled her tail like she was always game to be held.

"Petri doesn't like to be held," I said, a little breathless from Remi's kiss.

Neil continued, "She likes to eat Lego. I told her it's not food, and she ate it anyway. I had to open her mouth to get the piece out." Holding my cat with one arm, something I would never have attempted in a million years, he extended a battered purple piece. "She's sneaky. I didn't even know she was there until I heard chewing."

"Maybe put the cat down," Remi interjected. "Karla says she doesn't like to be held."

My cat purred. Neil looked down at her and they gazed at each other like they'd grown up best buds. "She likes me. Maybe I'm good at Lego and cats."

"You must be an animal whisperer," I said. "My cat does not like people."

"She likes me," he said.

Remi's timer went off. "That's our signal to leave." She reached out and tried to extract Petri from Neil's arms. Petri hissed and jumped free.

"She doesn't like you," Neil said.

"Thanks for that," Remi said wryly.

Neil turned to me. "That's sarcasm. She isn't really thanking me."

Remi walked to the door and gathered her coat and purse. "Neil's been working on social skills."

"So have I," I admitted, walking them to the door. "My family is always saying that I have terrible people skills."

"You're autistic?" Neil asked.

"I'm a scientist. I spend so much time around cells that sometimes I forget how to be nice to people and show them that I care about them more than my experiments."

"I think you're nice," Neil said. "But I think you should keep your cat away from the Lego."

"I promise to keep the door shut."

"I can get you a new purple two-by-six brick."

"I'd appreciate that," I said. Remi opened the door, and Neil walked out without another word. I wouldn't have noticed except for the expression on Remi's face. The softness was gone again and her guard up. I could hear her thinking that I could not provide new Lego sets to keep his interest indefinitely. Remi's expression conveyed the years she had spent straddling her world and Neil's. She had said that some could interpret her brother as competition. I had thought she meant people who wanted to date her, but now I could see that Remi herself interpreted Neil as competition. And probably saw my work as competition as well.

I wanted to tell her that there was no competition. I'd discovered that having my name on major papers or associated with a new drug was not the most important thing in my life. She was. I couldn't tell her all that with Neil waiting by the car, but I would figure out how to show her. "I really enjoyed seeing you again tonight."

The edge of her mouth moved up, but the caution didn't leave her eyes. "This was good for Neil. It's important for him to feel successful. The more stability he has in his life, the more he succeeds."

I understood that she was talking about me. "We could do it again, or another movie night. I get that you're a package deal."

"Yes, that would be great. Let's set something up next week."

My schedule flashed in my mind, and I winced.

"What?"

"I could do Sunday. Judy is sending me to another conference Wednesday." I felt none of the elation I'd had telling Valerie about the International Diabetes Association conference. I felt angry about how quickly the potential clinical trial was forcing me to travel again.

"There is only so much change Neil can tolerate. I cannot push him," Remi said.

"I get that," I said, realizing that my words about understanding they were a package deal were empty without the follow through.

"What's taking so long?" Neil called from the car.

Remi leaned forward to give me a chaste kiss. I wasn't expecting her to deliver anything smoldering in front of her brother, but her lips felt stiff on mine. She was still guarded. I watched her walk to the car, uncertain that I had made any progress at all.

CHAPTER TWENTY-EIGHT

"Why do you keep doing that?" I asked as Valerie repeatedly bent over to look under plants. I was panting from the pace Valerie set but didn't want to tell a pregnant lady she was walking too fast for me.

"Checking for goats, mate. Wouldn't want you to go running off to have sex with one."

"I never should have told you that," I groaned.

"No, I'm glad that you did. I wouldn't want you to destroy your career because you couldn't stay away from a stray goat."

"Judy said she didn't care if I screwed a goat."

"Oh, right. So you want me to let you know if I see one? Ah, brilliant idea! Since Remi isn't staying over, let's find you a goat. Emma's been talking about getting a pygmy goat for yoga. Since we'll have our hands full with the cricket, you can take care of the goat. Betcha you'll sleep like a baby with a goat around!"

"Have you seen my friend Valerie?" I huffed. "I was supposed to walk with her and get some sort of emotional support and advice on my career."

"Sorry. No more jokes. Promise. Would you really give up research? Right when you're about to step up and take over the renal program? Not to mention the retinal trial."

"I don't know if I want it. I didn't want to go to that last conference. I got into research because I wanted to help people, and the further I progress up the career ladder, the further away from people I get. I don't want to be like Judy."

We walked in silence for a spell, and then she was craning her neck once again. "Would you please be serious just for today?"

"Sorry. Thought I saw your little mentee off the footpath there."

I frowned, doubting the likelihood of Maricela being on campus. I had texted after her mother stopped being a volunteer and had heard nothing. I hadn't expected to ever see her again. Honestly, I didn't know if I even wanted to talk to her. "Keep walking. If she wants to see to me, she's going to have to work for it."

Instead of powering ahead, Valerie hollered "G'day!" and reduced her speed considerably. Seeing my glare, she said, "You said you wanted to help people. She's a person, and you helped her. You should talk to her."

Maricela stood off to the side of the footpath as we passed, wrestling, I guessed, with whether to follow through on her plan to track us down. "You said I could walk with you, even if I'm not gay or pregnant."

I didn't respond immediately, which earned me one of Valerie's elbows to the ribs. I had to admit she was trying, but that didn't mean I was going to let her off the hook. "From the complaint my boss got, I was pretty sure I'd succeeded in turning you gay."

Valerie poked me again. "You're always welcome," she said to Maricela.

I walked in silence, fuming about the letter that had turned my world upside down. Even though I rationally knew that any number of things could have thrown my relationship with Remi into a tailspin, emotionally I still blamed Maricela.

"I tried to keep my mom in the trial. I didn't want to mess things up…"

"I hear a but there!" Valerie happily nudged her to continue.

I glanced over to see a huge smile on Maricela's signature red lips. I blinked a few times. She looked so different, I blurted, "Are you pregnant?"

She stopped abruptly. "No!"

Valerie shook her head. "I agree she's glowing, but it's from love, idiot."

Maricela blushed deeply.

"The nurse worked out, did she?" Valerie asked.

Valerie was certainly having a good time catching up with my former mentee.

Maricela nodded. "Penny asked me out, and it was great and then my mom wanted to know where I was going."

"You could have told her you were taking a new class! Or that you joined a gym!" I started walking again, and both Valerie and Maricela followed.

"You're the one who said I should stop lying about who I am. That's why I told her who I was with and why. You were right, too. It's easier now that I'm not trying to hide that from her. She's pissed about it, but now it's like that's her problem. I'm not carrying around a bunch of guilt."

"Well, I'm glad someone's life is easier," I grumped.

"Don't let her get you down. She's got the shits about her work right now, but it's got nothing to do with you," Valerie said.

"Did you get in trouble because of my mom?" Maricela asked.

"No, I'm not in trouble. Uncomfortable talking about my sex life with my boss, but not in trouble. I'm not enjoying my job as much now that a lot of it is away from the bench."

"So you don't hate me?"

"I don't hate you. I just hate my job. I don't know if I can stay in Judy's lab."

"What?" Valerie barked. "You've got a drug that's about to put your name on the map. Everyone wants a name in research. That'll get you your own lab. I thought you wanted to be your own PI."

"I don't want to run my own lab." I stopped, stunned to put what I had been feeling into words.

"You can switch fields. Dr. Seonwoo would take you."

"You know how I feel about working with mice," I argued.

"Chang?"

"Are you kidding?"

"Language barrier?" Valerie asked.

"No, I could handle that, but not how he micromanages everything. Plus, breast cancer? I'd be doing cell culture all day every day. Boring."

"Arce?"

"Plants."

"Then what *do* you want to research?" Valerie's voice was rising.

"Nothing! I'm sick of research!" I yelled back. My words echoed in my head. "I don't want to do research anymore."

"That's not true," Valerie argued. "You don't want to do research for Judy. There are other labs."

"And every one of them is going to make the same demand on my time. I can't do it. I'm not you! I'm not Judy! I don't want to live at the lab!" My heart was pounding, and I was breathing heavily, but my head was clear for the first time in weeks.

"You should teach," Maricela said.

I'd forgotten all about Maricela and simply blinked at her. It took me several seconds to register what she'd said. "Where?"

"You could teach at my college. You were way better at explaining things than my teacher," Maricela said.

I looked to Valerie to see her reaction. Helpfully, she shrugged.

"I've never thought about teaching."

"But you're really good at it, and think of all the students you could get excited about research. I was a goner. I was so ready to drop out, and I ended up finishing Bio 101 with a B! If I'd had you from the beginning of the semester, I might have even gotten an A!"

I veered off the path and found a bench. "All I've ever thought about is research."

"But you've got to adapt," Valerie said. "Look at me and Emma. We only thought about her being pregnant, but when that didn't work…" All eyes turned to her bulging tummy.

"You think I should be a teacher?" I asked them both.

"I already said." Maricela shrugged.

I looked at Valerie. "It could make sense," she said. "You seem to know how to make it relatable to students, but I can't see you at a community college. You've done so much here at The Miracle Center, it's hard to see you leaving."

"What do I say to Judy?" Thinking about it made me feel so sick, I tucked my head between my knees.

"Don't say anything yet. You're a friggin' researcher. Go home and find out how hard it is to get a job teaching biology. Then make a decision. You've got to do that and sleep on it, or at least lie in bed with your eyes closed thinking about it, before you make any drastic decisions," Valerie said.

I sat a minute more until my head stopped spinning and then finished the walk. Maricela peeled off from us at the parking lot, and Valerie and I walked in silence toward my building. Her eyebrows were set in a straight line the way they always were when she wanted to say something but didn't want to hurt my feelings. "What?" I asked at my door. "Spit it out. I have to get back to work."

"It has to be for you."

"What does?" I asked.

"If you leave research. You can't leave because you think it will make Remi happy. It has to be the right thing for you. If it is, then telling Vogelsang will be a piece of cake. Like when I told Seonwoo about the cricket."

Finally, I smiled. "That makes a lot of sense. Thanks. For all of this."

"Come to dinner. I'm too tired making this baby to explain all this to Emma. You can tell her while the cricket and I rest."

I agreed and entered the building. For the first time, I walked up the stairs and swiped into the lab wondering whether it was the place I was meant to be.

CHAPTER TWENTY-NINE

I turned the recently purchased Lego figurine in my hand as I waited for the outgoing voice mail message on Remi's phone. I'd heard it too many times lately. I thought about hanging up before the beep but gathered my thoughts, knowing that we needed to talk in person.

"I'm back from the conference," I said lamely. She knew that. I'd texted her while I was away and again when I'd made it home, but I had only gotten a courteous, *Glad it went well* response from her. "My research has kind of taken a turn, and I'd like to talk to you about it. Would you call me? Please?"

I tucked my phone in one pocket and the figurine in another and rolled my shoulders. On the desk were the notes I had jotted down to make sure I didn't freeze when I went to talk to Judy. Of course, she was still in her office. I'd made up an excuse to walk past to make sure and had promised myself I wouldn't leave work before talking to her.

Judy's eyes danced from one monitor to the other while I stared out the window at the ocean, still looking for the right words.

"Karla!"

Although my presence was a surprise to her, I was the one who jumped. "Do you have a minute?"

"Certainly," she said, her eyes returning to the screen. "What is it?"

I walked into her office and perched on the edge of the chair that faced Judy. "I wanted to say thank you for the opportunity to represent the lab at IDA conference."

"Yes. I am particularly happy for you to get the experience when I'm so busy with the clinical trial."

It would have been so easy to continue the conversation following either vein of opportunity, but for me, the Band-Aid is best pulled off quickly. I filled my lungs and said a little prayer. "This conference was not the same as West Coast STEM when I came back invigorated about our research. This conference put things into perspective for me."

Judy's eyes left the monitor. "One of the Biotechs is trying to tempt you away with the promise of salaries in the triple digits. Is that it?"

"No! I'm not interested in Biotech."

Her level gaze told me she didn't believe me.

"Biotech would be as demanding of my time if not even more so. Each new opportunity means a new sacrifice of time. Putting all my commitments on the table, I don't have enough hours in the day to keep everyone happy. If I try, I know I will disappoint you."

"You're *quitting*? You've invested years in this research. You would throw it all away?"

"I can pass on what I've learned. Helping the community college student who was struggling made me think about teaching. I can pass what I know on to people who do have the amount of time a lab like yours expects."

"Or…" I could see Judy applying a new protocol to the experiment of me. She tapped the desk for a few moments and then smiled. "Yes. Teaching. A university like Stanford or UCLA would have great funding and resources to explore new possibilities. Of course you wouldn't be able to take our human cell lines, but if you…"

Her mind amazed me, and there was a time when hearing the confidence she had in my abilities would have been all the validation I needed. But when I heard Stanford and UCLA, I heard prestige and prestige came with time and money. It came from getting papers out yearly in publications like *Cell* and *Nature*. Prestige came with expectations, higher expectations than I could sustain without continuing to make sacrifices.

"I'm looking for something closer to home, maybe the Cal State in San Diego."

"Are they hiring? Do you have any idea how many people apply for a position at any educational institution?"

I didn't.

"Besides the question of whether they happen to be flying a position, a state school is not going to support your caliber of research. You are capable of substantially more than a state school can support. Berkeley. Princeton. A university with recognition."

Not so long ago, her words would have shamed me into listening to her direction, but that direction was what made her happy. It wasn't making me happy anymore. "I wanted to give you notice, so you have time to hire another research scientist."

She did not respond, and I guessed that the extended silence was supposed to invite me to take back my words. I stood. I was ready to go. When she still said nothing, I nodded to punctuate the end of our conversation and walked to the door.

"Karla?"

I turned at the doorway.

"This is a major decision. One that should not be made in haste. Sleep on it. We'll talk tomorrow."

I said okay even though I knew my answer was not going to change. My shoulders felt lighter than they had in years as I gathered my things and headed home.

I took the street that passed my parents' house and stopped at my place only long enough to give Petri a pat and check her food before heading back out again.

Rosa was waiting for me at the corner. I smiled at the look of surprise that greeted me.

"Gramma sent me to see if something was wrong."

"Why would something be wrong?" I slipped my arm through hers as we walked back to her house together.

"You're never home this early."

"I found a stopping place."

"I'm glad," she said.

"I am, too." When we reached the house, I told her I needed to call Remi and would just be a minute. My family would give me that.

I glanced at my watch and crossed my fingers that Remi would pick up. When she did, I felt like a leaf lifted by the wind. I was being carried by something out of my control with no way to predict where I was going. It was exhilarating and scary at the same time.

"Hey. Thanks for picking up."

"You're welcome."

I loved her voice. Even two words made my skin tingle. "I left work early, and I wanted to tell you I miss you and I wish we were having dinner together."

"Karla…"

"Not tonight. You have plans with Neil tonight, and my mom is staring at me through the window wondering what we're talking about. I called to invite you to dinner. Will you have dinner with me tomorrow?"

I heard her sigh.

I said the phrase I'd looked up on the Internet. "*Tu me manques*."

She laughed and repeated the phrase in her beautiful French.

"Are you correcting my pronunciation, or do you really miss me?"

"Correcting you," she said, but I heard humor in her voice.

"Maybe I need a tutor to help me with my French. Have dinner with me. Please?"

"Dinner sounds like a date."

"Would you be okay with that? I'd like to take you out again. I still have one more language to guess."

"That is true," she said.

"If I guess right, maybe you'll come home with me."

"We shall see how it plays out tomorrow. Text me the time and place?"

I agreed and joined my family, distracted by figuring out what I was going to say but present nonetheless.

I didn't mention my talk with Judy to my family. I didn't text Valerie to tell her I'd set the wheels in motion. When I got back home, I spent an hour exploring the Cal State San Diego website, checking out their class offerings and the human resources site. I didn't see any job listings for biology professors, so I looked up positions at Stanford and UC Berkeley, feeling again like I was getting further away from what I wanted. The magnitude of material on the university websites was overwhelming, but the only other thing that came to mind would be in Biotech, and I had already dismissed that idea. Frustrated, I closed the computer. It would not help my sleep to continue searching when I did not know what I was looking for.

I did my stretches. *Be well.* Joining my family for dinner had nourished me in a new way tonight. What a difference it made to get there without rushing and be greeted without the all-too-familiar needling about my work.

Be content. I felt good about my talk with Judy. Despite the points she had made to dissuade me. My brain started spinning on different schools, so many of them far away, and with them the responsibility of research. Like I'd said when I was talking to Valerie and Maricela, I didn't want to do research. I wanted to inspire people to do research, but how was I supposed to do that? My heart rate increased. I had to let it go for the night.

Be calm. Panic was exactly what Judy wanted me to feel, so I would return to the lab committed to her vision. But I was serious about needing a change in direction. I loved The Miracle Center, but I needed a job with regular hours. If only The Miracle Center had a position to help recruit people to science. Who was it that Maricela's teacher would have spoken to about the internship there? I pulled a breath deep into my lungs and let it out. That was a good question! My eyes flew open. The right question could make all the difference in finding an answer! I laughed out loud and felt my entire body relax with relief. I had a question. I had the right question.

Be at peace. My heart rate steadied, and I breathed easily for the first time in ages. It felt like stopping at the top of the stairs where Valerie and I could enjoy the view. I didn't know quite what I was seeking yet, but I had confidence that my question would lead me in the right direction.

I took myself to bed and dropped into the most restful sleep I had ever experienced alone. I slept without checking the time. I slept until my alarm went off. I slept, and I woke up rested.

CHAPTER THIRTY

We met at Valenti's Trattoria. I waited outside for Remi, having made a point to be early. I closed my eyes and replayed our first date. She'd snuck up on me the second I shut my eyes to think about whether we were in hug territory. We'd gone so far beyond that, yet I was still nervous waiting for her.

I recognized the Ferrari's purr and patted myself on the back. Remi would be coming home with me tonight, and I let my thoughts wander through all the wonderful things we could do.

"*Ciao*, Beautiful," Remi said, kissing me on the cheek.

Oh, yeah. I had a lot of plans. "So I picked right?"

"I have never been here before." She held the door open for me.

"But you speak Italian?"

"That is your guess?"

"My official guess. You drive a Ferrari and you greeted me in Italian."

"What if I Googled *how to say hello in Italian* after you texted me the name of this restaurant?"

"Then I don't think it would sound like that on your lips. Do you speak Italian?"

"I'm afraid not. I can understand a little, but my only Italian I picked up from movies which doesn't count."

My jaw dropped. I was wrong? I couldn't be wrong! What happened after dinner if I was wrong? Remi reached out to touch my chin, prompting me to close my mouth before something flew in. "But I was so sure! I had plans!"

"It appears those plans will have to be rearranged," she said, ushering me through the door.

I slipped my hand into my pocket and wrapped my fingers around the Lego figurine trying to think of a way to salvage the evening. Remi's words had pushed us back toward the tension over my conference trip. I sighed and recalibrated the evening. The conference wasn't a bad place to start, considering what I had wanted to talk about. "The conference was awful. I should have been with you and Neil."

She smiled to acknowledge my words but did not respond. She picked up the menu to scan the contents. I had already decided on the *manicotti* and used the time she took to choose to study her, her delicate cheekbone, the perfection of her eyebrows, the crisp cut of her hair that accentuated her jaw and always drew my attention to the places on her neck I wanted to kiss.

"You are staring." Remi set down her menu and placed the napkin on her lap.

"I was remembering how you captivated me from the moment I saw you at Rosa's science fair."

"You made it very difficult to focus on the content of the young scientist's project."

"And then you floored me by saying you had ideas about my sleep study." She held my gaze. "I was hoping to gather more data for that tonight."

"Is that why you invited me to dinner?" She twisted the stem of her empty wineglass, making my body ache to have her fingers on me…in me. I had to look away to regain my focus.

"I wanted to tell you that I told my boss that the conference clarified a lot of things for me."

Our waiter appeared, dressed all in black with a crisp white apron around his waist. Accentuated by his dark goatee, white teeth flashed when he delivered a basket of bread. Noah introduced himself, ran through the night's specials and took our order efficiently.

Instead of reaching for bread, Remi extended her hand, inviting me to continue. "If I follow the career path I am on now, there are tons more conferences like last week's, and I was bored out of my skull. I was trying to figure out why I enjoyed the STEM conference so much more. That got me thinking about Rosa's fair, and it hit me! I enjoy working with young people, with students!" I leaned forward. "I don't have a firm idea of what I'll do next, but I told my boss I'm leaving research."

Remi didn't smile like I expected her to. She was quiet until Noah had delivered our wine. She took a sip, savoring the deep red liquid before she set down her glass. "I did not ask you to leave your research."

"No, I know you didn't! But now I can see the stress it causes me. My mother has been pointing it out to me for years, and until now I have ignored her, thinking that I knew what I wanted to do with my degree. That science fair, helping Maricela pass her class, I want to be doing things to inspire young scientists!"

Remi took another sip of wine. "You do not have to leave research to be a mentor to young scientists." I opened my mouth to argue about how I didn't have hours enough in the day to see her let alone any spare time to volunteer. She stayed my thoughts with her hand and sighed deeply. "I have already suffered through my father's resentment after sacrificing his career on my brother's behalf. You have a PhD, Karla. You studied hard to earn your position, and I can't be the person who makes you walk away from that."

"I'm not making a drastic decision."

Her beautiful eyebrows lifted. "When did you tell your boss about not enjoying the direction of your work?"

"Yesterday. She said to sleep on it. I did, and I'm even more certain today that there is a better job for me. I just have to find it. And then I'll have more time for the important people in my life."

Noah delivered our food, which was delicious. We exchanged bites with each other, and I waited for the food to relax Remi to the point where she could hear my words and understand what she meant to me.

"Have you considered that you could change jobs, and things with Neil will not improve? What if his agitation continues to grow and he hurts himself worse next time?"

"That's not what I saw when he was at my house. What if having less demands on my time contributes to the stability he feels?"

Remi ate in silence, and I could tell that she was still sorting her thoughts. Finally, she put down her fork and set her napkin on top of it. "I cannot help wondering how long it will be until you miss the challenge of research. How will you feel when your lab puts out another paper, and your name is not on it? That question will always be at the back of my mind."

I reached into my pocket and pulled out the Lego figurine. The figurine had a ponytail, like I often did, and held a box of popcorn. I adjusted the arm, so it looked like the figure was offering it to Remi. "You're my Wyldstyle. And I'm Popcorn. I'll keep learning, with him and with you. Isn't that part of being in a relationship? What if that's the challenge I pick?"

"It is a big change, Karla. One I think you need to give more thought." She picked up the Lego figurine and held it out to me. "You are immeasurably more than Popcorn. Set her next to the scientist in the Lego lab Neil liked so much. You will see what I am saying."

Reluctantly, I took the figurine back. I could not argue with her words. I would only sound irrational if I did. I would have to keep my big-girl chonies on tonight and do as she asked.

CHAPTER THIRTY-ONE

"You haven't given an update about the sleep study in a while, mate. What's the data showing?" Valerie asked at the top of the stairs. Her pregnancy finally had her huffing about the same as I was.

I waved off her question. "No new data lately."

Valerie scowled. "What do you mean no new data?"

"Just what it sounds like. No sleepovers for me for a couple of weeks."

"It has NOT been weeks since you had sex!"

"I never said I wasn't having sex. I said I wasn't having sleepovers."

"That doesn't make any sense at all. You look happy and rested. Based on your studies, I took that to mean you were getting laid *and* getting a bunch of sleep."

"I am getting both, but I'm also sleeping alone. I guess I should add a new column for that." I started walking down the stairs. I didn't want to have more of that conversation in a building where I might run into coworkers, and I knew Valerie wasn't going to let the subject go.

"Why doesn't she want to sleep over anymore?" Valerie asked, doing the funny waddle that her belly made her do when she went downstairs.

"I guessed the fifth language wrong."

"Sorry, mate. I don't follow."

"The deal was that if I guessed the fifth language she speaks fluently, she'd come home with me. I guessed wrong, so she won't stay."

"You keep guessing wrong?"

A little embarrassed to admit it, I waited for her to look at me so I could get away with nodding. She wasn't letting me off easily. "Yes."

"What've you guessed?"

"Italian, Russian, German, Portuguese. Japanese, Korean, Chinese."

"Oof! You're lucky that she didn't say she wouldn't have sex with you until you guessed right!"

"I know, I know."

"Is she at least happy about your leaving research?"

"Not as much as I thought she'd be. She still thinks that her brother is going to make me change my mind about being together. I gave her the popcorn Lego figurine, which I thought would explain everything. If accepting the nickname Popcorn doesn't say 'I love you,' what will?"

"Do you?"

"What? Love her?"

"Yes, love her! Have you said the words? Because I'm not seeing a dramatic declaration of love in a plastic toy."

"I told her she's my Wyldstyle!"

"Still not seeing it. This is big, Karla. Are you in love with her?"

I swallowed, unable to say the words to Valerie but absolutely sure that she was right. "Yes, I am, but I can't tell her or she'll think that's why I decided to leave research."

Valerie tipped her head, agreeing. "What's she think of the new job?"

"I haven't told her."

"How's that? You've known for what, a week?

"I left her a message. I wanted to tell her in person, but she's been busy. She had to take Neil to get his burn checked out. I've been working late, too, training my replacement."

"Maybe the late hours make her think you're not really serious about slowing down?"

"Maybe." It didn't make sense to me, either. I hadn't pictured anything dramatic like us exchanging keys or anything, but I did think that she would at least show some excitement about the changes I was making. For someone who worked in education, she met my enthusiasm about wanting to mentor future scientists tepidly at best.

Though Remi's guardedness worried me, I thought of how Rosa's science fair had brought us together. Leaving the lab had been difficult that day, but it had been the right thing. It had led me to something that better suited me.

"Sometimes the answer is different than what you expect it to be. When Rosa stayed over when we were working on the sleep study, I had thought that it was her sleepover that made me sleep better. Now I wonder if it had more to do with how I was focusing on something other than work that made me relax. Since that talk with Judy, I've been sleeping fine. It might not be the result that Rosa expected, but it's one I can live with."

Valerie frowned. "You're a big fat liar."

I shrugged. "But it sounds good."

We'd reached the spot where we separated to walk to our respective buildings. Valerie's hug made me think of Maricela and her mom. For so long, I had thought it was her mother's population I wanted to help. Now, I was excited to help more students like Maricela and convince them of their potential.

Valerie must have been thinking of our walking buddy as well because she said, "Will Maricela be at your going-away party tomorrow?"

"No. It's just my lab mates and you."

"You didn't invite anybody else?"

"It's not that big of a deal. And it's for the lab to say goodbye. It would be weird to have anybody else there."

"But you invited me."

"Only because there's food."

"Free food!" Valerie smiled and waved over her shoulder "Okay. See you tomorrow."

Funny how any end, even a good one, feels tinged with sadness. I was closer to Valerie than I was to anyone in my lab, and I would continue to see her just as often, so there was no reason to feel sad at my farewell. Ashleigh had covered the break room with balloons and two small banners, one saying "Congratulations!" and the other "Good luck!"

I'd told her that since she had her own key lanyard, she wouldn't miss me at all, and she'd surprised me with a heartfelt thanks for my help when she first started. I was touched that what I'd thought of as a forgettable gesture she used as an example of why I was sure to excel at my new job.

Judy offered an unexpected farewell speech, which choked me up enough that it was difficult to voice how thankful I was for the confidence she'd had in me. Though I was excited about my new career path, and I knew that it would sting when I didn't see my name linked with the drug to decrease retinal damage, it was also a great relief to set down my guilt because I could not dedicate a hundred percent to the project.

Valerie kept everything from feeling awkward by trying to get everyone to eat as much as she did. I was lucky to have her as a friend. We'd had so many conversations about luck... My musings were interrupted by the profile of someone who looked exactly like Remi passing the break room. I shook my head, chastising my thoughts for circling back to her. As if I had the right to ask for more in my life.

The door opened, and she peeked in. I had a few beats to watch her before she found me, a few seconds to try to read why she was there. I set down my half-eaten cake and walked to the door.

Her eyes never left mine as she slipped inside. Her smile was tentative, and we didn't hug. She read the signs in the room and congratulated me, though her cheerful tone did not match her resigned visage.

"Remi. What are you doing here?"

Her eyes left me then, and when I turned Valerie was giving a thumbs-up, a grinning broadly.

"Valerie texted me and asked if I would come to your going-away party. I wondered if it was a new job when you said you had news to share."

"You didn't call."

"I wanted to give you space to think about the decision you were making."

"Didn't you hear me when I said how excited I was about working with students?"

"Yes. But I still worry that you will come to resent Neil and then me for making you leave what you love."

"You're not making me leave."

"You belong at The Miracle Center. What you do impacts so many lives."

The few colleagues who had lingered used my distraction to take their leave. After I said goodbye to them, I turned back to Remi. "But I don't have to leave! That's what I wanted to tell you." I bit my lip and caught Valerie's eye, pleading for help.

"Show her your new office. I'll clean up here," Valerie said.

"Come with me?" I took Remi's hand.

She looked uncertain, something I had never seen in Remi and earnestly wanted to erase. She was stunning as ever in her flowing black pants and tailored blue blouse that showed off every wonderful curve.

Her hand felt so good in mine, that I wrapped my other hand around it too. "I am so happy to see you." When we got to the sidewalk, Remi started to turn toward the parking lot. "This way," I said, pulling her the opposite direction.

"I thought we were going to your new office."

"We are! You're absolutely right about how much I love The Miracle Center. I remembered two things the night Judy told me to think about leaving research. When I was at Rosa's science fair, she wanted me to reach out as a liaison between that event and the lab. That made me think about how someone must coordinate with The Miracle Center's labs to set up the service-learning projects with community colleges. Maricela had such low confidence about pursuing a research career, and I helped her. I had an impact on her life. Now I'll get to work with that population earlier and grow their confidence to pursue careers in science."

We stopped in front of the Public Relations building.

"My new office is on the second floor."

She blinked. "You will be working with students like Maricela?"

"Yep! I'll be coordinating outreach with local schools, encouraging minority students to invest in science. Nine to five, normal hours. So I can spend more with you. And Neil. And my family, too, of course. But mostly you. Say you'll give me some of your time."

Remi looked toward my building. "No more lab coats?"

"You sound disappointed. I bet Judy will let me take the one with my name stitched on the pocket. Plus, I'll need it for touring students around to labs."

She placed her hands on my shoulders but still kept her distance. "I've been telling myself that it was selfish of me to want so much."

"It's not selfish of you! I've been trying to tell you that. How come it takes Valerie calling you for you to listen? It's the accent, isn't it? And how does she have your number? Should I be worried?"

She laughed then, and some of her sparkle returned. "It's not the accent. Remember the picture of you doing the Southern blot?" She waved her phone which made me cover my eyes with my hands. She pocketed her phone and pulled my hands away from my eyes. "It was not her accent at all. It was your sleep-study spreadsheet that convinced me."

My hands flew back up to my face. I said between my fingers, "She didn't tell you about the spreadsheet."

"She did. That is why I finally understand that you are not sacrificing your life's dream."

"All I had to do was tell you that I was sleeping fine, and you wouldn't have freaked out?"

"I did not freak out."

The words sounded funny on her lips. I leaned forward and was about to kiss her when I heard her question about Maricela. She had not shaped the "r" at the back of her mouth like she was saying "tiger." I reached back in my memories and heard her saying my whole name. She pronounced it with a silent "h." She gave the Spanish pronunciation, ehr-nahn-des. "You speak Spanish!"

A light shone in her eyes. "That is not a guess. A guess is a question."

"Why didn't you tell me on our ice cream date?"

"You did not say it was an official guess. You said something about needing more time to study my linguistic patterns."

"My studies have revealed more than linguistics," I ventured. "I love you, Remi. I want my days to be shaped by you. I want to know that when I crawl into bed, you'll be there."

She wrapped me in a tight hug. "I love you too. I should have said so instead of pulling away."

"I'll forgive you if you let us make up for lost time."

"Will you continue to log in whether we have sex or not?"

"I don't actually have a spreadsheet."

"Perhaps you will have to begin." Her fingers tickled the stray hairs that had come free from my ponytail.

"I think it would be best if we start with the 'how I sleep after sex' column," I suggested.

"Agreed."

She kissed me, and I burned for her down to my toes. "I don't think I can wait till tonight."

"Do you still have access to that darkroom?"

That surge of excitement and adrenaline zipped through me. "Are you serious?"

She stepped closer, her mouth so close to my ear that I felt her breath. "I am very, very serious."

I shivered and placed my finger over my lips. We retraced our steps back to my building to get a start on our joint research project.

Bella Books, Inc.

Women. Books. Even Better Together.

P.O. Box 10543
Tallahassee, FL 32302

Phone: 800-729-4992
www.bellabooks.com